As the Matzo Ball Turns

JOZEF ROTHSTEIN

BOOK PUBLISHERS NETWORK

Book Publishers Network
P.O. Box 2256
Bothell • WA • 98041
Ph • 425-483-3040
www.bookpublishersnetwork.com

10 9 8 7 6 5 4 3 2 1

Printed in the United States of America

LCCN   2012931538
ISBN   978-1-937454-24-1

Editor: Julie Scandora
Cover Art: Kayla Sharwell
Cover Design: Laura Zugzda
Typographer: Stephanie Martindale

The following story captures the spirit of actual events that happened to me. Some creative license has been taken for dramatic purposes. Modifications may include changes to lines of dialogue, alteration of the timeline, adjustments to identifying features of certain individuals to protect their anonymity, the creation of composite characters and the addition of commentary based on the opinions and the imagination of the author. This book should be read and was intended for entertainment purposes only.

Contents

What started out as a kick
in the rear end turned
into one big laugh. I hope
you enjoy it!

Jozef Rothstein

P.S. May this book bring
you the gift of laughter
Mr. Bob Elfant!

Introduction

After spending ten long, hard years as a struggling actor in Hollywood, I am convinced there are only two kinds of people living in LA ... the Steven Spielbergs, Harvey Weinsteins, and Angelina Jolies of the entertainment empire and all of the aspiring artists like me who serve them their lunch and get them their coffee. It's not that I moved to Tinseltown with the expectation of bringing Alice Cooper his morning Joe; it's just what I did for ten years while trying to become the next big thing in celluloid. I am sure I could think up a hundred reasons why I wasn't selected to join the royal class of Hollywood, like I am not a direct descendant of the Queen of England or I didn't have a rich and connected uncle who worked in the business, but I will spare you the grief. The following is a first-hand account of one man's journey (mine) into the belly of the beast of the entertainment empire and how I was shot out the back end into a very popular Jewish deli where I encountered hit men, hookers, celebrities, and angry seniors.

The names of the characters have been changed in order to protect the innocent, but the names of the celebrities have not. If the paparazzo who almost ran me over with his car in order to get an uncanny picture of Brittany Spears can make a buck off these overpaid ego maniacs who take themselves way too seriously, so should I. And for all the hard-earned money I spent fueling the Hollywood machine on acting classes, headshots, and mind-numbing, big-budget flops, I figured it's the least I can do for myself. Besides, it makes for a better read. So, without further ado, here is the beginning of my ten-year saga as told from within the confines of the matzo ball establishment.

The Dream (Before I Woke Up)

When I arrived in California back in the late nineties, I was about as bright eyed and bushy tailed as they come. I was certain that once Hollywood decision makers got a load of me my days of working in the restaurant business would come to a crashing halt and I'd be trading in my rusted-out Mazda 323 for a brand new Mercedes XL. I had just left a great-paying and cushy job as a pool bartender at a luxurious resort in Scottsdale, Arizona, to pursue a career in the arts. And because everybody and his brother who pursues acting in Los Angeles clings to his bartending job like a barnacle attaching itself to a fishing vessel, I would soon realize that I had a better chance of becoming the next Pope than I did of getting a good bartending gig in LA. Not knowing a single person in this large, lonely city didn't help matters either. Thank God, I did have some restaurant experience because if you are an aspiring actor in Hollywood and you can't wait tables and/or bartend you might as well dig yourself a hole and throw yourself in it. There is no other way to eek out a decent living while also maintaining a flexible enough schedule to audition at a moment's notice. Well, I lied; there is, but I don't look good in lace.

So, before I left Phoenix, I made arrangements to work at a sister hotel in Santa Monica, California, as a host so I at least had some sort of revenue coming in. Next, I rounded up the little bit of junk that I owned, crammed it into my beater, and began my trek for the Golden State. My hosting job was at a beautiful ocean-front property in downtown Santa Monica, which gave me the opportunity to generate a measly income while I charmed the managers of the hottest nightclubs on the strip in order to create a more substantial livelihood for myself.

Landing a job in the exciting career of mixology would enable me to uninhibitedly chase my dream while still maintaining a respectable standard of living. The plan was that they, the nightclub managers, would recognize me as a potential Hollywood heavyweight and would instantly hire me so that when I did hit it, it would bring even more notoriety to their local hotspot. The one minor detail that I happened to overlook was that just about everybody in LA, including the managers of popular nightclubs, is a failed artist, and if a dejected discotheque supervisor didn't make it in Hollywood, he sure as hell wasn't going to lend a hand to some half-dazed greenhorn traipsing around town with a cheesy smile plastered on his face. So while the bloodhounds guarding the golden gate to paradise were sniffing out my big dreams like a German shepherd rooting through Robert Downey Jr.'s luggage, I was paying my dues as a glorified talking statue in an upscale restaurant where I had my first direct contact with the rich and famous. Pretty exciting stuff for a small-town boy from Pennsylvania. Two of our biggest regulars were Donald Sutherland and Anthony Hopkins. We also dined the likes of Michael Keaton, Gary Busey, June Lockhart, and Kenny Loggins. It seemed that just about every other day a celebrity was either passing by our host stand or I was leading one to a table.

After a short month in LA, I began to feel as if everyone around me was either famous or knew somebody famous. One of the first employees I got to know at the hotel was a woman who was once married to Kevin Cronin of REO Speedwagon. This may mean nothing to you, but REO Speedwagon was everything to me growing up. I even had my first masturbating experience to the song, "Keep on Loving You." Anyway, Kevin's ex was a very nice lady, who explained to me how she helped write some of the lyrics to REO's songs but never received any of the credit or royalties. And, as I would unfortunately find out with the creative types in Hollywood, she may not have been making this up. More on that later, but one of the major highlights of my hotel-hosting experience came on a day when I was doing something as simple as putting plates away.

The dishes were kept in an overhead compartment of a large hutch that was enclosed by high, swinging, glass doors. I was right in the middle of this tedious task when I heard voices at the front of the restaurant. Lo and behold, when I rounded the corner, standing at the host stand was none other than Mr. Hannibal Lector himself, Sir Anthony Hopkins plus one. For some reason, on that day, Sir Anthony wanted to sit at a patio table, which he never requested. I politely led Mr. Hopkins and his guest towards the patio door. As we approached the cupboard where I had been putting plates away, I couldn't help but run the scenario through my mind where I asked him if he would like a glass of Chianti and some fava beans. My thoughts must have been screaming at him, or maybe he was trying to figure out twenty different ways to eat me because he was not paying attention to where he was going. As I reached out to open the patio door, I heard a thump and an "Ouch!" When I turned around, I found Sir Anthony Hopkins hunched over, rubbing his forehead. I offered to help him, which just seemed to make matters worse. Then the grim realization hit me that I had left the cupboard door open. As my job flashed before my eyes, the only thing I could think of saying was, "Would you like some ice?" Sir Anthony Hopkins was a very private individual, who never liked to draw attention to himself, so he simply replied, "No, thank you." I then nonchalantly closed the cupboard door to clear the way (and to cover my ass) and proceeded to lead him to a table.

A few days later, one of the servers later complained to me that "The World's Fastest Indian" never tipped above 15 percent, no matter how great the service was or how much work was involved. This gripe was uniform throughout our wait staff, and I was surprised to learn that someone as refined and sophisticated as Sir Anthony Hopkins was a tightwad. After learning this fact about someone who dined in our restaurant on a regular basis and who also required special service, I began to think of my serendipitous action as somewhat heroic. A loud message was sent to the world that day … even if you were knighted by the Queen of England, if you are someone of social importance and you have a nice stash of cash yet you only tip 15 percent to the little peons fawning all over you, you will get a cupboard door upside your head. I only wish I could have wheeled that large wooden cabinet around with me everywhere I went.

One other regular who frequented our ocean-front property was Chris Penn. Yes, that Chris Penn from *Reservoir Dogs* and brother of Sean Penn. Hardly a night went by when Chris wasn't bellied up to the bar for a bowl of loudmouth soup. I watched him stumble in and out of the restaurant for months at a time and never once heard him utter a hello or goodbye, despite the fact that I greeted him on almost a daily basis. It was hard as an aspiring thespian to watch a guy who had so much going for him act so obnoxiously and so irresponsibly while at the bar. One of the weekly performers at the restaurant was a man by the name of Ray Johnson. Ray was a classic. His brother, Plas Johnson, played the saxophone on one of the most renowned saxophone pieces of all time, the Pink Panther theme song. Ray was quite the entertainer when he joked with the crowd from behind his grand piano, but unfortunately for Ray, his tickling of the ivories didn't match the skill level of his witty banter. Ray emulated Nat King Cole in just about every way, including the manner in which he dressed. Ray also featured many Nat King Cole songs in his repertoire. Regrettably, most of the songs came out of Ray like a drunk uncle hijacking the family piano on St. Patrick's Day. Ray's draw was more about his charm and sense of humor than it was his about musical genius, but it was great having him serenade the eclectic dining crowd anyway.

Things would always get interesting (and usually on a weekly basis) when Chris would want to go up and sing with Ray. Chris may have been a decent actor, but his singing voice was far from pitch perfect. His speaking voice was already too nasally and high pitched for my liking, and it became even more piercing when he began to sing. Add to the fact that he was usually three sheets to the wind when he got up before an unsuspecting crowd, and you have a disaster in the making. Every week, Chris would at least attempt to get up and sing his favorite song. Ray would sometimes be able to stave off his request, but other times, Chris was just way too determined. I don't know if I simply can't remember the name of Chris's favorite number or if it's some sort of auto-defense mechanism protecting my central nervous system by erasing it from my memory, but I can't remember the name of the song he always sang or how it went. The only thing I can remember is that it sucked whenever he sang it. People were literally uprooted from their peaceful dining experiences whenever Chris took the stage. To my satisfaction, it was the unfortunate duty of the restaurant manager to respond to the complaints when the piercing shrills got so bad the guests were on the verge of tossing up their evening feed. Eventually, Chris was banned from the microphone. It was around this time when there was also a noticeable descent in Chris's behavior. I don't know if it was from the realization that he would never have a singing career or if his personal demons were really starting to take control of him, but something was going on with this guy.

One of the last things I remember about Chris before I resigned from the hotel was the physical condition he was in the night he came into the restaurant after being beaten up a few days prior. He had several fresh gashes on his face and a black and blue eye. It turns out that he had been jumped by a group of guys who had struck him with a baseball bat. Since he never talked to me, I didn't really get the full story of what had happened, but he did tell a bartender it had something to do with Las Vegas where he also ran a business. Unfortunately, Chris was never able to get his act together and passed away at the young age of forty.

The hotel restaurant provided a nice atmosphere and some interesting experiences, but in order to survive the high rent in LA, the expenses for headshots, gas costs, acting classes, and my mounting credit-card debt, I would need a little bit more than a minimum-wage job to pay for it all. That's when somebody strongly suggested the name of a high-volume, high-profile Jewish deli that could be my ticket to a discussion with a famous director looking for the next "it" man or, at the very least, a slot on the ever-revolving casting couch with an older, hard-up female casting director. Unfortunately for me, I would have no such luck in either department, but that will become self-evident as the story continues.

As for gaining employment at this notorious deli, it would take countless phone calls and even a few surprise drop-in visits that screamed "remember me" to work my way up from the bottom of the stack of applications, which included every new arrival and wanna-be actor in Los Angeles, to a spot on the top of the pile. Before long, my persistence paid off, and I would soon have my first waiting gig in a fast-paced restaurant with over eight hundred menu items that catered to an extremely picky, if not crabby, clientele.

My "day job" or I should say my "graveyard job" of serving all of the drunks and undesirables of the LA nightlife scene was now on the fast track. My acting career was also moving along as I was studying acting at not one, but two of LA's most prestigious acting studios, thanks to a referral from Phyllis Carlyle's office (producer of the movies *Seven* and *The Accidental Tourists*). I, like many before me and I am sure many after me, have learned and will learn, there is a fine line between being persistent and being a royal pain in the ass. My whole strategy to launch my acting career revolved around pestering people so much that they would have to cast me in something in order to shut me up. In hindsight, this was probably not the most effective way to win over insiders, especially, when a role called for a short, black, elderly woman in her eighties and I was a tall, Caucasian man in my twenties. Hey, but you never know, they could see the role in a whole different light. Anyway, it didn't matter. Even though Phyllis Carlyle's office stopped taking my phone calls, I was chasing the golden carrot with vigor.

Meanwhile, back at the deli, the only carrot I was even remotely close to catching were the four and only four miniscule carrots I was permitted to put in the matzo ball soup. You see, we had a general manager who didn't really know much about running a restaurant, but she sure knew how to monitor the various menu items we assembled in the food-prep areas. She would pick us off one by one for some sort of infraction as we tried to leave the kitchen. I will call her Gus because she was big and mean and could beat most men in arm wrestling. She also dressed like a guy and from behind (or, for that matter, the front) looked like one. A half-senile, elderly Jewish man stopped her one day with an "Excuse me, sir." When he realized his mistake, he retracted his statement with, "Oh, I'm sorry," to which she replied in a deep voice, "It's all right." Gus was a no-nonsense brute who spoke in a very condescending tone.

I know it's probably hard to believe that a Jewish deli would hire someone so fanatical about portion control, but this was indeed the case. Yet in the same breath, the sandwiches were stacked so high that you would have to step on them to squash them down enough to fit them in your mouth. But I am not here to judge; I am just here to report the facts. Countless times I was stopped by the floor Nazi for putting too many carrots in the soup, slicing up pita bread instead of serving it whole, piling too much ice cream on top of a sundae, serving too much dressing with a salad, not carrying a drink on a tray, etc., etc., etc. My moment in the sun finally came one day when Gus was scrutinizing a bowl of matzo ball soup that I was preparing in the soup station. "Do you know the meaning of three to four pieces of chicken?" she asked. "Is that a philosophical question?" I smugly replied. But because Gus was referring to the maximum number of three to four pieces of chicken that we were permitted to put in the matzo ball soup, I received a blank stare as if she was deciding whether to slap or strangle me. Then, after a brief uncomfortable stare down, I spun around and proceeded towards my table with their enormous bowl of doughy ball soup, which, by the way, was large enough to hold the whole Olympic swim team. Oddly enough, Gus never questioned my portion amounts again.

My first two years chasing the Hollywood dream were spent searching for the perfect agent. You know, the one who was going to believe in me even if it meant throwing himself in front of a bus or putting his own life on the line to get my career on the fast track, the one who would spend countless hours hounding Tarantino just to get me in for an audition, and naturally, the one who didn't exist. No agent was too big to say no. I went for them all ... William Morris, ICM, and CAA. It didn't matter that my only acting experience was from a second grade recital where I played the role of the oven in *The Gingerbread Man*. I had balls and something to say to the world, and nothing was going to stop me.

The process of submitting yourself to an agent goes something like this ... First, you spend your whole week's slave-labor earnings paying for your headshots. Then you spend your next month's rent buying envelopes, copies of your headshot, and a trusty agent book. Then you steal a shopping cart from the local grocery store to wheel your two hundred-plus headshots to the post office where the guy behind the counter wants to pull out a shotgun and shoot you because you are looking at him as if you are going to be the next big thing in the cinema and he should be honored to be in your presence. In the meantime, he's the one who has to wheel your truckload of trash, along with the thousands of other envelopes he's carted off by forty other saps just like you, that in his opinion, are going right to the shredding machine anyway, to the mailroom. But, away you go from the post office, and away the envelopes go to their desired destinations. Then you sit by your phone all week and wait for the phone to ring. If you're lucky, one, maybe two, agents will call. But not the week you spent sitting by the phone or checking your voicemail every ten minutes. It'll come right before you are about to hang yourself from the shower rod in your rundown apartment.

As the phone rings, you decide to unwrap the cord from around your neck and take the call. It's a personal assistant who offers you a five-minute time slot with the agent whose trainee accidentally threw your picture in the yes pile. You calmly book the appointment, set down the receiver, and then start bouncing off the walls because you think someone finally sees your talent in an eight-by-ten photograph. You call your friends, share your excitement with your acting class, and write yourself a postdated check for a million dollars. You rack up more credit-card debt buying a new outfit for yourself and just for the hell of it throw in a pack of new tube socks to replace all of the old, crusty ones with holes in the toes filling up your drawer. You take off work the day before your big agent meeting so you can get a good night's rest. But unfortunately, the night before your big meeting, you're so excited that you can't fall asleep.

You finally crash two hours before you need to wake up. When your alarm does go off after a couple of hours of tossing and turning, you spring out of bed in fear that you've overslept. You take a nice warm shower until your eyelids finally unglue themselves open. You put on your new outfit and practice introducing yourself to yourself in the mirror. On your way to the meeting, you stop by Starbucks to pep up with a triple red eye. You go to the address scribbled down on your overdue gas bill, but there's no building there. You realize you're on North Whatever Street and you need to be on South Whatever Street. Now you're running late and dripping with sweat from your overdose on caffeine. You finally get to your destination, and it appears they've rented out some hole-in-the-wall theatre in a sketchy part of town. There is a line of ten people waiting outside who look exactly like you. One is even wearing the very same outfit as you. You park your car, walk past the line, and attempt to enter the building. As you open the door, you can't see a thing because it's dark inside and your eyes haven't adjusted to the lack of light yet, but you hear a "Close that door; we'll get you when we're ready."

At this point, you realize nothing is going right so you try to strike up a conversation with anyone outside who will listen, minus the guy who's wearing the same outfit as you. Finally, after you've lost ten pounds of water weight from leaning up against the hot brick building you are exhaustively waiting to get into, your name is called. You enter the theatre and see the outline of a figure that looks like a melting tarantula. You realize it's the agent. You try to introduce yourself, but she's already had a long day, and you better do something just short of walking on water, or else she is going to clearly instruct you to never approach her again for representation because if you do she will file a restraining order.

It turns out she has a piece of paper in her hand, and after just a few seconds of your boring biography, she wants to hear you cold read. She hands you the paper with the most idiotic thing ever written by a human being on it and asks you to quickly look it over and then hit your mark. You ramble through the piece the first time, and you can tell she's not feeling it. She gives you an instruction like, "Give me more energy," which feels impossible because of (a) the moronic text you're reading and (b) the fact that you're trembling like a junkie due to your overdose on caffeine. But, you line up again and like someone out of a Crazy Eddie commercial start delivering the most exciting pitch for a double cheeseburger the world has ever seen. You're flying high, and your endorphins are rushing when without rhyme or reason you forget your next line. You look down at the paper, which seems to be written in Arabic. You can't find the line you need, and it feels as if someone has just let the air out of the room. The agent says not to worry about it and promptly thanks you for your time.

You exit the theatre mumbling to yourself and speed past the line of people waiting to go inside. You then spend the rest of your car ride home reciting the one line out loud to yourself that you flubbed in the audition. This, in turn, draws odd looks from the people sitting next to you at a traffic light, whom you don't even notice. When you finally get home, you throw yourself down on your bed. You sleep for the next twenty-four hours straight, and when you eventually awake from your depression, you still hold out hope that maybe she will call. A week or two go by, and the only feedback you get is the 30 percent or so returned headshot submissions that didn't make it to the addressee. You sit down and attempt to figure out the various reasons why your stunning glossy was sent back. These explanations include everything from the addressee leaving the business (probably for such criminal acts as fraud and embezzlement) to agents escaping the hordes of mail they receive on a daily basis by moving to an undisclosed location. So you go back to your trusty agent book and mark down which agents moved and are no longer located at the address listed in your book. You then call Samuel French bookstore every day to find out when next month's updated agent handbook is due for release. And so the process continues.

When the mail-in submission approach doesn't get you the results you are looking for, there is always the good old agent workshop. In any other occupation, this sort of arrangement would be considered highly unethical, not to mention illegal. That is, paying someone to consider you for employment, but not in Hollyweird. It seems that not only is paying someone to interview you, who has no interest in hiring you or representing you, the norm; it also is standard operating procedure. I mean, how else are these heavyweights of the midway supposed to pay for their second mortgages and their poodle's grooming appointments? In theory, these workshops are supposed to be an actor's best friend because the actor picks the material that he/she is most suited for. This would be fine and dandy if every actor had some sort of grip on reality and understood the type of roles he/she might be cast in. Couple that with the fact that most of the agents who attend these highway robberies have their slates filled for years to come and you have the perfect Saturday afternoon. So, you may ask, how do I know that most of the agents have their slates filled for years to come? Ancient Chinese Secret.

Okay, I'll tell you.

I, being the rambunctious soul that I am, felt disenfranchised after spending hundreds of dollars without receiving even one follow-up phone call to say, "No way in hell." I felt I was emitting true emotion when I kicked a chair through a window, and I wanted to know why no one appreciated my "work." So the following week, I went down the list of agents who attended my academy-award-winning showcase. I got no further than the first agent on the list when I encountered my first problem. When I called this agent's office, I was told that the agent I was trying to contact was busy and that he wouldn't speak to me if I wasn't a client. I went on to explain that I was attempting to become a client. That's when the person on the other end of the phone treated me as if I were a second-class citizen. I took down his name and made him aware of his error in judgment. I went on to write him a letter informing him that he and his agency had just missed their golden ticket and that his greatest accomplishment in life would be telling his grandchildren how he shot down Jozef Rothstein. When the agent I auditioned for caught wind of this letter, he immediately contacted the organization (TVI) that had set up the workshop and asked them, "What in the hell does he think he is doing?" and "Who the hell does he think he is?" My response to TVI was that I was only kidding. When the smoke finally settled, one of my key contacts at this "actor-friendly workshop service" told me that I WAS someone that particular agent might have signed a few years down the road when something opened up, but ... When something opened up!? Why was the agency even at the workshop to begin with if there were no spots available on their slate? Of course, now that I had done what I had done, there was no way in hell this agency, which no longer exists anyway, was going to sign me. Oh well, I guess we both lost out on that one.

The Price of Fame (and the Pastrami)

My first week of training at the deli was the equivalent of a military boot camp for food-service workers. My indoctrination into the way of the matzo ball included tagging along with a stout, brooding woman who had over twenty years of emotional deli battle scars and who ended every other sentence with "I am going to kick your ass." I am pretty sure she also delivered at least one of her babies sideways, but you didn't hear that from me. My training included written and oral tests, the managing of several tables at a time (which was especially difficult for me since I had never waited tables before), and physical adjustments such as, "No, you take the ice cream scoop and you drive it in there!" She highly recommended the foccacia sandwich for my employee meal and warned me that if I failed to pass the final exam, the whole process would start all over again. I felt more pressure taking my final deli exam than I did my quantum physics exam during my most stressful semester in college. I mean, come on, I needed this job as a launching pad to superstardom. Considering the fact that the only food service experience I had prior to this job was setting beer nuts on a counter, I had my work cut out for me.

Training was brutal, but I was told I would see a countless number of celebrities (as if that was some sort of incentive), and I was certain that, once I got through this rite of passage and broke free from my oppressor, I would be well on my way to peace and prosperity. It turns out the training phase of this coercion was simply a warm-up to what was in store for me next. The only bright spot in my whole first week of initiation was actually waiting on someone that I had idolized as a kid.

The problem was I didn't recognize him without his makeup. And no, it wasn't Richard Simmons. It was none other than the man who would pass around a cup for everyone to spit in so he could drink it himself, Mr. Alice Cooper. I remember wanting to see his show as a kid but being told by my father that I wasn't allowed to go because Mr. Cooper was planning on sacrificing young children from the audience as part of his act. Once these mental wounds healed and I began interacting with other children again, I took a renewed interest in his music. It's probably a good thing that I didn't recognize Mr. Cooper until I ran his credit card and read the name Alice Cooper on the bottom of it because I probably would have spilled coffee all over his lap. It must have been a strange experience for an aging rock star to look up and spot a grown man, wearing a name-tag, ogling him like a lost puppy dog. But hey, what can I say? He performed the childhood anthem that blared from our school buses once a year, "School's Out for the Summer."

One reason why I may not have recognized Mr. Cooper as the devil himself was because of his polite and gentle nature, which was in harsh conflict with his on-stage persona. In short, he was a breeze to wait on and was very courteous. When he wrote, "No More Mr. Nice Guy," he was completely full of shit. And if you don't believe me, "You Can Go to Hell." He was a 180-degree turnaround from the rest of the hawkish clientele who didn't care if it was my first day or my ten-thousandth day on the job; they were going to make it my last if they could.

This became a recurring theme throughout my deli career. I began to realize that most of these spoiled ingrates had no problem flipping out on me for one of three reasons. Either (a) these adult babies had already been yelling at their assistants all day long, and I was just one more person in a long line of saps who, in their eyes, was begging for one of their tongue lashings; (b) they were the assistants getting hollered at all day long, and now these office whipping boys needed someone else to wail on; or (c) I happened to stumble upon a deal Mr. Inferiority Complex had been working on for the past ten years of his miserable life, and he wasn't about to let some clown who didn't know the difference between corn beef and pastrami screw it up for him.

I miraculously passed my written final deli exam, thanks to a disgruntled waiter who had a slow section and got tired of me slamming my pencil down on the table. With his years of knowledge and my desire to remove the previous week's torment from my life for good, we were able to complete the rest of the test in less than five minutes, and he was able to stop the heavy sighs and other annoying sounds emanating from me. It was a win-win for both of us. I wanted to frame a copy of this lifetime achievement award on my refrigerator, but under no circumstances was a copy of "The Test" to leave the building.

After barely escaping the raging and impatient customers of my first week, I was now ready to fly solo. I soon came to realize that I had been very sheltered during my first week of training because if there ever was a problem or I didn't know the answer to a question, my potato pancake mentor was always there to bail me out. I was also surrounded by the best cooks and servers the restaurant had to offer. The managers also left me alone because they figured if I screwed anything up the person responsible for my tutelage would straighten my sorry ass out. But now, my world was about to change. I was trading in my security blanket for a swift kick in the pants. One of the first things that I began to notice when entering the lions' den of the graveyard shift was how glaringly red the restaurant was. From the vinyl booths to the carpet on the floor to the paint on the walls, everything was bright red, including the large, bright red, deli store emblem. In scientific studies, the color red is known to elicit anger. I truly believe this color scheme was chosen on purpose in order to rile up the customers. The draw of the restaurant was now coming into view. It was a place for people to complain about everything from the prices of the sandwiches to the quality of service they received, and it gave them a place to vent their life's frustrations on you. Besides the blazingly red interior, many other factors encouraged hostile reactions from our patrons. I'll go ahead and take the liberty of naming a few. These examples are by no means meant to be a complete list as there is not a library in the world large enough to hold all of that information. The following is being used for illustrative purposes only in order to show, well, how screwed up this place was.

One of the first problem areas that come to mind was the layout of the joint. The pizza kitchen was in the back of the building, the deli was on one side of the building, the kitchen was at the center of the building, and the salad area was on the opposite side of the deli. The soup/sundae station was located in an entirely different area from all of the other stations altogether. It was not uncommon to need three of yourself to put one order together. The soda fountain was across the restaurant from the bar, and the milk machine was across the restaurant from the soda fountain. To make a Brooklyn egg cream you would have to sprint to the milk machine, side shuffle to the soda fountain, and then enter into a series of back handsprings just to get to the sundae area for the syrup. On a busy night, this turned into a free-for-all, and somebody was always wearing something chocolaty on his wrinkled black and whites.

The second problem was the fact that none of the finished dishes had a ticket showing what belonged to whom. I'd have to write a whole separate book to detail the bloody battles that took place when one of ten servers on the floor mistakenly took a part of someone else's order as part of his own. A typical scenario would work like this. Server 1 would see most of his order up. He would ignore the type of burger he was grabbing from the window and would erroneously snap up burger A, which just so happened to be lying next to the rest of his order. He would put it on his tray along with his other items, and away he'd go. Then Server 2 would enter the kitchen and realize that her order was up, minus burger A. She would scream at the cooks about how she needed burger A, not burger B, and would then insist that they made the wrong one. The lead cook would have to step away from the avalanche of tickets spewing from the printer to figure out what in the hell just happened. The cooks would quickly decide that the fastest thing to do would be to turn burger B into burger A. Server 2 would then leave with a replica of burger A as Server 1 re-entered the kitchen with a bite out of burger A, which he accidentally took. He'd spend a few seconds looking for burger B then sheepishly tell the cooks he needed burger

B, which had now been turned into burger A. The cook would flip out on Server 1, and as burger B was being freshly prepared, the customer would flip out on the manager because burger B was now taking way too long and everybody at the table had eaten their dinner and he hadn't even received his crummy burger yet. The manager would in turn yell at Server 1 who initially took burger A, and Server 1 would in turn yell at Server 2 for taking the replica of burger A, which was originally his burger B. Server 2 would then direct her anger back at Server 1 who took the wrong burger (burger A) to begin with, and the restaurant would grow redder and redder and redder as the night went on.

The third problem was the location of the fixings for all of the different menu items. These accompaniments were placed in either completely opposite areas from the drop-off zone of the host dish or in very hard-to-reach places. For instance, a hamburger required coleslaw. The hamburger came up on the kitchen line, and the coleslaw came from the deli area. The salad dressings were stored in a refrigerator below the kitchen line on a shelf that was just inches above the ground. This refrigerator was always jam-packed with things you didn't need. To get a container of Cajun dressing, you would have to remove a majority of the useless items blocking your way just to get a scoop of this rarely used item. Then, if you had an accompanying soup to go with the order, you would have to travel to the soup station located in another far-away land. Once you finally got there, you'd sometimes forget that your customer wanted toast instead of the standard bagel chips (which were located in the soup station and typically garnished all soups), so you'd have to run all the way back to the kitchen after making the soup to start toasting the bread. In the meantime, the customer at the table was wondering if you'd gone to New Orleans for his Cajun chicken salad. The whole process was essentially the equivalent of a monkey trying to hump a football.

The blintzes required jelly, apple sauce, and sour cream, all of which had to be scooped from individual containers. As a result of bad karma or the fact that I must have been a serial killer in my past life and was serving my sentence in hell, we would be out of at least one of those items. So, I'd have to run to the back of the building to the walk-in cooler where I'd have to shoulder press a fifty-pound bin of bread pudding off a five-gallon sour-cream container in order to scoop out a small portion of sour cream into a soufflé cup before either (a) my muscles gave out or (b) someone else took one of my food items off the line as part of their order. Other times, I'd do a mad dash to the pizza kitchen in the back of the building to pick up a pizza. Upon returning, I'd weave through some prep guys, then hightail it to the dishwashing area where I'd have to hurdle over a mountain of pots and pans and a bag of used towels in order to initiate a scavenger hunt through a myriad of plastic bins in order to unearth a pizza spatula. Then I'd lay out a few ovals, assemble the platters and—bam the fourth problem … the bus boys.

God love 'em. They come to America with a dream and send most of their hard-earned money back to their wives and five kids still living in Mexico. They are very nice people and for the most part laugh at anything you say, even when you're not trying to be funny. They are always happy to see you and go out of their way to joke with you the second you walk in the door. Now for their downside. They are not the most self-motivated people on the planet. They like to hang out in groups, usually by the back dumpster where they smoke *mota*, or for the non-Spanish speaking readers, pot. Then, when you really need something, they miraculously can't speak English or Spanish. No matter how many years of kitchen Spanglish you study, they are the only south-of-the-border employees who will never understand a word you are saying. For my case in point, I would like to introduce you to Subject A. I will call him Jose G. because nine out of every ten bus boys in Los Angeles went by the name of Juan or Jose.

Jose G. was one of the most interesting stewards of the dish-removal occupation I had ever encountered. He didn't respond to you in words but rather in grunts and moans, much like Scooby-Doo. He always played the same joke on you by asking you for twenty dollars at the end of the night when he knew his tip, at maximum, would be twelve to fifteen. Having a conversation with Jose G. was always strangely fascinating because he would make the most obscure observations. One day, with a fluent Spanish speaking server on hand to decipher his ramblings, Jose G. started commenting on a baseball game that was playing out on one of our restaurant's many TVs. Until this day, the translation is still a little murky, but it had something to do with the pitcher digging a large hole in the pitcher's mound as if he was installing in a swimming pool (I think) to which he laughed hysterically. I can't even begin to tell you the multiple times I would send Jose G. on a task that would end up going completely awry. And as frustrating as this was on a busy night, I couldn't help but watch in amusement as Jose G. wandered around the restaurant aimlessly while trying to complete a request for one of my now infuriated customers.

There were so many memorable Jose G. experiences it's hard to pick just one. For starters, I'd spend countless hours explaining the table numbers to him during our downtimes. During these slow spells, I would quiz him on his newfound restaurant knowledge, and to my surprise, he would generally match all of the table numbers with their respective locations. I would say, "Where is table twenty?" And he would walk over to the table and say "Uh … *aqui*." Then, as a reward, I would throw him a bone and pat him on the head. His new, self-assured confidence made me feel that if I was ever in a pinch on any given night he would at least be able to drop something off to a table. Only, of course, after spinning him around, pointing him in a general direction, and then kicking him in the ass. It wouldn't be long until Jose G. would get his opportunity to perform, under live bullets, his understanding of table numerology.

On one particular busy evening, I asked Jose G. to deliver a glass of ice to table twenty-three, which I also pointed to and said, "*A la dos hombres* (to the two men)." I then handed him the glass of ice, and away he went. I took a second to make sure he was at least heading in the right direction. Of course, when I went out to my section, one of the men at the table emphatically waved me over and, with his face as bright as the red interior, roared, "Where's my ice?" Upon searching for the culprit in this foiled operation, I took notice that halfway across the restaurant, in another section, on a large party's table was the glass of ice I ever so gently placed in Jose G.'s hands. I gasped in disbelief at the *vaso con ielo*, or glass of ice, that was sitting on the edge of the table like an unwanted stepchild. When I picked up the ielo, a woman from the group softly remarked, "I was wondering why he brought that to us."

Then there was the time I was leaving the kitchen with an oval full of food while another server, Mike, was gathering his prepared dishes for a large party. When I felt someone behind me after entering the floor, I spun around to notice Jose G. hurriedly rushing to catch up to me with one of Mike's trays. I shook my head no and pointed for him to go back into the kitchen. I assumed he took this order but when I arrived at my table, Jose G. was standing behind me with the tray of food. Again, I said, "No, it's not mine." I had to go to another table to pick up an empty glass for a refill. He followed me again still offering Mike's vittles. This time I said even more sternly, "NO," and something like, "Dude, you are starting to creep me out." I looked over to the kitchen where I saw Mike standing in the entryway with a puzzled look on his face. I pointed at Mike, and when Jose G. looked, I quickly looped around the server station in an effort to shake him. Jose G. overrode this instruction and quickly closed the gap and converged on me once again with the oval full of grub. At that point, I had no other choice but to lead Jose G. back to the kitchen where Mike was waiting in the wings to hopefully intercept my stalker. In hindsight, I think it was the actual physical process of returning Jose G. to the kitchen that unlocked the never-ending loop in his brain. After Mike's tray returned from its psychotic joyride, Mike later confessed to me that he couldn't figure out for the life of him why Jose G. took off with his assembled platters after he gave Jose G. the verbal warnings of "*Alto* (stop)" and "No! Wait … get back here … that's mine!"

The last and maybe most memorable Jose G. moment came when he was assisting me at a table and I made the grave mistake of asking him to bring me a side of coleslaw. I could tell from his deep blank stare that my words were not registering. After checking his vitals signs and then undertaking a massive campaign to explain to him what coleslaw was, which included pointing out the side dish on another customers plate and having a women at the table who spoke fluent Spanish describe it to him, Jose G. began his mission back to the kitchen. When he returned, however, he had in his possession a giant side of mayonnaise. This stumped the table, especially the woman who spoke fluent Spanish. After a few seconds of listening to the woman reassure her friends that she actually did speak fluent Spanish, I told him, "No!"

and ripped the mayonnaise from his hands. I then stormed back to the kitchen. On my way back out of the kitchen, I passed Jose G. and once again showed him what coleslaw actually looked like. Then I told him in Spanish, "*Necesito este*," or "I need this." I dropped the coleslaw off to the woman who requested it and made sure everyone had what they needed. Since everyone was content for the moment, I seized the opportunity to check up on my other tables.

When I returned a few minutes later to make sure their food was prepared correctly and that everything tasted okay, Jose G. appeared again, this time out of the blue, with another jumbo side of mayonnaise. I watched in pure awe as he made his way over to the woman who had ordered the coleslaw. As she tried to explain to him that she didn't need the mayonnaise, the table was screaming with laughter. Jose G. was overwhelmed with this new information and was frozen like a deer in headlights. I instructed him to put down the mayonnaise and thanked him for his effort, which drew even more cackles from the group. I don't know if it was due to the sheer entertainment value of the incident or if the group actually took pity on what I had to go through working with this imbecile, but I received a 25-percent tip, and Jose G. finally got his twenty-dollar tip out at the end of a very busy night. After Jose G. finally received the tip he'd been clamoring for for so long, he began upping the ante by jokingly asking for one hundred dollars, or *ciento,* at the end of every shift. This, of course, was followed by his usual laugh. My response each time he said this was, "*Cuando las vacas vuelen,*" or "When cows fly," to which he would respond "*Que?*"

Okay, back to the scenario where I am leaving the kitchen with a tray of food and I desperately need a bus boy. Even though these masters of the midway were required in Article 1 Section 3 of the Deli Employee Handbook under the bus boy job description to carry all food trays for servers to their respective tables, finding one of these underachievers in your time of need was next to impossible. Typically, one would appear roughly 33 percent of the time. I can't tell you how many times I looked out into a bus-boy-free zone where not one of these key ingredients to the service experience was to be found. This would put me in the precarious position of leaving the kitchen with two large ovals, one on each shoulder. And when I finally got to the desired table with some of the food still on the plates, I would have to ask an elderly woman to help me lower one of the trays before I dumped it on her granddaughter. My frustration with these guys never ceased to amaze me, but it also got me into trouble.

One such instance came on a day when I specifically remember having a five-minute conversation, entirely in English, with our lead bus boy, Juan. About an hour later, I was in the weeds in a very busy section when Juan nonchalantly breezed by me. I was in desperate need of some help so I urgently asked him for a bottle of ketchup. Miraculously, the English Juan spoke an hour ago vanished into thin air. He also pretended to act as if he had suddenly lost his hearing and went scampering off to his favorite rest area under a TV set, leaving me with a sudden rise in blood pressure. I jokingly turned to my table to avoid breaking down in tears and said, "It's funny how he speaks perfect English until you need something." This attempt at humor went over like a lead balloon, and the man who did all of the ordering for the group glared at me with disdain. He barely said another word to me throughout the duration of their meal. Unsurprisingly, he left me a lousy tip.

Later that evening, a manager pulled me aside and told me the man complained to him. He was upset because he was with a group of Spanish guys who couldn't speak English, and he found my comment very insulting. How he made the connection between someone who could speak perfect English but suddenly forgot to his situation where his friends maybe wanted to speak English but couldn't amazes me to this day. But it affirms my earlier point in this book that these customers would try to get you fired just because it made them feel important. I am further convinced that these very same people should not be allowed out in public. These agitators would try to ruin your life just to get their rocks off on your misfortune, and the previous example proves that this is not a hypothesis but a concrete theory.

Let's keep my list of gripes rolling by entering into the next castrating element of this one-star dining establishment, the Rosanna, Rosanna Danna Principle, which states, "It's always something!" This covers everything from the never-ending list of supplies the restaurant was always out of when you really needed something to the most illogical and impossible demands made by our deli's management team. Since I am going to devote at least an entire page to the latter, let's take a closer look at "what we were out of and why."

I would say the hub of the restaurant's dysfunction started with one word … "Harry." Harry was so old he was in Moses's yearbook. He had the personality of a lump of coal and was so crotchety he made Ebenezer Scrooge look like Jay Leno. This one man had the sole responsibility of ordering goods for the entire restaurant and for anticipating its needs. Hardly a position for a person who got the job because he knew the owner's great-grandfather and who spent his entire two-hour shift looking up the skirts of young girls. With Harry at the helm, it was not uncommon to run out of turkey on Thanksgiving Day yet have an over abundance of fried fish sticks on that very same day or to receive ten pallets of to-go boxes when we were, and remained to be, completely out of straws. Necessities like ketchup would be gone for most of the week, and things, like plates to serve the food on, would be completely out of stock.

But let's not put all the blame on Harry when there was plenty of blame to go around. Sometimes, I didn't even know whom to blame, but I knew it was pretty damn hard to serve a soup or a drink when there weren't any bowls or glasses to put them in. Then when you finally did find soup bowls and you thought you were in the clear … bam, we were out of soup spoons. This type of problem usually reeked of ineptitude from none other than the dishwashing department. What made this scenario even more infuriating was when you'd walk back to the dishwashing area and the dishwashers were squirting each other with water or eating a mistake off the line while, in the meantime, they were surrounded by a mountain of dirty dishes. Or worse yet, you'd walk back to see what in the hell was going on back there, and nobody was even around. This was especially stroke-inducing during the middle of a rush.

Again, it would be appropriate to mention the manager's role in all of this hilarity and high jinks, but I will address that shortly. Of course, the customer doesn't understand any of this; he just wants his tongue sandwich. But, that takes me to my next problem area … the customer.

Sure, some, if not slightly over half of the customers were complete angels—generous, understanding, and polite. If these customers were my only concern, I would have had the greatest job in the world. Unfortunately, for me and everyone else in the profession, this was not the case. Some very common idiosyncrasies will be pointed out, and then some glaring examples of how not to treat others as thou wouldst not want to be treated thyself will be made self-evident. Let's begin with one general rule. Waiters do not drop down from the ceiling to your table just because you are ready to order. This rule also applies to those who sit at the counter. There is this concept of "other people," and sitting at the counter does not grant you a special license to start cackling like a jackass just because you want to order. And for God's sake, if you walk into a super-busy restaurant, please do not tell your waiter that you are in a hurry and need to put your order in because you are trying to catch a movie that starts in fifteen minutes. Simply go to McDonalds.

While we are on the subject of the counter, why is it that you, and you know who you are, choose to sit in the seat with the dirty dishes in front of it when the rest of the counter is completely clear. Is it because you figure that seat is warm or that particular area has seen some recent activity lately and will mean faster service so you can catch your movie that starts in fifteen minutes? Or do you simply enjoy watching other people slave in front of you, working to create order in your otherwise disorderly world? Dirty dishes are like some sort of magnet that draws in the socially unrefined. It is now completely obvious to me that most people really do need the help of a professional to lead them to a clean table. By "professional," I meant "host." Why, what did you think I meant? Anyway, waiting tables in this establishment was basically an underpaid and underappreciated baby-sitting job. People whining, "We're hungry, we want our food, we want this seat not that seat, I spilled my milk, I don't like this, my table's dirty, you're ignoring me, listen to how funny I am …," Jesus Christmas, just sit down, shut up, and eat. And when you are done with that … LEAVE.

Now for some prized moments in customer service. I will call Exhibit A Frank and Sue. This mother-and-son team had a notorious reputation around town and put the fear of God into those in the restaurant business. On the exterior, this duo had the makings of two close family acquaintances you would invite over for Christmas dinner, but on the inside, these two next of kin were pure evil. I was introduced to them by a very vile co-worker named Elizabeth. More on Elizabeth later, but because of Elizabeth's lazy nature and her mean, vindictive spirit, with a smile as wide as Texas, Elizabeth walked Frank and Sue to my section after proudly announcing to me that she was giving me a table. She returned after seating them and told me they were very nice and that she used to wait on them herself. Oh, how sweet. Then she began laughing when she told me that she told them they would like me much better. Great. What was she up to? She then informed me that they could be "a little demanding" but tipped very well and were, once again, "really nice." But, something seemed a little off. Anyway, it didn't matter. I convinced myself that I was in LA to succeed in the entertainment business no matter what, and no one, especially some seventy-something-year-old woman and her momma's-boy son were going to ruin it for me, so I decided to step up to the challenge.

My initial impression of them was a pleasant one as I felt a warm glow emanating from their table. They assured me they were in no hurry and that I could take my time bringing them their order. This seemed fair enough as I was very busy. After I brought them their fruit punch and diet coke as per their request, they were ready to order their starter, a chopped salad, which they intended to share. They told me they wanted extra garbanzo beans, extra corn, extra scallions, extra ranch dressing and extra tomatoes all to be put in little side cups with easy cheese on the salad and an extra bowl so they could split it. Okay, now the order was becoming a little presumptuous, but I figured once I entered it into the computer, it would be all downhill from there. This assumption turned out to be a huge miscalculation.

When I returned with their specialty salad, there weren't enough garbanzo beans, and there was too much cheese. "Should I take it back?" I asked, to which Frank politely replied, "If you don't mind." When I returned with the corrected salad, Frank said, "It looks good," but they just needed some extra dressing and a few more napkins. Frank was now well on his way to becoming a royal pain in the ass so I ran off to do a couple of other things before I tended to his latest task. When I got back with Frank's most recent request, in the most courteous way possible, Frank asked me for more fruit punch. I quickly refilled his drink and returned to find their menus folded. They were now ready to order. "We would both like the chicken parmesan platters, but make sure they are hot," Frank insisted. And I guess what he meant by "hot" was "cook them until they reach the core temperature of the sun." It appeared the old lady's taste buds no longer gauged thermal gradations and only the results of nuclear fusion registered as warm on her palate because even though I picked up their entrees directly from the line immediately following their completion they were still not hot enough.

I became aware of this fact when out of the corner of my eye I observed the ancient fossil tasting her chicken and then abruptly shaking her head no. After Frank leaned down to sample his, he waved me over in the most courteous way possible and asked me to "nuke" their platters. Since we only had one microwave, this running of the chickens entailed me taking the entrees back to the soup station where I battled for supremacy on the re-heating mechanism. I'd heat up one dish and then run it back to the table before any air had a chance to touch it, all while leaving the other plate smoldering in the microwave. Over time, no matter how scalding hot these dishes came out to their table or how much I zapped them before I served them, they were never hot enough. The only thing that seemed to satisfy these two inbreeds was when I had to wear oven mitts to deliver their plates to their table. And the thing that over time really pissed me off about this whole ridiculous process was the amount of time it took for them to eat their platters once they received them. Week in and week out, they would literally take over an hour and a half to nibble on their recurring entrées even though at least fifteen minutes into their whole annoying routine their meals had to be ice cold.

After the first two or three weeks of their circus act, I was able to overlook this minor detail, but after a month or two of these two traipsing in every Thursday night, requesting me and only me as their waiter and then pulling this same stunt over and over again, I began seething with anger. After another couple of months of this nonsense, I was bringing their lunacy home with me where it would linger in my psyche for two to three days. Yes, they would tip me eight to ten dollars on a forty-dollar check, but they were starting to appear in my dreams, and I was waking up from my sleep in a cold sweat. I knew this was self-destructive so I started challenging myself to see if, for just one time, I could serve them their meal without any glitches. When this failed, I thought I'd try to kill them with kindness. So much kindness they would puke up their chicken parmesans. Then I tried being rude. They told me they wanted to make me a Democrat, and I told them Richard Nixon and Ronald Reagan were my childhood heroes. No matter what I did to counter these two dimwits, I could not slip them. I started dreading coming into work on Thursdays. When I switched shifts, they would leave and come back on a night when I was working. These two were haunting me like the Ghost of Christmas Past and I knew I had to do something before I sawed them into little pieces and put them in their chopped salad.

I now had some very difficult questions to ask myself. As I searched deep inside, was I finding that, after just two years of pursuing acting in LA, Hollywood was already starting to get the best of me? Could I not even handle this aging predecessor and her coddled son? Then a realization! For my own survival and for the sustenance of my dream, I had to pawn these two deviants off on someone else. But who would be gullible enough and who did I despise badly enough to pass these two devil's spawns off onto? It didn't matter. I just wanted to get through a Thursday shift that entailed someone else toiling over these two despots. I will always remember that final Thursday as "The Last Supper," and the lucky winner of these two ingrates was the first person I laid eyes upon who looked like he wasn't busy. It just so happened to be a new guy, Andy, who was as smart as a box of hammers and who would have no problem telling these two ass wipes where to go if they pushed him far enough. He was perfect!! I approached him and asked him to do me a huge favor in which he agreed. His section was slow, and he just wanted to make some extra money. Plus, I explained to him how I had waited on these two crackpots for over a year and how I just couldn't stand them any more. He laughed and said no problem.

The next phase of "Operation Dump These Two Retards Off on Someone Else" was informing my manager of my intentions. I couldn't believe his reaction when he simply replied, "I don't care what you do, as long as they get a waiter." What? You mean I could have done this a year and a half ago? As sweeping as this realization was, I didn't want it to rattle me because I could see the light at the end of the tunnel. The last thing I needed to do in order to set my plan in motion was to inform the host that these two still joined by an umbilical cord were to be placed in Andy's section, not mine. The host placed the unsuspecting croakers in one of Andy's booths, and presto, the plan was set in motion. I'll never forget the knot that formed in my stomach when I saw the panicked look in Frank's eyes as Andy approached their table. I remember Frank explaining to Andy with every ounce of energy in his body how he wanted me as their waiter. To Andy's credit, he was able to hold off the firestorm for a good twenty seconds or so before he turned around, looked at me, and with a simple gesture of his hand, asked me to fill his spot. I shook my head no and wanted to run through the wall directly behind me and out onto Ventura Boulevard where I would hopefully get run over by a tractor trailer. But in order to keep my job, I came to the more rational conclusion that the best thing to do would be to explain my sudden about face directly to Frank and Sue. So, I walked up to their table and said, "Listen, I really like you guys a lot, but I just can't wait on you any longer." The reality of this statement all but dislocated their jaws. As I walked away from their table, a shell-shocked Frank jumped up and pursued me while badgering me for answers. He pleaded. He grew angry. He teared up. He kept following me … demanding that I tell him what was going on. And like a Disney character at the end of his shift who must beeline for the underground tunnel to escape the mauling children, I fled to the kitchen to break away from this raving lunatic.

I implored a couple of my fellow servers to watch my tables for a few minutes while I sat in the walk-in cooler praying to God this man would just return home and settle for the milk from his mother's tit for the evening. Or if not that, at least learn to accept Andy as their new indentured servant. When I finally felt safe enough to come out of the refrigeration unit, and after developing a slight chill, I returned to the floor. To my relief, Frank was gone. I looked around and nothing. As I grew braver, I once again built up enough courage to walk over to where the Manson family was sitting. They were nowhere to be found. When Andy spotted me from across the restaurant, he was grinning from ear to ear. As he made his way over to me to fill me in on the events that had transpired during my sit-in, he approached in what seemed like slow motion. As I looked over at the manager in the front of the restaurant who was positioned like a royal guard, defending 10 Downing Street, something felt very wrong, and a sudden panic rushed over me.

Then, with an explosive burst, the front door swung open, and Frank once again emerged. Like Jason Voorhees from the *Friday the 13th* movies, Frank just wouldn't die. The manager that night, Bill, stepped in front of this hound from hell and confronted him with discourse. Bill, who was a muscular and intimidating man who looked like Mister Clean, was fighting a losing battle in trying to deter this sociopath from confronting me. When even Big Bill couldn't handle the wrath of this nutcase, who thought he owned the rights to my soul, I knew my escape to freedom was not yet complete. I nervously stood by as Bill threw in the towel and made some sort of compromise with my pursuer who desperately wanted to know why I wouldn't take his crap anymore. When Bill arrived, he asked me to speak to the seething madman at the front of the restaurant. But for one of the only times during my ten-year span at this grind house, did a manager take my side when I said, "I can't. I have nothing more to say to him." Bill returned to the front of the restaurant and, while respectfully engaging Frank in conversation, used his free arm to sweep Frank out of the restaurant and out of my life forever.

The pair never returned and have not been seen at any local eateries since. They may have left the state. Intelligence as to their whereabouts is unknown. They may have changed their identities or may be wearing some sort of disguise. If you are a waiter and they appear at your restaurant, they are to be considered armed with ignorance and very dangerous. Please be on the lookout.

My next example, Exhibit B, returns us to my earlier theory (which again is no longer a hypothesis but a concrete theory) that some of these disturbed mental units who dined in our establishment liked to pretend that they were something they weren't so they could realize a power they were never able to achieve in their daily lives. Exhibit B blew in one night during a modestly busy evening. We had a smaller than normal staff on duty that night, and unfortunately for me, Exhibit B landed right in my section. Exhibit B was alone and was the type of customer who knew exactly what she wanted when she wanted it because she had eaten at our deli every day since the age of three. She wanted gefilte fish as an appetizer and was willing to commit bloody murder to have it. Then after she inhaled her gefilte fish, she was going to chase it down with a chicken liver sandwich with plenty of onion. She placed her order as if she was performing some sort of sacred ritual that involved drinking the blood of young children.

But before I continue, I would like to freeze the frame for a moment here and make a point. In any given week, I would wait on anywhere from three to five hundred people. I found it impossible to appease every person who walked through our doors, but I would, on the other hand, at least try to get their order right and make sure each guest had what he or she needed to enjoy their food. And, believe it or not, every once in a while, I would even make a mistake. But only because I desperately needed this crappy job to rise through the ranks of Hollywood was I willing to admit my mistakes and, at a minimum, attempt to correct them. Let's continue, shall we?

We'll fast forward to my arriving at Exhibit B's table with pickled herring instead of gefilte fish. I could immediately tell upon setting this planktivore down that something was incredibly wrong. I thought maybe Exhibit B was yakking on a bone as her eyes grew to the size of half dollars. I rarely ever served gefilte fish and had no idea it drew that kind of reaction. "What is this?" Exhibit B clamored. "Gefilte fish," I replied. "No it's not," Exhibit B insisted emphatically. "That's what I rang in," I shouted back. "Well this isn't it," she retorted. "Don't you know what gefilte fish is?" she prodded. "Well, I don't serve it that much," I sheepishly replied, and just as I was saying, "I'll—," she interrupted me with, "I can't believe this. This is ridiculous. This is the worst service I've ever had in my life."

Seconds later, I shot back towards the deli with flames shooting out of my Payless slip-resistant shoes with the mistaken fish plate in hand. "What is this?" I screamed at the deli guy. "Herring," he responded back. "I need gefilte fish!" I retorted. "We're out. How long have you worked here? We only have gefilte fish during the holidays," he snickered. "Great," I said to myself. As I made my way back towards Exhibit B, I knew the conversation was not going to go well. She was anticipating my arrival and had already informed the manager of my incompetence. The manager was now watching my every move. My relationship with Exhibit B suddenly took on a whole new dynamic. It was that of "just get me my freaking sandwich, you stupid moron, so I no longer have to deal with your inadequacy … and … I don't want my damn gefilte fish now anyway because after speaking with your manager I know that you don't have it."

I was motivated to avoid any further collateral damage by just getting the sandwich out to her table as quickly and quietly as possible. Although, back in the kitchen, if I could have written a book at that point in time, it would have been entitled, *Just Give Me the Damn Sandwich*, not unlike the book written by former pro football player and notorious blockhead Keyshawn Johnson entitled, *Just Throw Me the Damn Ball*. This one table was now monopolizing my time, and I had to ensure for my job security that the sandwich was prepared exactly the way Exhibit B had ordered it and in the most expedient way possible. As Exhibit B gnawed on her sandwich, I took a step back to catch up on my other tables. It seemed like a good time to do that because at least with a mouth full of food Exhibit B would not be able to verbalize her dissatisfaction with me. But, when another server picked up her empty glass for a refill, I thought her head was going to spin around and she was going to start projectile vomiting green chicken liver at me.

I quickly darted over to her table only to be met with "What's wrong with you that you have to get other people to do your work for you?" She then proceeded to scold the server who bailed me out when she returned with the fresh drink. I now knew no matter what I did or didn't do, I would not be able to reach Exhibit B's unattainable standards. I thanked her for signing her credit card slip, even though it contained the amount of zero dollars and zero cents as my tip. I was at least relieved that I was able to dodge yet another bullet by a big shooter who was looking to ruin my life and my goal of earning a golden star on the Hollywood Walk of Fame inscribed "Jozef Rothstein."

Exhibit C was yet another typical customer who knew everything that you were doing wrong because she was once a server and never did things as badly as you were doing them because she was so much better than you were at it. The only thing more asinine than this assumption was when a customer purported to be a close friend of the owner and threatened to call him at three in the morning just because he had to wait an extra ten minutes for his tuna melt.

At first, this threat of knowing the owner was a Clear and Present Danger. But, by the three-thousandth time, I started to assume that either the owner had over a thousand extremely close friends or these people were completely full of shit. Would these alleged close friends really call the owner in the wee hours of the morning just to tell him that their meatloaf sandwich was cold? Would you do that to your friend if he owned a restaurant? As a matter of fact, I'd be surprised if most of them had ever met the guy. I worked there for ten years, and I never met the guy. He seemed to be more fiction than reality. If I went to the corporate office for something, I'd overhear a receptionist tell someone, "He's in a meeting." Or, if I caught wind the owner was in the restaurant, by the time I could locate him, I'd be told, "He just left." I mean who was this guy, Mr. Snuffleupagus? Anyway, if I had a nickel for every person who knew the owner and was going to rat me out to him for some ridiculous reason, I could have retired ten years ago. But aside from this little detour, let's get back to Exhibit C.

I bring up Exhibit C only because it was the one time during my decade-long stay at the Matzo Ball Hilton that I was ever on the verge of tears. And it wasn't because I was sad or because my feelings were hurt. Oh no, it was quite the contrary; it was because I never wanted to choke the living shit out of someone so badly. Again, I was faced with the inner conflict of spending my life behind bars or having a chance at superstardom. And my vain side won out. Exhibit C came with all the bells and whistles of your typical unruly customer minus one fact: It was New Year's Eve, and the restaurant was closing for the first time ever due to the Y2K scare. I had plans to party with some friends over in Phoenix, Arizona, and after just one year of living in LA, I desperately wanted to escape the fast life and hang out with people who weren't trying to stab me in the back because I might ruin their chances of appearing on an episode of *Friends*. The thing that made Exhibit C different from the rest of the jerk-offs who knew everything about everything was the fact that she could smell that I wanted to leave early.

Although I gave good service and was respectful to this pariah, she was going to extend my stay until she completely crushed my holiday cheer. Exhibit C exemplifies another condition that made serving in this hostile public arena that much more difficult ... oppressive RULES. I'll get into this category soon enough, but one of the rules needed for this example was that no drinks—and I mean NO drinks—were to be served a half-hour before the legal drinking hour expired or, in this case, a half-hour before the restaurant closed. We were to shut down at 6:00 p.m. on this particular evening, so using Laplace's theory of transformation and some straightforward Chinese arithmetic, that made the cut-off time 5:30 p.m. The thing that would have made this situation much more server-friendly is if someone would have mentioned this minor little detail to me. You know, the one acting as the liaison between the bar and its loyal minions on National Alcoholics Day. But since I didn't normally work that shift, and the restaurant never closed early because it was a 24/7 operation, I failed to give my tables a last call. Shortly after 5:30 p.m., the manager sprung from his office like a bird from a cuckoo clock and announced that no more drinks were to be served from the bar since it was past the allotted time. In this restaurant that meant everything. God himself could appear at 5:31 p.m. and be refused a drink.

Of course, when I returned to my table, it only made sense that Exhibit C would insist on having one last cocktail for the road before she closed out her bill. At first, I was going to work with Exhibit C to see if I could negotiate some sort of deal with the bar, but when she elevated her demeanor to hostile after being rude in every way, shape, and form since entering the building, I grew firmer in my position. That's when Exhibit C wobbled over to the bar to take matters into her own hands. I watched in disbelief from a distance as the bartender broke the restaurant's number one sacred rule and complied with her request for a drink. The satisfaction she obtained after pouting mercilessly to get her way was palpable. As she waddled back to her seat, her body radiated with the sense of one-upmanship that she had achieved over me. This loaded her arsenal and gave her even more of a reason to treat me like the dead animal that was rotting in the sewer line underneath our building that all too frequently stunk up the restaurant.

She now was completely certain that I refused her a drink because I wanted to leave early. And yes, she was right. I did want to leave as soon as humanly possible, but that was not why I refused her a drink. I watched one by one as my fellow co-workers left the building. First, it was the servers; then, it was the cooks and bartenders, followed by the bus boys. I grew more and more livid as only myself, the manager, and the cleaning crew remained. At first, I casually cruised by the table every ten minutes or so to subtly drop the hint that it was time to settle up, but it wasn't until the cleaning crew started putting the chairs on top of the tables that I finally asked Exhibit C to pay the bill, "You know, the one that I laid down in front of you over an hour ago?" She simply ignored my request and sat there for an additional fifteen minutes to prove her point. It wasn't until the manager eventually told her that we were about to lock up for the evening and then started turning out the lights that Exhibit C finally decided to close out her tab. If you are reading this book and you are that person, thank you so much for the wonderful lesson in life. You are a miserable troll, and an eternity in a lake of fire would be too kind for you. And by the way, Happy New Year to you too!!

The last exhibit, Exhibit D, is mentioned just to show you that every cloud has a silver lining and that there is the possibility of retribution when these out-of-control whack jobs cross the line … only to return back over it again the next day. In case you were bothered by the past few examples, this one will get you rooting for the underdog once again. This little saga took place in the most hated region of the restaurant, the patio. There are many contributing factors that made this desolate barren wasteland of a dining area so despicable. For one, it was the furthest point from the kitchen, and every time someone requested something, you would have to pack for two days to be sure you had enough supplies to make it to the kitchen and back. This post also attracted smokers who produced toxic clouds of gas that made the former Bethlehem Steel look like an oxygen tank. This station also entertained representatives from every corner of the globe, and the only prerequisite for these foreigners to loiter in this part of the joint was that they were not allowed to speak English (or so it seemed). Even customers who dined in this sector from allegedly more modern civilizations like the United States of America made special-needs children look like Albert Einstein and mumbled in incoherent sentences. There was also a direct relationship between the patio patron and the low tips one received while working in this section. In short, the amount of labor that went into keeping this area from erupting into all-out chaos was immense and wasn't worth the crummy tips you received. And the only thing worse than waiting tables on the patio was waiting on large parties on the patio.

The patio, just for the record, was the station where all new servers were expected to pay their dues and where I spent most of my first two years. There was no room to move while serving in this obstructed region, and the door to this loathed area sprung open and shut like a bear trap. I've seen hands, trays, and even a small dog get caught in the door, and for the whole ten years I worked there, I never saw it get fixed.

Exhibit D was the largest party I ever served in that area, and for not speaking any English, they sure found a way to run my ass off. Their bill reached almost two hundred dollars, and because someone told me that this party was part of a royal family from Saudi Arabia, I thought I would take my chances by skipping the automatic gratuity. That was before eighteen of their citizens allegedly flew large planes into some of our buildings. But, what the hell did I know? Saudi Arabia equaled oil, which equaled money in my eyes, so I was confident my tip would be extraordinary. But when I went back to pick up the credit-card slip for the almost two-hundred-dollar check, I observed a line through the tip space and then spotted a five dollar bill on the table. I was fuming. I couldn't get over my shock as I mumbled to myself. I also reflected on the fact that some of the members of their party were regulars who should have known better; especially if they didn't want a logier in their burger.

Well, of course, being the low man on the totem poll, I was once again assigned to this wretched area the following night. The only thing that made this deplorable twist of fate even remotely bearable was the resurgence of this clan of stunads that same evening. I felt my prayers had been answered as they piled into my designated area in small clusters and took it upon themselves to set up shop. I was now captain of team payback and I was going to make sure that this merry band of misfits learned what 2-percent service really looked like. And since their vocabulary was limited to get me (food item) and get me (another food item), what were they going to do—call my manager over, point at me, and shake their heads no? One of the more fluent English speakers from their group immediately let me know how hungry they were and how badly they wanted to order. I interpreted this in their language as, "We are going to need more time because even though we are hungry we are willing to starve ourselves to death due to our lack of appreciation for your wonderful service last night."

So I gave them twenty minutes or so after sitting down to really think about what kind of beverages they wanted. When I finally came back to take their drink order, they were clamoring that they wanted to order their food, but I explained to them how I had to bring them their liquid refreshments first. As I was walking away to complete this task, one of the girls in the group stopped me by calling out, "How is whitefish salad?" to which I shrugged my shoulders. She then pointed to the item on the menu and asked, "Me try? Little?" to which I responded, "Sure." When I returned with their drinks twenty minutes later, the crowd was furious. The girl asked me where her whitefish salad was, and I said, "I'll go get it." Ten minutes later, when I returned with her whitefish salad, I also asked them if they were ready to order. Some of them had already started chewing through the table. They responded with a passionate "Yes," which again translated back to me as "Take the order but wait all day to ring it in and then let it get cold in the window before you bring it to us." When I checked back on their drink levels twenty minutes later, a few of them had asked me to cancel their orders. Many stormed off. I saw this as a good thing because at least my tip percentage was going up according to their five-dollar standard. A five-dollar tip on an eighty dollar check is much better percentage-wise than a five-dollar gratuity on a two-hundred-dollar check.

After another half-hour passed and the pressure of the cooks screaming at me to remove my food from the window finally over-whelmed me, I hand-delivered each meal to them one by one. I would bring one dish to the table and then run back to the kitchen for the next. I repeated this procedure until every one in the party had received their entrée. I watched this dwindled-down group devour their crusted-over dinners with such incredible vigor that it brought a tear to my eye. And to think that it was I who provided them this once-in-a-lifetime dining experience. They went on to express their appreciation with a forty-dollar tip on an eighty-dollar check. Until this day, I still have no idea whether it was something as simple as someone else from the group settling the tab or if the service they received that evening was considered exceptional in their homeland, but I found redemption in the form of a large gratuity for less than adequate service. And maybe just maybe, these barbarians learned a very valuable lesson that evening that teaches thee not to mess with those who bring thee thy food. Thank you, God. Praise you, Jesus!!!

We've all heard the Golden Rule that states he who has the gold makes the rules. The Golden Rule also applies to hostile work environments where the wait staff, already facing great odds, has to deal with new and oppressive policies sent down on a weekly basis from their invisible overlord, Mr. Snuffleupagus. After being cooped up with a couple of political conspiracy theorists and, in the same breadth, watching how things ran in this totalitarian eatery, maybe the idea of a group of power elites dictating policy to our elected leaders who in turn force these policies onto us isn't so far fetched after all. What I mean is, Poof, the Almighty Lord of the Matzo Ball gets an idea while sitting on his throne in the corporate office, and voilà, the regional manager's scrambling, the general manager's barking out orders, and the floor manager's running around with the expression of the *Home Alone* kid while the rest of us are wondering what the hell is going on. Turns out the corporate office, a.k.a. "Snuffy," doesn't think we should have a middle coffee station even though this saves countless tons of rubber from wearing off the bottom of our shoes. And once this draconian policy's set in place, we're the ones having to deal with long lines, coffee shortages, and coffee pots being left in places where I wouldn't take my mother.

Then just when you think it can't get anymore daffy, another week goes by, and kazam, "No drink is to be carried without a tray." Never mind the fact there are a total of five trays in the entire restaurant, and most of the time you'd have to run completely across the length of the floor to grab a tray in order to return all the way back across the floor to snag the drinks so you could run all the way back across the floor to deliver them. Talk about a clusterfuck. To someone observing from an outside window, we must have looked like a bunch of chickens running around with our heads cut off. On a busy night, it was not uncommon to sprint through the restaurant in a mad dash to comply with all of the ridiculous rules and regulations the management team imposed on us. And when I say "us," I mean all of the other rejects I was thrown into the bottom of the Hollywood caste system with. Unfortunately for me, it wasn't the cast system of the entertainment industry, which is an entirely different caste system onto itself.

Our caste system was made up of all of the people in Los Angeles who joined the bottom rung of society to work as food service workers. We got tarred and feathered in the town square and then got kicked in the rear end by just about everyone who passed through the village. Don't get me wrong. The people I am about to mention had a pain tolerance beyond belief and a mental toughness that would make Evander Holyfield look like a Girl Scout. But we all must have suffered from some sort of personality deficiency or reeked of some other ineptitude that drew us to this drama unit and allowed us to endure the punishment bestowed upon us for so long.

As I announce the starting lineup, one should keep in mind that these were some of the initial characters that I encountered when I first started my ten-year sentence in Matzo Hell. Many others will appear throughout this text without any rhyme or reason. So, ladies and gentleman, boys and girls, may I present to you your Los Angeles deli staff rejects.

Hailing from an undisclosed location in New York City and living under an alias because she testified against the mafia … wearing employee number 2424 on her key card … Head Server and Queen Bitch "Elizabeth."

Also, tripping on the power of being a head server in a dysfunctional deli, originally from the Bronx, New York … the guy who takes ten minutes to respond to your question even though you're standing directly in front of him and repeat the question a countless number of times, sporting key card number 7745, Henry.

Known as the Pit Bull, this prematurely balding woman in her early twenties stands four foot something and hates you just because. She automatically assumes you're an idiot simply for asking her a question … five-year veteran of slinging nasty insults at anyone who looks in her direction, key card number 6666, Hilda.

After sneaking through five different countries to enter the United States illegally, this Columbian refugee learned to speak English by watching cartoons. He's known to be a practical joker who intentionally messes up your side work so he can laugh at you while you're being reprimanded, carrying key card 0001, Julio.

And last but not least, the team's token "crazy" black man, who purposely talks politics and religion to his tables so he can start an argument. The guy who never shuts up and who has a meltdown every night because he takes on more tables than he can handle, key card number 1212, Chester.

More bench players will appear throughout the remainder of this text, but these starting five are special to me because they played such a key role in my inaugural misery.

Elizabeth was the most brutal of the bunch. She was nicknamed the Queen Bee during her run with the mob. She went on to confess to me during a slow evening that she ordered some of the most ruthless acts carried out by the crime family that she married into. She argued irrationally about side work and demanded that her most frivolous requests be carried out in full. One of these odd demands entailed her running her fingers underneath the lip of the stainless steel counter top located in the shake station. If anything felt sticky, she would insist that you scrub the whole counter … underneath, along the sides, and around the back. Side work that usually took fifteen minutes to complete would take two hours under her supervision. She enjoyed wielding her power over you and tried to brainwash you into believing that she held your job in the palm of her hand. And what made her threats somewhat believable was the community of managers who turned a blind eye to her bullying tactics, like corrupt prison guards in on the scam.

She was also responsible for the nightly server break down. She consistently put herself on the easiest and most lucrative stations while the newer people were placed in the most difficult and least profitable areas, usually the ones furthest from the kitchen or worse yet, all the way out on the patio. This was hardly a place for a struggling server who had trouble finding the Coke button on the computer. And even though we were promised during our interviews that we would have no more than two closing shifts per week (from 11:00 p.m. until the morning crew arrived at 7:00 a.m.), Elizabeth was generous enough to grant Chester and me everybody's closing shifts, which put me at a grand total of three and even sometimes four closing shifts per week.

I can't explain to you the wretched feeling that came over me after working all night in that brutal, bright red environment, only to drive home the following morning with the hot blazing sun beating through my car window. Once I got home, I usually found myself lying in bed and staring at the ceiling as the neighborhood kids screamed at the top of their lungs while gathering for school. Once the decibel levels of these little hollering hellions returned to non-piercing, I would drift off to sleep, only to suffer from bouts of uncontrollable sweating as the afternoon sun set in. To cure this, I would plug in my broken AC just in case it decided to work.

Back at the deli, the more we argued with Elizabeth regarding her injustices, the more misfortune she placed upon us. At that point in time, all we could do was hope for a new crop of recruits who were just as naïve and just as enduring of her torture tactics as we were. Ill-fatedly for us, that blessing would take many more months to manifest.

When there wasn't Elizabeth, there was Henry. Henry wasn't as confrontational as Elizabeth, but he sure enjoyed swinging that head-server position over his head like a battle axe. Henry cared about one person in the world, Henry. You could talk with him, plead with him, gouge your eyes out in front of him, and he still wouldn't acknowledge a word you said or a thing you did. But every once in a while, he would call you over to say something like, "Who said you could … (insert the violation of corporate policy of your choice)?" And you'd say, "No one. I checked everywhere, and we don't have any more lemons." And he'd say something like, "I don't care. All water glasses get a lemon. Don't do it again." And you'd say something like, "Henry, there was a deep freeze this winter that killed most of the citrus plants in California, and the restaurant is too cheap to buy any at the current market prices so, therefore, we don't have any." And he'd say, "I don't care. Don't do it again."

In case I didn't mention it, Henry was, and I'm sure still is, black. Saturday night was, right from his own lips, "act like a black guy night." On these trend-setting evenings, Henry would sing anything from old school rap to Michael Jackson. And these songs didn't come without a dance accompaniment. Ringing in an order next to the sixth member of the Jackson Five could be a daunting task, especially considering the level of conviction Henry sang with. He had this funny sort of speech impediment along with a uniquely high singing voice for someone who spoke in such a low tone. And I'd be lying if I didn't say he made me incredibly uncomfortable while standing next to him in the middle of one of his *American Idol* type outbursts, especially when the restaurant was busy. Particularly, when five minutes earlier, he was giving me a hard time for putting too many pickles on a pickle tray.

But his trademark quality came out in full force once the restaurant slowed to a crawl and all of your side work was done and you just wanted to go home. You'd say something like, "Henry, can you sign my time card? I want to go home." And he'd look up from the newspaper he was reading and would just stare straight ahead for a minute. Then he'd look back down at his paper. You'd wait a few more seconds and then interrupt him again with, "Henry, everything's done. Do you need me to do anything else?" Suddenly, he'd get up and disappear for a few minutes. After looking everywhere for him for a good ten minutes or so, you'd finally see him in the back of the restaurant flirting with one of the waitresses. So, you'd walk back to him and say, "Henry, do you mind if I go?" Then he'd look at you and say "Is everything done?" And you'd say, "Yeah?!" From there he'd carry on his conversation with the waitress for another minute or so while dangling your time card in front of you until he finally scribbled something down on it that resembled the letter *H*. It didn't matter whether you said goodbye or not; he was done with you, and he wouldn't engage you in another one-way conversation until you committed your next infraction.

As I mentioned in her introduction, if there was one word to describe Hilda, it would be pit bull. I guess that's two words, but you get the idea. Hilda is short. Not a midget but almost. And she is female. So, I guess that gave her the right to bite your head off anytime she felt like it. For ten years, I forced myself to be nice to her so I wouldn't drop kick her through a window. And God forbid if I asked her something that she knew the answer to but I didn't. It got to the point where I'd rather lie on the floor covered in flames than ask her for a fire extinguisher. And if you accidentally bumped into her or mistakenly took one of her food items, she would let out this piercing shrill that released all of the bats in the Western Hemisphere from their caves. I came to find out that this hard outer shell was just protecting the miserable bitch inside of her that was looking for any reason whatsoever to be unleashed. I remember getting severe neck pains every time I pulled into the parking lot for a shift, and I'm sure Hilda can be given most of the credit.

And for being one of the dullest tools in the tool shed, Hilda sure worked hard at coming off as a superior intellect. Maybe her harsh attitude towards humanity was responsible for her male-pattern baldness or vice versa, but I certainly know I am happy to be three thousand miles away from this rabid animal.

In hindsight, Julio was a lot more fun to work with than I had realized at the time. That was probably because I wasn't maimed or injured during one of his spectaculars. His practical jokes teetered on the verge of hazardous and usually got really old, really fast. You always had to be on guard to protect yourself against one of his shenanigans. There were a couple of harmless but humiliating incidents that I, only now, find somewhat amusing. One being the time that I was working the counter area and, every time I passed by the patrons sitting in this section, I'd hear bursts of laughter. One guy couldn't even swallow his food he was chuckling so hard. His face was beet red, and at first, I didn't think it had anything to do with me. But after cruising by a couple more times to erupting chortles, I finally had to ask these misfits, "What?" Of course, they pleaded the Fifth. It was almost time for my break so I decided to make an early exodus and head out to my car for a few moments of tranquility. As I got into my vehicle, I noticed that my apron string was stuck on the outside of the doorframe. As I unhooked the string and reeled it up to my lap, I discovered a pacifier tied to the end of it. Then, the realization hit me like a tidal wave, and I finally knew what all of the hilarity was about.

Julio must have made a living in South America as a pickpocket because you could never feel him tying anything to your apron strings. These objects ranged from ketchup bottles to chairs, forks, knives, and even other people. Yes, that's right, other people. One day I was ringing in an order next to the largest woman on our wait staff, known to everyone as the "Penguin." The Penguin stood about five feet two inches and weighed about 250 pounds. Then, like something out of a *Three Stooges* episode, when we both split off into different directions, we were suddenly yanked backwards. We collided into each other and nearly pulled each other to the ground, but fortunately for both of us, we somehow caught our balance. We both wanted to smack one another but instead just studied each other for a few seconds like two Sumo wrestlers about to engage. The tension was broken when someone pointed out that our apron strings had been tied together. We all knew who the culprit was, especially after spotting Julio across the restaurant bent over in stitches.

Julio also liked to throw banana peels under people's feet as they walked through the sundae station. This provided comic relief to him, especially if someone slipped on one. He also loved to take the Penguin on thrill rides through the restaurant during her cash outs. He would sneak up behind her, grab the wooden chair she was sitting on, spin it around, and then start pushing her down the aisle as if they were entering a bobsled run. In no time, they would be whisking around corners and picking up steam through the straight-aways. Her shrieks indicated to everyone that she was scared to death and wanted her wild toboggan ride to end. But Julio only pushed faster. This would enrage her even more, prompting her to furiously call for him to stop. For those of us watching, it only heightened the comedy. Julio was relentless and didn't comply until they arrived back at their original destination, hockey-stop fashion.

If you went to use the restroom while Julio was working, you would have to hide your apron because, if something wasn't tied to it when you returned, something was squashed up inside it. His humor not only matched the sadistic nature of the place but also magnified it. One night after completing all of the requests imposed on me during one of Elizabeth's dictatorial side-work tantrums, I was on my way to seeking final approval for release when I heard the blender turn on and then come to a screeching halt. When I arrived, Julio was cracking up as strawberry smoothie graced the entire area that I had just spent the past hour scrubbing. Red goo was dripping from the ceiling, the walls, and all over my once-immaculate station. After composing himself enough to quickly pour his concoction into the glass he was holding, he swiftly whisked away. Of course, the most comical thing for him to do, in his skewed opinion, was to take off, deny responsibility for the mess, and leave the disaster detail to me. Oh, but in the restaurant business, paybacks can be a bitch.

A few nights later, I spotted Julio cleaning the always-messy and very time-consuming dressings' area. I watched from a casual distance as he fussed around while putting the finishing touches on his assignment. I calmly waited for an opening. It came just a few minutes later when Julio left the kitchen to make his final rounds on the floor. I quickly occupied his post, and when I was sure there were no potential witnesses in the vicinity, I got down to business. I grabbed the first thing I could find, which happened to be a one-gallon tub of ranch dressing, and poured it all over the inside of the crawl-in cooler he had just spent a huge chunk of time cleaning. I was done for the evening so I urgently scampered out through the back door before Julio returned. The unfortunate part of this payback was that I would never get to see the look on Julio's face when he returned only to find his beloved side work drenched under a gallon of ranch dressing. Nor would I have the satisfaction of watching him toil for another hour re-cleaning it. Julio was not the kind of prankster you wanted to escalate a war with so I felt leaving the scene look like an accident caused by someone else on duty was my safest bet. On my ride home, the mere thought of retaliation from Camp Julio gave me the feeling that my joke on him could turn out to be not so funny after all.

Julio and I did, however, have one last laugh together before he quit and tried to get rehired, only to find out that our upper management didn't want him to ever return again. It was a couple of days before

Christmas when Julio was giving this one particular table the best service I had ever seen him give. In short, he must have really needed the cash. Anyway, he was courteous and accommodating, and to be quite honest, it hurt me to watch him act so hospitably. I watched him run back and forth continuously from the server station I was positioned in, which was located directly behind the table he was humping it for. No matter how mundane the request, Julio fulfilled it dutifully and with a pleasant smile etched on his face. At the end of the meal, Julio dropped the check to the table and came over to where I was standing to chat about something. As we were talking, I curiously watched this mother of three sign her credit card slip and gather up her children. As she made her way towards where we were standing, she was grinning from ear to ear. When she finally reached us, she gave Julio a gentle tug on the arm. She handed him the folded up slip and, in the kindest, most sincere way possible, uttered the words, "Merry Christmas." This caught Julio completely off guard, and I thought he was going to melt. I couldn't believe the man actually blushed. All he could do in return was reply with a very appreciative "Merry Christmas," which he followed with a slight bow. I found this exchange to be very odd, especially for Julio. I wasn't sure if they were saying their goodbyes or they were going to start mating in the middle of the restaurant. As soon as Julio opened up the slip, I was already hovering over his shoulder to sneak a peek at his grand prize … a two-dollar tip on forty. I started laughing the second I saw it and didn't stop for three whole days. Every time I walked by Julio, I would greet him with a very sincere "Merry Christmas," to which he would respond with a heartfelt "Merry Christmas." This went on for months and finally cemented our past grievances into something more beneficial … a good laugh for both of us.

The last but not least member of our original starting five was Chester. Every establishment needs one crazy black man, and Chester was our representative. This man never stopped talking and got under your skin like a bad rash. He had an opinion on everything. And if you didn't have a topic for him to have an opinion on, he would graciously provide one for you. He offended more people than a Catholic priest and did everything in his power to ensure the most unstable working environment possible. He loved to hoard tables and monopolize the bus boys. He ordered them around as if they were his own personal servants while everyone else suffered the consequences. He was notorious for his "Happy Birthday" solos, which he would sing at the top of his lungs while his voice buckled under the duress of his poorly trained vocal chords. And I thought Chris Penn was bad. Chester was like an unruly contestant on the *Gong Show* times ten. You know, the type of contestant the celebrity judges used to let sing so they could make their goofy faces and show everybody in TV land how funny they were just before they smashed the gong to kingdom come with their giant matchsticks. When Chester bellowed out a birthday melody, elk in Colorado started mating and whales began beaching themselves. Chester was our go-to conspiracy theorist, and whenever someone called him out for a wrongdoing, like grabbing the wrong entrée from the window, he would respond with a "Sure, blame it on the black man."

Chester would get so amped up on his supplement shakes that he would actually get up in your grill for simply asking him for a pen. And I've seen him almost land a flying drop kick to the face of a fellow waiter who was innocently doing an impression of him. Chester was a loose cannon and was ranked number one on our "People Most Likely to Go Postal" list.

The final and key ingredient to a chaotic and dysfunctional restaurant is its management team. I am sure at least one of the prerequisites for introduction into this incompetent circle of confusion had to be a minimum of either a year in a state penitentiary or two years in a mental institution because those who were hired to fill this thankless position made the Menendez brothers look like model citizens. To excel in this role, one had to have a knack for ridicule and a true passion for ordering people around. And as part of their training, I am sure that they also had to be proficient in 1950's style management techniques. The final litmus test for acceptance into this underpaid and underappreciated position must have been to say in the most convincing way possible, "Because I said so!" Meanwhile, these power brokers had to be able to kiss the ass of upper management while staying sane just long enough to come off as stable human beings.

I already introduced one of our managers, Bill, earlier, and although his heroics on the night of "The Last Supper" probably make him seem like somewhat of a noble character, don't let this rare flash of compassion fool you. I am sure Bill had some sort of ulterior motive that night, like he wanted the guy to take a swing at him so he could kill him. Bill was big and he was mean. One eye was looking at you while the other one was looking off to God knows where. You sometimes didn't know which eye to look at, especially when both were wandering off in different directions. Anyway, he had a shaved head and loved to tell you, "Because I said so." He was filled with rude comments, designed to belittle you and rob you of whatever little self-esteem you still had left after dealing with a long line of unruly customers, who were on a mission to make your life as miserable as possible.

My biggest nemesis at the deli was also a very proud member of the gay mafia that filled our restaurant's chain of command. She was a woman (somewhat) who I'll refer to as Sardine. Sardine looked like Roy Orbison's dopier and taller brother. She dressed like a pirate and had the personality of a lump of shit. The gay mafia and, hence, Sardine got a free pass to behave any way they wanted, as long as they swarmed the queen bee, Gus. The same applied to the plethora of she-males the deli hired on an all-too-regular basis. Non-gays were definitely a minority in this organization, and we were an unwelcome one at that. Sardine will get her day in hell, but until that time comes, she has to be one of the stupidest and most annoying idiots to ever grace the planet. Her pants never reached down past the top of her shins, and she treated everybody as if he were a retarded second grader, most likely a phase that she never grew out of. Her outfits looked like ratty pajamas, and I, later in my career, kept a journal of all of the violations of corporate policy Sardine perpetrated against me. I may list some of these offenses in later chapters, that is, if I can even stomach to mention her again. But for now, I'll bury the hatchet with the management team until I bury it in Sardine's head at some later point in this book.

After two years in Hollywood, I was already spending, like this second chapter, way too much time at the deli and not enough time working on my acting career. So, it was time to get serious. Up until this point in time, I had actually been represented by a few small-time agents.

One of these 10-percenters was Dale Garrick, who was a pretty successful agent back in the 1980s but who was twenty years past his prime. When I entered his office for the first time ever, I immediately recognized one of his client's pictures on display as the young girl from *Family Ties*. I was also able to place a few other recognizable faces that graced the paneled walls of his once lush suite. When he invited me into his office, he talked to me for a good two minutes or so before he signed me to a contract. Probably, the same method he used on every other client he could actually get to show up for an appointment. I'm guessing Dale was probably around eighty years old when I signed with him, and his trademark phrase was ending every phone call with a crackly "God bless." Dale's assistant was an elderly man who appeared to be ten years older than he was. Dale's assistant passed away within one month of my signing.

Whenever Dale called me with an audition notice, he would repeat the address twice on my answering machine. And both times, he would read back a different street number. If I actually had him on the phone I would say, "Did you say 5545 Vine?" And he'd say, "No, 12545 Vine," and I'd say "12545 Vine?" And he'd say "15425 Vine." Usually on the day of the appointment (this was before I owned a computer), I would realize that there were no five-digit street numbers on Vine. After driving up and down the city block for twenty minutes, I would spot the casting office at 1245 Vine. This happened almost every time. Finally, after growing tired of circling the city five times every time I had a commercial audition for the role of a guy who smashes a beer can off his head, I decided to call it quits with Dale. God bless him, he tried his best for me, but I was studying acting with the best teachers in the industry. We focused intensively on the great playwrights of the theatre, and I had to draw the line somewhere. Was I really stupid enough to believe that Hollywood had artistic integrity and that I would get the opportunity to audition for roles that had some sort of social significance? Was I on crack?

During this same time-frame, I was also represented by an agent by the name of Jack Scagnetti, who signed me because I listed the pogo stick as a special skill on my résumé. Jack reminded me of an over-the-hill used-car salesman. Jack didn't send me out on one audition during the four months he represented me even though I went out of my way to provide him with some of the leads. He had one rotary phone in his office, and his desk was completely surrounded by mountains of boxes packed with headshots. How he ever found anything in that suite I will never know.

And sometime before Jack, I also briefly obtained a commercial agent who signed me because of a cover letter that I had sent to him written in crayon. In a child's penmanship, I wrote that if he wanted to represent me he should check the "Yes" box and if he didn't he should check the "No" box that I courteously provided. The agent thought that this was creative. After failing to receive a single callback after well over twenty auditions, I believe the agent began to question my mental state and released me from his roster.

As they say, and as I can attest to, there is a price for fame. And a hefty one, I might add, especially on my measly salary. One of the largest price tags came in the form of acting classes. The price of acting class didn't only come with the lofty toll of humiliating yourself week in and week out in a room full of other grown adults who were also behaving like little children, but in the college-like tuition prices these self-proclaimed gurus charged for their time. I made it my business to promote myself, Jozef Rothstein, to as many top agents and managers as possible. As I mentioned before, I was able to squeeze out the names of a couple reputable acting coaches from a contact that I had developed at the Carlyle Production Company. That is, before they stopped taking my phone calls. It is also worth mentioning that not all of these top purveyors of talent gave up on me so quickly. Oh no, a few of them realized that a man with as much zeal as Jozef Rothstein must have had something worth taking even if it was his intellectual property, or his very soul, for that matter. Other parts of the machine simply enjoyed the slow grinding-away process of a fresh, young, bright light that was supposed to result in its eventual dimming. But these sadists only win if you let them, and my quest for thespian knowledge was real, and it was voracious.

The two acting studios that I was referred to were the Barry Finn Acting Studio and the Herbert Ross Acting Studio. I chose to dabble in both. At the Barry Finn Studio, audits were quickly approaching, and you had to call to reserve a spot along with mentioning your referral's name. At the Herbert Ross Studio, audits were forbidden, and there was a waiting list to get in. I was able to sidestep this little nuance by signing up for a cold reading class that was being held at the personal residence of one of the instructors. If everything went according to plan, I would take scene study at the Barry Finn Studio and cold reading from a teacher at Herbert Ross.

Let's first take a look at the inner machinations of the Barry Finn Acting Studio or, as I like to call it, mini-Hollywood. There was one implied rule at the Barry Finn Acting Studio, and that was that Barry Finn and the late Uta Hagen (the famous actress from New York who authored the book, *Respect for Acting*, that the studio used as a religious doctrine) were not mortals but actually gods, gods to be worshipped and prayed to every day. One wrong move, one question of authority, and you could find yourself not only blackballed from Barry's scene study class but from the entire industry as well. Or so he would have you think. I mean come on; this guy got called up to work on set with some of the "Bigs." He didn't have time to deal with a bunch of little wannabe actors, who were taking up his precious time. This coming from a once bald and overtly heavyset man who spent the money he robbed from his brainwashed students on expensive toupees and liposuction.

But back to the indoctrination process at the Barry Finn Acting Studio. You had to apply by a certain date to be invited to the audit, which I did. You were then supposed to receive a phone call to let you know whether or not you were invited to this preview, which I did not. I called the studio several times right up until the day before the audit only to learn that the list was almost full. If I missed the audit, it would mean that I'd have to wait months before I'd get another chance to enroll. I couldn't let this happen. My philosophy since entering Hollywood was to market myself as a great actor and then bust my ass to become one as soon as possible in order to back up my bold claims. I figured it would take a while to get some sort of legitimate shot, if one at all, but every second not working on my craft meant that I was setting myself up for some kind of possible failure down the road. So I convinced myself to show up to the audit with no invite.

When I arrived at the location, much to my surprise, my name was on the list. What was this, some sort of test, or did Mr. Finn hope that I just wouldn't show up? I guess I'll never know. A personal assistant checked off our names as we entered the room and then briefed us on the very serious nature of the audit along with the audit rules. I sat patiently with all of the other new hopefuls in our seats as we waited for the master himself to arrive for the be-all and end-all "master class" session. I remember how uncomfortable I felt watching the actors warm up. A warm-up to me meant doing a few stretches or repping out with some light weights, but a warm-up to this group had a whole new meaning. To them, it meant giving each other a massage, even if it was guy on guy. I started to wonder if I would turn gay from taking the class. I knew Hollywood was strange, but when our guest of honor arrived, it got even weirder.

The actors lined up in rows as Mr. Finn shouted out his instructions. As his zombie-like students fell deeper into their trances, they began shouting out tongue twisters, making jerky movements, and barking out strange noises, all at the command of their mentor, Mr. Barry Finn. If someone would have walked in off the streets, he would have assumed the Finnbots had Tourettes. Once the scenes began … they were generally boring, and I thought to myself, "Even with no acting experience at all, I have to be at least a little more interesting to watch than these brain-dead drones carrying on with an annoying air of self-importance." Arrogance seemed to be either a trend in Hollywood or a contagious disease. Of course, I kept these thoughts to myself as I didn't want to risk being beheaded. To Mr. Finn's credit, he did have a lot of insight into the craft of acting. He gave very sound, a.k.a. harsh, feedback to the actors stinking up the stage, which was enough to convince me to try his beginner's class.

The class was generally fun, and I learned quite a bit in the eight-week intensive, including the fact that our teacher was gay. As the rumors swirled, I remained hopeful, in a non-gay way of course, that I would get to continue studying with Mr. Finn. But the reality of studio politics seeped in, however, when it came time to learn which teacher I was assigned to for the next level of classes. Only the connected in Hollywood, the students who studied at the studio for a very long time (a.k.a. paid a lot of money) or the boy toys (i.e., Barry's own personally handpicked students) were allowed to study with Mr. Finn. The rest of us peons would get stuck with the cannon fodder that was swept in off the streets and given the title of "Acting Coach." My particular agent of Satan was named Gail.

Gail was a miserable New York JAP (Jewish American Princess) in her fifties who suffered from so many mental illnesses a shrink could spend a lifetime diagnosing her. Her claim to fame was a guest appearance on *Night Court*, and she knew as much about acting as Helen Keller knew about bright colors. I would equate her coaching technique to that of an abusive stepparent who tries to toughen you up by criticizing and beating you constantly, hardly the type of person you wanted guiding you in a vulnerable state of suggestion, especially when the whole idea behind the craft of acting is to develop a technique that allows you to open up and make yourself more emotionally available. This woman made me want to slam the door shut and throw away the key! I sat in her class for months on end until one day I felt like my head was going to explode. I finally had enough of her illogical critiques, her constant nagging, and worse yet, the details of her horrible dating experiences. At Herbert Ross, the cold reading teacher had liked my work and asked me to join her scene study class, to which I gladly obliged. I later found myself excelling in it. There was no need for this self-inflicted torture anymore. As I removed myself from the Barry Finn Acting Studio, I was warned that once I left the studio I could never return, to which I proudly replied, "Don't worry. I won't."

Herbert Ross was the place for me. I studied there for a total of five years. That was probably two years too many, but I really wanted to squeeze the juice out of that place. I couldn't get enough stage time. I am certain that many potential Hollywood A-listers left the industry for good after watching me flounder with the same material week in and week out. The teacher rewarded hard work and encouraged it from everybody. After a few years, I think even the teacher got sick of me. Because her critiques were very tough and no one wanted to fail in front of her, I was able to find a ton of stage time in not just one but in many of her other varied level classes as well. All I had to do was drop in on another class and track down a scene partner. Once that was accomplished, we'd work on the scene until it was ready to bring into the respective class I was crashing. To me, her critiques were the most important part of the process, and I was getting several per week.

Her teaching method catered to the self-starter, and no one fired up his engines more than Jozef Rothstein.

Life in an acting studio can be very cliquey and caddy but only if you get consumed in it. I blew in like a force of nature and left the gossipers and nay-sayers with lots to talk about. Their disdain for me didn't slow me down one bit. As they sat on their asses praying for me to fail, I simply viewed them as lazy couch potatoes who were satisfied with their careers as professional acting students. These haters were the type of dimwits who parked themselves in acting schools for years, hoping their teacher would recognize their dedication and talent and would at some point call Steven Spielberg on their behalf. As they sat there waiting for their big break, they were unknowingly funding the Hollywood industrial complex and perpetuating the legendary status of the all-powerful, all-knowing acting teacher.

Although I am convinced there was no better coach in the business than the woman I studied with at the Herbert Ross Studio, one does not make a living instructing others on how to play make-believe without having a few character flaws. I don't know whether it was from boredom or as a way to numb the pain that she endured while watching grown adults humiliate themselves week in and week out in scenes that she must have seen a million times, but this woman loved to eat. And she wasn't shy about doing it in front of her disciples either, which leads me to her next flaw, the use of her students as her own personal servants.

Our teacher had the proverbial carrot dangling in front of us, and boy did she use it. We all knew that she had the connections and that she knew acting very well, so I am sure we all figured, by default, that if she wanted to make or break any one of our careers at any time, VAVOOM, it could be done. The problem was she had no intention of doing that, and she knew it. But she wasn't going to let us in on her dirty little secret. Not when she could connive most of her students into walking her dogs, scooping up their poop, repainting her house, fetching her food, or even donating a kidney for that matter. I am joking about the last ... well, sort of.

I saw through her façade as soon as I joined the studio, but thankfully for me, I made a commitment to myself the second I stepped foot in LA that I only wanted to learn how to act and that I didn't want to involve myself in any of these institutions any more than that. In other words, I would make my own career happen without reducing myself to a stagehand or some other sort of brown-nosing assistant. But I couldn't help but get pissed off at our guru when she hosted a fundraiser at her new cultural center and roped all of us students off from the industry elite in attendance. It made her supposed understanding of the human condition that she squawked about from her pulpit appear pretentious and fake. It turns out acting teachers weren't the only ones to watch out for.

Wiser people than I had warned me of Hollywood's tricks and schemes and stated that if I ever had to pay an agent or manager for anything, I was getting ripped off. The theory behind this philosophy was that if an agent felt you had the potential to generate a lot of revenue for him, he wouldn't have to charge you for such trivial things as coming to see you audition. The bottom line was that in order to get my career moving I felt that it was essential that I obtain a good agent, even if that meant going against the most simple and reasonable advice anyone had ever given me. After paying for showcases and submitting headshots until I was blue in the face, I decided to ignore such sound advice and instead tried to buy my way into some decent representation. That's where Joe Fox's casting office came into play.

For a very long time, Joe was situated in the ever so popular Cahuenga Studios on Cahuenga Boulevard. As a matter of fact, he is probably still there today and will most likely be there until the day they find his rotting corpse hunched over in his swivel chair. I can see the Hollywood propaganda headlines now, "Star maker who casted such memorable classics as *Dead Men Don't Disco* and *Cadaver Creek* has passed away in his office. He was 83." Lord knows you have to have an impeccable eye for talent to carefully choose the actors necessary for such meaningful pieces of cinema. At the time of my naïve thinking, the charge for his service was around three hundred dollars, and to qualify, you basically had to be able to read. He would hand you a vague script from a courtroom scene and ask you to make a strong choice as to who your character was. Was he guilty, not guilty, or was he hiding something? Once you passed this litmus test, you paid your ransom and got a personal recommendation from Joe in the form of a letter. You then also got to audition for one agent per week. At that time, Joe's letter of recommendation and a dollar ninety-nine could buy you a cup of coffee at Denny's. In his contract, Joe agreed to get you an agent or your money back, kind of like those loud, late-night commercials that jolt you out of your recliner because they're a million decibels louder than the program you fell asleep to.

Upon viewing Joe's upcoming agent list, I grew ever so hopeful after seeing the decent list of players he had put together. In hindsight, I am sure all of the participating agents inked some sort of backroom deal to sign a certain number of actors in order to receive an agreed-upon portion of the proceeds. Agencies are ranked like grades on a report card. The A agents find you when "it's your time" because they are the big money people, and they come to you when you are in a position to make them some serious dough. These agents would never even consider showing up for such a worthless event. The F agent would steal the shirt off your back, then try to sell it back to you. They are too corrupt to be invited to something even as low level as this because if they were invited they would immediately expose themselves as the cons they are and reveal the whole scam. All of the other agents were somewhere in between those two extremes with most of the agents on Joe's roll call listed as B and C agents. Not bad for three hundred dollars and the experience of auditioning. That's what I told myself anyway. I have no doubt that many of these usual players crossed paths at similar events, which I am sure provided them with a nice side income.

So the time finally came to audition for these shallow twits. I was going to enter the fighting pit with my best foot forward, and I would do so by choosing the best possible material available for someone of my "type." This decision landed me in a play by John Patrick Shanley entitled, *Danny and the Deep Blue Sea*. To sum up the plot, two lowlifes meet in a bar. The guy thinks he killed someone in a fight, and the girl feels bad because she sucked off her father. The guy almost kills her by choking her to death, and after she is able to breathe again, they decide to go back to her place and have sex. Her room is a closet in her father's house where she admittedly sucked him off. The next day, they wake up after a night of infidelity and decide to get married. I know what you're thinking, maybe not the most suitable material for a television agent who makes a living booking his clients in McDonald's commercials. But hey, what can I say? I had to follow my artistic voice.

And as this relates to doing a scene for an agent, I'm sure most would agree that it is best to have someone at least read the other character's part so the agent not only understands the scene more fully, but so he can get a feel for how you interact with the other actor as well. But because you had to pay to play to enter Joe's office, the possibility of bringing along a more suitable female lead was non-existent. So, I was to play the role of Danny, and the aging casting director, who sounded like Casey Kasem and looked like the lead singer from Blue Oyster Cult, was to play the female. I can still remember the horrified look on some of the agents' faces as I hovered above the very man who graciously invited them into his office and threatened to kill him. Weeks went by without a single response. I was beginning to doubt that the man who promised me the sun, the moon, and the stars for only three hundred dollars was going to be able to deliver. Then I began to wonder whether I should really attack him to either (a) sell the scene a little more or (b) get my three hundred bucks back. Then, a miracle happened. One agent, who in appearance, resembled Bill Gates but had the bedside manner of Richie Cunningham, found the entire scene hilarious and even asked me questions after the audition. He didn't have an agent ranking because he was a new kid on the block (not literally), but he told me that I reminded him of Ed O'Neil and that he wanted to meet with me. I thought about ignoring his initial request in order to hold out for a better agent, but when he insisted that I come down to his office to sign with him, I decided to give him a whirl. At least by having representation, I would finally be auditioning for paid assignments, not middlemen.

When I arrived at the high rise in Korea town that accommodated Jeffrey's office, I took the elevator to the twenty-seventh floor (a pretty tall building for LA). I walked into the suite and was greeted by a receptionist who instructed me to sign in. Lo and behold, sitting in a chair along the wall was yet another actor who looked like me and dressed like me. Our matching attire included khaki pants and a tight black shirt. But in this case, I actually knew the actor from the

Herbert Ross Studio so I went over to strike up a conversation with him, wish him good luck in his interview, and of course, compliment him on his outfit.

The entire suite was shared by many different businesses, each of which must have chipped in for the one receptionist fielding the avalanche of phone calls that kept pouring in. The phone would ring, and in one fell swoop, the secretary would recognize the lit-up line on her console while assigning the correct company name to her greeting, "Hello, Ziegler's Insurance." A second later, the phone would ring again, and she would greet the caller with a "Hello, Starmaker's Talent Agency." By the end of the day, this poor woman must have been mumbling to herself in the hallway and screaming at invisible people in the elevator.

When I entered Jeffrey's office, there was no office furniture. That's right, NO office furniture. Jeffrey was sitting on the floor Indian style, and I was waiting for him to offer me a peace pipe. He asked me to sit down, and I told him I was fine standing. The phone rang, and after excusing himself for a moment, Jeffrey rolled over on the carpet until his outstretched arm reached the receiver of the phone that was buried under a stack of papers. He yanked the phone out from beneath the clutter and raised the receiver to his ear. During his diatribe on the phone, I studied the boxes of headshots and papers that were randomly scattered throughout his suite. When he finally hung up the phone, the only thing that I remember from our lengthy conversation was that his uncle was once the producer of the Grammy Awards show and that he wanted to sign me as a client. I had no idea what this would bring on, but by this point I was willing to try anything.

A Hit ... a Fire ...
and a Sting

Much to my surprise, my new agent was on the move and sending me out on almost a daily basis. I danced around a prop dummy while auditioning for a Vidal Sassoon commercial, I pretended not to have a fear of heights while reading from atop a tall ladder for a Coke commercial, and I went from acting serious to becoming downright loony when a fellow office worker wheeled in a cart of Boston Market to our conference room. It was only a matter of time until I would book my way out of six nights of crucifixion a week at the deli. (Or so I hoped.) But until that time, some very interesting things transpired while slinging matzo ball soups into the wee hours of the morning.

For one, I experienced my first earthquake while collecting drinks at the soda fountain during a very busy graveyard shift. Back in 1994 when I first entertained the thought of moving from Phoenix to Los Angeles, I was getting ready for an interview as a sales rep for a company that sold plastic drums in Sherman Oaks, California. As I was primping myself in anticipation of my five-hour-plus drive to Los Angeles, a news story flashed on the television that revealed the severe damage that had been done to the I-10 freeway due to a major earthquake that had just pummeled the area. After the realization gradually hit me that I was supposed to travel on the I-10 freeway that very morning, I started paying closer attention to the broadcast. As the story unfurled, it became apparent that a major quake had struck the vicinity that I was traveling to (it would soon be known as the Northridge Quake). The region affected was in shambles so I called the recruiter who had set up the interview and asked him if my appointment had been officially cancelled. In a tone that screamed, "No shit, Sherlock," he confirmed that this was indeed the case. It would take another few years until I finally built up enough courage, once again, to try to uproot myself from Phoenix and make my big move to Los Angeles.

As I felt my feet wobble underneath me, I questioned the sanity of my decision. As tea boxes fell from a high shelf and the whole restaurant rolled like a ship on a tidal wave, I quickly made my way to the exit. As if standing outside would be safer. The power on the whole block went out when a transformer blew less than a hundred feet from where we all congregated. A combination of fear and excitement swept through the crowd. Store regular and extension of the bright red upholstery, Bert (who sat at the counter every night and looked like a homeless person even though he allegedly had millions of dollars left to him by his mother and father who once owned a lumber yard) began probing me regarding my earthquake experience. After admitting that I was a virgin and that I just had my cherry busted, Bert took center stage to reminisce about the '94 quake. He set the scene as if it were happening right in front of him. As he reached the crescendo of his grand finale, he proceeded smoothly into his eyewitness account of a house that slid down the side of the mountain and landed right across the street from the deli. "Bullshit" was the first thing out of my mouth. But when other restaurant regulars confirmed Bert's assertions, I finally gave his story some credence. One person was killed in the mishap, which just so happened to be a man sleeping in his bedroom while his house made its double black diamond run through the Hollywood Hills.

Once the lights went back on and the danger seemed to have passed, we attempted to get back to business as usual. It was at this time when I noticed some of my customers either used the earthquake as a diversion to skip out on their bill, or they ran to their cars and sped away with their tires screeching because they felt it would be safer to drive at high speeds down a road that could split in two at any second. But either way, a few of my tables were long gone. The place was in disarray, and the computers were all rebooting after going blank during the initial power outage. The archaic computers we used at that time did reset themselves, but they did so without saving any of our previous transactions.

To a person more dishonest than I, this would have been the perfect time to rob the restaurant blind by not turning in some of the money collected from our pre-earthquake sales. Luckily for me, I kept a printed version of each and every phase of every meal that I rang in, starting with a copy of the first item(s) on the ticket all the way to a printed version of the final bill. My apron looked like a stuffed garbage can by the end of any given shift, but at least my records were complete. I am still planting trees as my penance for destroying the Boreal Forest due to my high paper consumption, but at least I was able to recall my sales amounts with pinpoint accuracy. Others weren't so lucky and were bullied by our regional manager, Sal, into over-reporting any sales amounts they did not have records for. Sal also threatened to fire anyone he found falsely reporting walkouts for customers who actually paid their servers. In reality, he probably had no way of knowing who did what, but he could be such a prick you didn't want to chance it. Even when we did get our computers updated, for the many years I remained on the job, I carried around a final copy of every bill just in case a system failure like the one caused by that quake ever blindsided us again.

One thing is for certain. I'd rather be thrown into an active volcano from a helicopter than find myself face to face with Sal, who was one of the most unfriendly and unappealing people you'd ever want to meet. He stood about five feet five inches and had these poorly implanted hair plugs that made him look like a Cabbage Patch doll. He never looked at you, even if he walked right past you, but he expected you to jump whenever he asked you to do something. And whether you jumped or not, he would still find a way to insult you during the process. I tried to avoid Sal at all costs for the whole ten years I worked there as I was nauseated by the mere sight of him.

Bert, on the other hand, was a different story. I was nauseated by just the mere smell of him. This guy would wear the same ripped up shoes and dingy clothes every night of the week, yet he was supposedly worth a fortune. He didn't have a job at the time, and I'm pretty sure he never had one. Bert would walk through the same side door at exactly the same time every night. Then he'd meander through the restaurant for his meet-and-greet until it was finally time to sit at the counter, where he refused to purchase anything. Not only would Bert horde the seat of a potential paying customer who could turn around and tip you, but his grungy appearance kept anyone from sitting anywhere near him. But that didn't bother ole Bert. He sat at the counter religiously as if he were a paid performer brought in to entertain his adoring fans. For years, the management team let him get away with this crap as if he was part of the memorabilia that graced the walls. And for every free meal someone offered him because they felt sorry for him, you could feed a whole continent.

Bert always politely refused these meals, but he loved playing this little game of creating an unknown mystique about himself. His whole charade revolved around the fact that people who met him for the first time were supposed to think that he was homeless, but the goof on them was that he was really well off, something he casually leaked to the most boisterous member of our wait staff, Chester. If Bert was really loaded, I found him to be a complete jerk for tricking people into opening their hearts and wanting to help someone in need even though he wasn't in need. But I also found him to be a complete jerk even if he wasn't loaded but pretended to be because he wanted you to laugh at people who wanted to help him. Yet he would never fully answer you when you asked him whether or not he was really worth anything. I wanted to strangle him. He drove this hunk of scrap metal called a car whose exhaust pipe left a carbon footprint the size of King Kong's. And the pisser about this guy was that when I would catch him eating at another restaurant, he would show no remorse for not patronizing our store. In fact, I was supposed to find it funny that I actually witnessed him stuffing his face at another eatery. He even had the audacity to explain to me how he dined at Sizzler every Tuesday, Thursday, and Saturday night. Then he'd babble on about how he'd always order the salad bar where he ate exactly twenty-one meatballs because twenty meatballs weren't enough and twenty-two meatballs were too many. Insert his annoying laugh here, which resembled that of a drunken department store Santa Claus staggering home from Macy's on Christmas Eve, and you have the makings of a complete douche-bag. He even had the straggly grey beard to boot.

There's not too much more to say about the guy other than the fact that he hung out with the most annoying late-night people (next to him) that frequented the joint and that he debated with the logic of an idiot savant. "It's either black or it's white, right? Right? It's either black or it's white. It can't be both. It has to be black, or it has to be white. Right? Right?" Insert his idiotic laugh here. Then he'd splinter off into how he'd buy the cheapest toothpaste in the store no matter what brand it was as long as it was the cheapest. It had to be the cheapest. Then when he was finished with that drivel, he'd ask you if you'd seen the Lakers game. Then he'd debate you as to whether Phil Jackson was the greatest coach of all time or if he just coached the greatest players of all time, as if any of it mattered or as if I really cared. This creature from the underworld would go on to haunt me for the whole ten years I worked there, not because he enjoyed getting under my skin. Oh no, he did it because he simply couldn't fall asleep at night. Yes, that's right. Count Bert preferred to sleep during the day, leaving him enough energy to suck the life right out of me during the graveyard shift. So, to sum it all up, I was forced to deal with this enigma named Bert for an entire decade all because he was too afraid to go beddy-bye at nighty night. Awesome!

I can't remember if the smelly cretin was actually in his usual crusted-over position at the counter the night an eleven-year-old boy sat there unaccompanied. As I bustled in and out of the kitchen into the wee hours of the morning, I remember finding it odd that a young kid was out that late; especially in our restaurant and especially on a school night. When I didn't see a parent with him, I guess I just assumed he was the prodigy of one of our fine employees who often dragged their offspring out to the workplace for a complete eight-hour shift when a baby sitter wasn't available. It turns out that a news story kept flashing on the multitude of television sets that were strategically hung at every viewing angle in our restaurant. The ongoing alert featured a missing Pasadena boy the police were on a frantic search to find. It didn't even dawn on me until the police cars arrived and the news crews came charging through our front doors that the missing boy on the TV was the very same kid guzzling down milkshakes at the front counter, courtesy of our manager, Bill.

Bill, being the attention whore that he was, only recognized the kid because he had nothing better to do than to look up at the TV every few minutes. Not only did Bill keep his discovery to himself, but he kept the kid sipping on free milkshakes until the peace officers arrived. I am certain that Bill remained silent in order to take sole credit for his heroics that night, which in all fairness I guess he deserved. So, in return, Bill got a nice thank you from the Los Angeles Police Department and his fifteen minutes of fame on the local LA news stations.

As the story unraveled in a most surreal way (surreal not because of the odds of something like this actually happening in our store but surreal because Bill actually smiled during the segment), we learned that the kid made his way to our restaurant because his parents were getting a divorce and the little man was upset. And because his parents used to take him to our chophouse for dinner, when things got rough between his folks, the boy decided to go to the only place he could think of where … he liked the food? But that wouldn't explain why he came to our place. But, in any event, he jumped on a few city buses and ended up at the old familiar deli. Thank God, the boy was returned safely into the caring arms of loved ones who had been tirelessly searching for him rather than into the hands of the riff-raff that stumbled into our late-night cesspool at all hours of the morning. And thank God Bill wasn't sleeping in his favorite booth as he usually was during the graveyard shift.

Speaking of the counter area, no sunrise would be complete without the morning rituals of Harry. Harry would rumble in at seven every morning and head directly to the coffee machine. God forbid, if there wasn't fresh, hot coffee waiting for him. I truly believe his daily dose of mud was the only thing keeping him alive, and you could at least stave off a few derogatory comments if you could provide him with this one simple luxury. Once he had his coffee in hand, he'd look over the stock levels around the counter area while mumbling under his breath. Then he'd wander to the back of the house to resume his duties.

One morning, Harry's routine was about to be severely interrupted.

As Harry plodded his way to the back of the house one particular AM, a gunman was awaiting his arrival. The man urged Harry to take him into the office so they could access the safe. With a loaded gun pointed at him, Harry had no choice but to comply. As Harry nervously and reluctantly dug his keys from his pocket, a cook named Jose stumbled upon the hold-up. Using the element of surprise, Jose tackled the gunman who discharged the weapon. The assailant took off running while the gun lay on the floor. Jose chased the man briefly, but the retreating burglar had already made a fleet-footed escape. When Jose arrived back to check on Harry, he spotted a bullet hole in the walk-in cooler and a trembling Harry, who was shaken but unharmed. Later, when Harry was finally able to speak again, he said he had been sure the gunman was going to kill him once the money changed hands.

As a reward for Jose's heroics, he received a two-week paid vacation. Now for the part of the story that I always love to tell. This exemplifies the amount of loyalty this establishment had for even its most valued employees. Two weeks after Jose returned from his paid furlough, he was fired by the company for showing up late for a shift. Never mind the fact that he had just saved the life of the owner's friend and also saved the restaurant thousands of dollars, but how dare he violate the company's tardiness policy. I think maybe the owner was just angry because Jose knocked the gun loose from the robber, which in turn left a bullet hole in his walk-in cooler. This made absolutely no sense to me or anyone else on staff. I guess the lesson to be learned here is that if you ever stumble upon a gunman about to kill Harry, let him do it. At least this way, you'll have enough turkey on Thanksgiving Day and enough supplies to get you through the week. Unbelievable!!!

Even more unbelievable were the clients who would show up at all hours of the morning, announcing their most intimate secrets. If only those walls could talk. A small minority of our late-night crowd included hit men. It always amazed me how openly candid some of these professionals for hire were. A few of them would even carry on their conversations with the volume and detail of someone adamantly telling a friend about their tumultuous day at the office. One night this turned out to be a grave mistake for the man involved. I'll never forget when Sandy, a dramatic but pretty young waitress in her midtwenties made a plea for us, her fellow servers, to help her stall one of her customers in the event he suddenly tried to leave the restaurant. She also asked us not to do anything that would expedite his service because she needed to buy some time. She couldn't give us any of the details, but as it turned out, an undercover detective was randomly seated next to a contractual killer who was discussing the nuances of his latest assignment with an acquaintance.

As I said earlier, I'd witnessed this type of bravado before, but when I would overhear someone boasting of a hit they had pulled off, I assumed it was the testosterone talking and the guy running his mouth off couldn't kill a fly with a fly swatter. But in this case, the specifics checked out. The detective left the facility to place a call to his department, where all of the information he picked up on was verified. The detective anxiously waited outside the building for his backup. The hit man, in the meantime, finished his meal and was ready for his check. Sandy was becoming increasingly nervous as the undercover officer was currently out of visual range. As backup cruisers arrived in the parking lot, the detective quickly briefed them and then re-entered the store. He casually sought out Sandy and asked her to drop off his check (wink, wink), which also meant she could cash out the hit man. The detective pretended to make his way to the restroom but instead hid around the corner, out of view, as the contractual killer settled his tab. I could see the police officers, with their guns drawn, covering both exits. As the hit man got up to leave, the detective loosely followed him. As the two confidants neared the main entrance, two police officers with their hands on their weapons were standing at the front door. The two officers then asked the suspected murderer for a word outside. As the self-professed assassin looked behind him he spotted the trailing undercover cop and finally realized what had happened. The officers then guided the man to the parking lot where he was handcuffed and placed in an awaiting police car. That night, an evening out at a Jewish deli cost a man more than the amount of his overpriced meal; it cost him his freedom. As for Sandy, not only did she receive a generous tip out of the deal; she also earned one heck of story for her grandkids.

Like all memorable events during our lifetimes, as long as we were cognizant, I am sure we all remember where we were the day of the 9/11 attacks. I, personally, was in my bed sleeping after a late night at the deli. When I picked up my phone around noon to see if my agent had called with an audition notice, I ran across a startling voicemail from my buddy Steve in Arizona who alerted me that "Some planes have been hijacked by terrorists, and they're on their way to California ... Wake Up!!" I immediately thought to myself, "What the hell is he talking about?" I shot out of bed, and after stumbling around my apartment for a few seconds, I made my way over to the front window, where I peeked through the blind to see if I noticed anything different. The sun was shining, and everything appeared to be normal, so I retreated back across the room and flopped back down on my mattress. I lay there for a few moments, trying to ignore this panicked community bulletin, but my curiosity finally got the best of me. I had to find out what the hell was going on.

So I leaned over, grabbed my phone, and called Steve back. When he picked up, he frantically cut to the chase and asked me if I had seen the news. Since just a few minutes ago, I had been sound asleep in my nice comfortable bed, coupled with the fact that I didn't have a TV set in my apartment, the answer was obviously no. He rambled through his version of the story at breakneck speed. Since a few hours had gone by since he'd left his urgent public service announcement on my voicemail, he assured me that all of the planes had landed but we were probably still going to go to war. After I got off the phone with Steve, I immediately called Henry (a) to see if what I heard was true and (b) to find out if we'd still be open. As I am sure you've already suspected, Henry confirmed everything and reinforced my notion that even if the deli was at the epicenter of a nuclear blast we'd remain open. Both responses were answers that I didn't necessarily want to hear.

It wasn't until I arrived at the deli later that evening that I finally witnessed the footage of the planes crashing into the towers over and over again. My co-workers and I stared at the screens in shock as did many of our patrons. Well, except for one ... Chester. Chester broke up our hypnotic trances with, "Man, you don't think the government did that, you crazy." What the hell was he talking about? I mean, I grew up believing in the American system. And not only did I have to hear it from him, but foreign customers, who I couldn't tell whether they were Israeli, Middle Eastern, or both, sang and cheered during the re-broadcasts. I had never wanted to hold an uzi in my hand so badly. And regardless of whether you like America or not, innocent people were murdered on that day, and it was hardly a time for song and celebration. Nor was it a time for radical black-man conspiracy theories either. And, of course, there was nothing I could do except swallow my anger, ignore my fears, and suffer through this dreadful yet memorable night.

There was high tension in the air for weeks. Hollywood royalty was spreading rumors around town that they were probably the next to be attacked. This made me laugh because they actually thought they were important enough to be targeted. This delirium heightened during the anthrax mailings. I was pretty unscathed by it all, and I even sent out headshots in envelopes that read, "Caution: Highly Flammable Actor Inside." I couldn't believe it when I actually got a meeting out of that one.

Back at the deli, I was accused of not giving a woman good service because she was Muslim. I told her not to be offended, that I didn't give good service to anyone, but she insisted on speaking with a manager to make an issue out of it. We were very busy that night, and honestly, I had no clue she was Muslim. She could have been a Zulu tribal woman for all I knew. But, nonetheless, I was working in a Jewish deli where all kinds of prejudices were emerging during this very stressful time.

As all of these significant events were unraveling in the world, my acting career was sinking in the mud. I was getting tired of dancing for the man in commercial auditions that were more appropriate for an actor with the IQ of a box of raisins than they were for someone as intelligent and focused as myself. Besides, I wasn't getting any callbacks, and my agent just had his AFTRA-SAG eligibility revoked after he stole one of his client's paychecks. So, it was time, once again, to take matters into my own hands. If Hollywood didn't have an appropriate role for me, I decided I was going to create one for myself.

So, I bought every screenwriting book that I could get my hands on. I went on to read and absorb everything in them and then began penning vehemently. At that time, I didn't even own a computer so my first script was actually written in pencil. I was so excited when

I finally finished my first screenplay that I unhesitatingly picked up the phone and started giving my million-dollar pitch to any studio executive or studio executive's assistant who would listen. I wasn't expecting an immediate response or, for that matter, any reply at all, but within just one short hour after my first batch of phone calls went out, a major studio gobbled up the story line and contacted me for a copy of the script.

I could hardly breathe, and I had stars in my eyes. They asked me if I had an agent, and I reluctantly had to tell them no. Then they explained to me that they'd send me a form that, basically, said, "If we steal your script from you, you can't sue us." I was so excited that a big Hollywood studio was interested in my story that I couldn't sign the form fast enough. It also dawned on me that I probably shouldn't send them a script written in pencil. Now, not only was I re-reading the story for content, I was trying to figure out how I was going to turn my lead-based screenplay into an acceptable and professional document in a short amount of time. I was now wishing that I had kept my big mouth shut until I had thought things through a little more.

So I called up a friend who worked as a secretary for MGM. She snuck me into her office every night for two weeks straight until I could bang out a typewritten copy of my screenplay. Even though she helped me with this monumental task, it still took us the entire two weeks to complete it. Every time we changed something, we had to go back and change all of the page numbers as we didn't have a screen-writing program at our disposal. This process seemed to take forever, but when the transcript was finally finished, it brought new hope to my sputtering Hollywood career.

I was now attacking Hollywood with a deadly one-two punch. I was combining my new writing prowess with my ever-improving acting skills. Soon, not even Spielberg would be able to say no to me. And the very same character that I brought in to Joe Fox's casting office was now engrained in my DNA. By now, I had been working on the character of Danny for a year and a half, and I was ready to take my show on the road. The only problem I had was that I had been through five different scene partners who thought I was a little too into the role of a violent madman who thinks he killed somebody and who, in turn, tries to kill her. Also, finding someone to play the dysfunctional female who sucked off her father was turning out to be a real challenge.

Getting people to come out to see a play in Hollywood is like putting a pedophile in a retirement home. But, I was determined to be proactive about my career. Then, another miracle happened. Hidden in the back of the room at the Herbert Ross Acting Studio was a pretty, buxom, and soft-spoken young blonde named Mary who had a slight crush on me and who wanted to work together on a scene. She was the last person in the world I thought would've been able to pull off the role of Roberta, but as it turns out, she was even crazier than I was and had the exact background (minus the sucking-off-her-father part) to play the character in the piece.

She also had a few other things going for her. For one … she had just gotten a divorce from her husband. Two … she liked the play. Three … she liked me. And four … she wanted to put a little cash into her career and hence the production. Since just a few months earlier, I couldn't even find anybody to work on the scene with in class, let alone split the cost of a self-produced theatre production, she was a welcome addition to the team.

So Mary and I started working on the material and started dating. I can't remember which of the two came first, but after six months of intense fighting, both inside and outside of rehearsal, we were ready to perform our little three-week show. The amount of preparation it took to perfect ourselves was astounding. We worked with an Alexander Technique teacher to flush out the characters' physical traits, took dialect lessons from a linguistics expert to nail down the play's lower class Bronx vernacular, and hired a director to block out our movements and to keep us from killing each other. I give my partner a lot of credit for the emotional and physical commitment she made to the material when she did decide to work on it, but trying to get her to put any kind of effort into the show was like pulling a continent up a mountain. Each and every time I wanted to rehearse, it would turn into a knock-'em-down-drag-'em-out fight in order to get her to participate. I believe she innocently thought that she could simply buy her way into being a good actress or maybe even thought she was good enough to just wing it. But either way, I wasn't busting my ass at the deli or the acting studio to get up on stage and look like a hack. I refused to let my one opportunity to show the industry what I was made of stink up the theatre like a giant turd, so the battles ensued.

Our director, Katya, was the perfect fit for our dysfunctional relationship on stage and off. To begin with, she was referred to us by our Alexander Technique teacher who had seen a play Katya had directed at UCLA. He told us that she had some edge. That would turn out to be an understatement. The more we got to know Katya, the more we discovered that she was a much looser cannon than the both of us combined. We first noticed her instability when she started showing up late for rehearsals. If her excuse wasn't that her tires were slashed (which they really were), it was because she sliced off the tip of her finger at her job (which she really did) or that she had to find a new place to live (which was also true).

Katya moped around endlessly and barely said a word during rehearsals due to her severe bouts with depression. Then out of nowhere, while we were practicing, she would grow agitated with our performance and start screaming at us at the top of her lungs. Other days, she'd pass out on the studio prop couch from exhaustion. As she got more and more comfortable around us, she later revealed to us that she used to work as a prostitute and that one of her clients was Verne Troyer, a.k.a. Mini-Me from Austin Powers fame, who she claimed wasn't so mini. She was getting fed up with her financial condition and complained to us that if things didn't soon improve in her life she was going to become an assassin. She grew up in the former Soviet Union and was the result of a broken and tragic home life. So, why did we keep her on as our director? She did it for almost nothing when everyone else wanted a ridiculous sum of money to do it. Plus, we felt it would be better to put someone's name on the production other than the two actors who were starring in it, even if we did what we wanted anyway.

We rented a little hole-in-the-wall, black-box theatre in downtown Hollywood for three weekends in the fall of '02. The space held about thirty people, and because it was a non-equity playhouse with fewer than one hundred seats, the author of the play refused to let us advertise. Not only could we not promote our little two-person show that we had worked so tirelessly on, but also our production ran smack dab into the middle of the World Series, and one of our shows actually coincided with a World Series game. As you might imagine, most people didn't want to come out and watch a bunch of "no names" perform some obscure and unadvertised three-act play, let alone during a World Series game. So, in short, for all of the time, hard work, and energy that we poured into our little three-week spectacular, not one professional from the industry or the media came out to see it. Not all was lost, though. Mary knew some people who were producing a low-budget movie, called *Living with Uncle Ray*, that could potentially lead to my first role in a feature film. So maybe, just maybe, I would get the break I was looking for.

The very next thing to happen to me wasn't really as much of a break as it was a sign from God. At that point in my silver-screen career, I had been at the deli for almost three years, and my quality of life had somewhat improved. I now had an apartment with a working AC and a great gal to come over and bake me muffins. But I still hadn't booked an official acting gig in Hollywood, and I was stuck in a perpetual state of living paycheck to paycheck. On one particular morning, I left the deli at around seven after finishing my graveyard shift as a closer. I had turned the restaurant over to the very capable hands of the breakfast crew and its brute of a manager, Gus. On my bleary-eyed ride home that morning, I could feel the outside air rapidly heating up. I couldn't wait to get home to my new and improved apartment with a working air conditioner. By now, I had my daytime sleeping routine down to a science as the inside of my living quarters resembled that of a deep, dark cave. I blocked out the light by closing all of the blinds and by draping heavy blankets over the windows. I was basically living the life of a Hollywood vampire.

When I awoke from my slumber that afternoon, I had several red-alert messages from my co-workers telling me that there had been a fire at the restaurant. And no, I didn't do it! As the calls kept pouring in, I was having 9/11 flashbacks. As I put bits and pieces of the staff members' stories together, I was able to deduce that after I had left that morning, the vent, which Gus failed to make sure was clean, took in a high flame from the grill and sparked up like a dried-out Christmas tree. That, in turn, set off the sprinkler system, which water-logged all of the old Hollywood photos and memorabilia that blanketed the walls of our restaurant. Would the next logical step, after being briefed by my fellow serfs, be to call Henry? Or would it? I mean, I had the feeling I'd get more verbal clarity out of a mime. Anyway, this was the course of action I decided to take, and when I asked him if there was a fire at our jobsite, he said with the utmost certainty, "Yeah, you're probably not going to be working tonight." I thought to myself, "This must be serious if the deli is actually going to shut down for a day." I mean, couldn't we still roast hotdogs on the burning ashes of the building and continue to make a profit?

It turns out Henry's response was a bit of an understatement. The restaurant remained closed for two years. When I drove by the scene of the crime later that day to witness the devastation firsthand, I was surprised to find that it appeared as if nothing at all had happened to the building as there were no signs of any structural damage.

People were scurrying in and out through the side entrance with armloads of stuff, and the parking lot was closed off with yellow caution tape. The early reports from Mr. Snuffleupagus and Co. assured us that we would re-open shortly. Then, after a few weeks went by, they reassigned us all to sister restaurants throughout the Los Angeles area until our store was ready to re-open for business. The time-frame for this festive event changed on a daily basis. First, we'd re-open at the end of the month, then it was the end of the year, then it was next week, then it was next year, until I started to think, "Are they ever going to open again?" But, I'll tell you, the timing of this travesty couldn't have been any better.

Mary was asking me to move in with her, and this temporary setback in my restaurant career provided the perfect reason to do it. She wanted me to quit working as an indentured servant and felt that she could hold us over with the money that she had tucked away from her divorce. She also wanted to spend some quality time with me when I wasn't tweaked out from dealing with all of the drunken ignoramuses that stumbled into our late-night eatery on a regular basis. She saw how burnt out I was getting, but I, on the other hand, wasn't ready to give up my manhood or my cash flow quite yet.

She romanticized about how we could both work on this upcoming movie project together and how it could help open doors for both of our careers. She did help me, Jozef Rothstein, get a role in the project, but it wasn't that of a lead or supporting actor. It was that of an assistant to an assistant working on the set. I didn't even get a credit at the end of the movie. But, I had never so much as stepped foot on a film set before, so I guess this experience was better than nothing. Well, it almost turned out that way.

One day, on a pre-production run for *Living with Uncle Ray,* I had to pick up some paperwork from a producer who was putting the finishing touches on a low budget movie that he was working on. The scene I dropped in on was being shot at Sunset Gower Studios and I wasn't allowed to enter the sound stage until the take they were filming was in the can. The producer I was there to meet was a short trolley man by the name of Weasel McGovern. Weasel talked a good game and got his rocks off on playing the part of a Hollywood big shot. The only problem with this little hobgoblin was that he was in the game to rip off anyone he could, especially any clueless sucker gullible enough to put his trust in him. After being pointed out to Mr. McGovern, I approached him and told him who I was and what I was there to pick up. In an effort to impress me, he told me not to look right away, but to nonchalantly look on the set as I was about to leave the building and I would see Faye Dunaway.

When my head naturally and instinctively turned right towards Ms. Dunaway, Weez dropped to the floor and pulled me down with him. I asked him what the hell he was doing, and he emphatically replied, "I told you not to look right away." He went on to tell me that earlier that day Ms. Dragon Lady had gone ballistic on a crewmember whom she accused of looking directly into her eyes. The film really needed Ms. Dunaway for her name value, and Mr. Big Shot's actions that day showed me that he was willing to compromise himself, or anybody else for that matter, just to keep a Hollywood "name" attached to their very sorry excuse for a movie. I learned a very valuable lesson that day; any cheap, low-budget movie can get almost any former superstar actress you can think of as long as you have a few thousand dollars of cold hard cash to throw at her. Just don't expect her to respect you, your project, or anyone else involved in it for that matter.

Leading up to the filming of *Living with Uncle Ray*, I decided to stay with the restaurant to keep the funds trickling in. My re-assignment would land me at the Beverly Hills chapter of our Matzo Ball Fraternity, where I would once again be assigned to the graveyard shift. On paper, being placed at our Beverly Hills store seemed like a real step up in the world if not an utter blessing. Palm trees, Rolls Royces, and Hollywood movie stars, right? During any other shift, this would probably hold true, but something very unusual happened every weekend once the clock struck midnight.

First of all, every check after midnight had an automatic gratuity added to it no matter how small the check total was. In many cases, this resulted in a double gratuity. The money at this location was twice as good as what I had been taking in at the other store, so what was the problem, you may ask? It's what I didn't tell you that transformed this step up in pay into a double-edged sword. This Beverly Hills venue turned into a war zone after midnight. Every gangster, pimp, and hooker in Los Angeles turned up at this hotbed of criminal activity on the weekend. We weren't far from Compton where most of these gangstas and wannabe rappers "represented" from after finding their way from the Hollywood strip located just a few blocks away. Note: This was not the ideal scene for a tall, white, Jewish guy named Jozef Rothstein. On most weekend nights, you could barely move through the large crowd, making this place a recipe for disaster. Even with armed guards on hand, all kinds of violent episodes would break out, not to mention shootings. After around a month on the job, a huge riot broke out during my shift.

People were standing on tables, throwing chairs, and smashing glasses. While many were cheering on the melee, some clients took the opportunity to use the chaos as an excuse to skip out on their bills. Once again, Sal was there to remind us that he would fire anyone he caught trying to pull one over on the company. I swear he must have had a twin brother because he always seemed to be at the wrong place at the right time. Sal was starting to sound like a broken record. When I thought about how working in this hostile environment put me in harm's way yet Sal was more concerned about collecting company revenue, I reached my boiling point. What also made this belittling speech by good ole Sal unacceptable was the fact that I knew that I had a little wiggle room if I decided to leave the deli business behind me. Putting up with this kind of crap was becoming intolerable. I was at the end of my rope, and the next event would all but seal the deal.

One night, a couple of weeks after the riot and at the end of a very busy Saturday night shift, I was helping a pretty young black girl close up the patio area when a male gang banger came up to where I was standing and told me that he wanted my attractive co-worker to serve him. I politely told him that we were closed and that she was unable to help him. He said, "No, I want her to serve me." And I guess what he meant by "serve me" was that he wanted her to perform a sexual act on him. When his "homey" exited the restaurant and stumbled upon the scene, he immediately caught wind of what his boy was up to. They now both found the solicitation hilarious, and of course, with the additional encouragement, Snoop Jr. persisted on. While pretending to play dumb, I once again told him, "Sorry, we're closed. We can't help you," and "You should probably get going. It's late." That's when all of a sudden, Lil Suge Knight started to take great offense to my lack of cooperation and instantaneously became my mortal enemy. The jokes suddenly stopped and now Smallsie Bigs was just staring me down. After his useless posturing, he whispered something to his friend, and they walked off to their car and drove away.

About a half-hour later, as I was closing out my checks, I noticed their ghetto cruiser passing by the front of the restaurant. It circled back around, driving very slowly. What I don't think they saw were the fifteen or so members of the LA County Sheriff's Department snacking on some late-night pastries. The management team had no problem allowing the sheriff's deputies in after hours as this was a nice trade-off for their protective services, especially when the money was changing hands. I watched cautiously as the *vato* who had been talking smack on the patio got out of their low rider and walked towards the restaurant. I quickly scampered off to the back of the house before Cripland could spot me, and I waited there until he was gone. The hoodlum with a score to settle was wearing a large, baggy coat, and

I am certain until this day he was coming back to shoot me as some sort of vendetta. Boy N the Hood probably would have hung around a little longer had it not been for his shocking discovery of the multitude of sheriff deputies sitting at the front of the restaurant. Mr. Thug Life circled the place once, and when he didn't spot me, he made his way back to the awaiting gangster mobile outside. I deeply pondered my place in life and what that deli truly meant to me. When I came up with "absolutely nothing," I decided to have a nice long talk with Mary. She informed me that she had had a dream a couple of nights prior that I got shot while in the line of matzo ball duty as she sat there helplessly and watched. She urged me to quit. About an hour before my next shift was supposed to start, I decided that I didn't want to die while slinging matzo ball soups so I informed the restaurant that I would not be coming into work ... ever again. I also explained to them why. They told me that I couldn't just quit on them, and I told them, "I just did." It appears that I made the right decision. A week later, a car drove past the Beverly Hills store and sprayed gunfire into the restaurant. One person was killed.

So now that my schedule was fully open, I was eager to get onto the set of my very first film project and learn all that I could. The movie, however, was cursed from the beginning. It also broke the old Hollywood adage that warns one to never work with kids or animals. This one had both. And one of my many tasks involved wrangling both. The script for these first-time filmmakers was interesting enough, but the execution of the entire production was terribly flawed as no one really seemed to know what the hell they were doing. The whole film was designed to be shot in one location, which is a wise move for any first-time filmmaker, especially these hacks who had a hard enough time managing one location, let alone several. *Living with Uncle Ray* was about a troubled Vietnam vet who returns home and finds himself fighting another war ... this time for the family TV. One of the movie's first-time actors, Steven Christopher Parker, has since gone on to star in movies, like *Rebound*, and TV shows, like *ER*. He also played bit parts in films, like *Little Miss Sunshine*, *Blades of Glory*, and *Juno*, and has been featured in many national commercials. The only other notable talent in this movie was Frank Payne, who was the host of a reality show, called *Big*, which ran several years ago. Each week on *Big*, the team would design and assemble the world's largest whatever. One week it was the world's largest popcorn machine; the next week it was the world's largest motorcycle. No matter what it was, these guys were on a mission to build it. And Frank, being the BIG guy that he was, fit the profile perfectly to host the show. Don't remember it? Well, on second thought, how many big things can you build before the world runs out of resources? Needless to say, *Big* didn't run that long.

It was almost comical to watch the producer/actor/writer/director/casting director/set designer/etc. Gene Duffy try to accomplish his vision for the piece while no one else seemed to give a crap. One of the gaffers left the set to work on a porno, and the DP was more concerned about always having a chilled bottle of water in the refrigerator than he was about setting up a well-lit shot.

The owner of the property was also an interesting case study. Simply put, the man was a ferocious drinker. Allegedly, the only reason he rented out his house for the production was that he was in trouble with the IRS. This same man, however, was his own studio supply store. I don't think the producers even realized the amount of random junk this man had on hand when they signed the location agreement. But whenever we needed some obscure prop, the land owner had it in a shed or a drawer somewhere. The first time I saw the location, the downstairs was completely empty and was one long continuous room. The production team, made up of about three people, rebuilt the entire downstairs into a full three-room set in about two days. And from what I heard, not a minute went by without the owner of the house criticizing every move they made. But usually the worst of it started after three p.m. when the bottle of vodka was attached to his hand.

When we got to the set on the first day, everybody chipped in to put the finishing touches on the newly built living room set where we were supposed to shoot our first scene. During an off camera rehearsal, one of the kids jumped up off the floor, shouting, "Eeew, maggots!" He was right. There were maggots crawling up through the carpet … and lots of them. As a matter of fact, there was some sort of infestation problem at that house, which also included black widows and the thousands of flies we found dead everywhere. Because the owner and his five kids stayed in the house during the three-week shoot, we had to let them know one day in advance where in the house we would be shooting the next day and at what time so they could adjust their schedules accordingly. The producers told us the owner would okay just about anything we needed for the production as long as we got his permission one day in advance. This would have been fine and dandy if the man holding the title to the success of the film wasn't completely annihilated every time we asked him for something for the next day. The production ran into a host of problems due to the owner's memory lapses. About halfway through filming, he was on the verge of shutting down the whole production and kicking us off his property because he felt that we were disrespecting his wishes. The day we were supposed to shoot in the owner's actual bedroom is a day I'll never forget.

On this particular morning, we had to be on set two hours before the rest of the crew arrived to prep the room. We needed more like ten hours. The dirt on the floor was about five inches deep, and one of my fellow PAs had to go to the hospital for dust inhalation. We found parts of sandwiches, a whole unwrapped beef jerky, and a ten-year old newspaper buried underneath all of the filth. We did the best we could to turn this pigsty into presentable film set, especially after being one person down, but there was only so much we could do, especially with Captain Caveman watching our every move. Every time someone criticized the proprietor's housekeeping habits, we'd turn around to see him standing in the doorframe. There was nothing at all glamorous about being on my first film set, and in the midst of this experience, I wondered if I'd ever want to be on one again.

Like father, like son. The owner's son also had a bit of an addiction problem as well, only his poison was heroin. I first suspected the gangly teen's vice when I was prepping his room for a kid's scene that was to be shot the following afternoon and found razor blades stuck in the carpet next to his bed. "Junior" also accused us of stealing a bag of his stash from his room and said that we were lucky that he couldn't go to his father about it because of the nature of the missing substance. But he still demanded that we return it. By the looks of some of my colleagues, I am sure at least one of them had a good time at his expense. And yes, this was all happening on the set of a family-themed movie.

Part of my animal handling expertise involved transporting the film's leading man, "Rooster," to the set. This was especially awkward for me since I had never handled a farm animal before. The owner of the property not only provided the rooster but also gave me a few pointers on how to subdue Rooster for transporting, which basically involved grabbing him by the feet and holding him upside down. I started to become very attached to this magnificent bird and found him to be more enjoyable than most of the people on set. That's why I was very saddened to learn of Rooster's untimely demise a few weeks after filming.

The producers caught wind of Rooster's fate when they went back to the owner's farm to see if the gamecock was available for pickups. That's when they were told he had been eaten by a coyote. That was the official story, but I wouldn't be surprised if the owner ate him for dinner. Either way, that's when I got a call from the producers requesting my assistance once again. This time they needed me to find a matching bird to replace the one I had grown so attached to during the original shoot. I was still out of work, even though a year and a half had gone by since the fire at the restaurant. In the meantime, I had written another screenplay while applying my firsthand movie-making knowledge acquired on the set of *Living with Uncle Ray*. But besides that, I didn't really have much going on, so I agreed to help.

Before I started my search, I had to revisit a picture of the good ole boy so I could remember what he looked like. Once I had his image burned back into my brain, I began my quest to find a matching fowl. I first crashed all of the local feed stores in Los Angeles County. Unfortunately for me, at that time, many of the regional birds were suffering from bird flu, which made roosters very hard to come by. I tried everywhere and came up with nothing. Time was running out, and I was on the verge of giving up when I randomly passed by a slaughterhouse in the middle of nowhere while traveling through Sylmar, California. I decided to pull in and give this neighborhood grind house a whirl. As I strolled onto the property, I couldn't control the knot that formed in my stomach as I passed by all of the sickly animals awaiting their horrible fate. I still can't figure out for the life of me how I didn't become a full-blown vegetarian from that day onward.

When I walked into the main office, I interrupted a man sitting behind the front desk from staring deeply and blankly into space. This gentleman was typical of most LA residents in that he didn't speak very good English. He also seemed to have an immediate disdain for me, which was magnified one-hundred-fold when I asked him if I could buy a rooster. I could feel his contempt, not only for me but for the animals we marched past as he mumbled under his breath on our way to the rooster pen.

When we stepped inside the room that housed the chanticleers, I was horrified to discover that there were around twenty large cluckers crammed into a three-foot by ten-foot pen and they hardly had any room to move. I wanted to open the gate and free them all as I perused the selection, but with the California Chainsaw Masochist studying my every move, that fantasy was not even a remote possibility. I was convinced that the Mad Butcher would not even think twice about throwing me into a food processor along with all of the other animals he mistreated for a living.

In the middle of the flock, I saw what appeared to be an identical twin to the majestic fowl that we had used during the filming of *Living with Uncle Ray*. I pointed him out to the cold-blooded killer, who opened the gate to the pen. He briefly studied the bird and in one fell swoop reached in and snagged the cockerel. He pinned it down so hard while capturing it that I don't know how he didn't break its neck. As he approached me with the fluffy feathered creature, I unfortunately realized that he had grabbed the wrong cock. "That's not the one," I politely explained. The man psychotically scowled at me as if I had just shit on his shoe. I felt that at any second he would just drop the bird, and instead of plucking out its feathers, he would pluck out my eyeballs. The former innkeeper of the Bates Motel now gave me a good looking over before he returned to the cage.

When he got there, he ordered me, "Come here." When I arrived, in broken English with a Farsi dialect, he prodded, "Which one you want?" I pointed to my bird of choice and replied, "The white one." Like a lion on the hunt, he began eyeing up the rooster that I had singled out. He studied the bird carefully until he sensed the exact right moment to spring on him. Then, within an instant, he was knocking feathered creatures out of the way until he could grab the legs of the fowl that I had selected. He yanked the desired male chicken out of the pen so forcefully that it sent the remaining inhabitants into a flurry. He was very proud of his catch. He demonstrated this fact to me by holding up his beaked trophy like a little boy who had just won a fishing contest. As I inspected his latest conquest, I noticed that there was something terribly wrong with this bird. I also realized that the shoot was taking place the following morning and that it was far too late in the game to find a closer match.

As all of these facts rushed through my mind at breakneck speed, I just nodded my head and said, "Yep, that's the one." The man briskly snapped back, "Six dollars. I kill it and have it ready for you tomorrow." A sudden panic rushed over me as the animal grim reaper appeared ready to break the bird's neck. I swiftly cut him off before he could do any further damage to my animated prop, pleading, "No, I don't want you to kill it. I want to take him home with me." The man's confusion turned to anger as his maniacal gaze pierced a hole through my forehead. Dr. Kerchickian then suddenly tried to hand me the bird, from which I instinctively pulled away. I asked him if he had anything to put it in. Brutus was running out of patience, and I knew this was probably my last favor. He left the room and came back with a cardboard box, which he threw on the ground. He stuffed the bird in the box, and I handed him the six dollars. I thanked the man for his assistance and scurried out of the door as quickly as possible. I rushed to create a distance between us as I kept the surgical slayer in my periphery at all times. As I neared the end of the property, I steadily picked up my pace to an all out sprint. When I reached my Mazda 323, I tossed the bird in the backseat, fired up the engine, and gunned it for the nearest freeway. It wasn't until I was about halfway home that I gradually slowed down enough to fall within the posted speed limit. It was at this point, when I finally wiped the sweat from my brow and reveled in my accomplishment.

When I returned home, unfortunately, my partner, Mary, didn't view my achievement in quite the same regard. This was because a neighbor had recently knocked on our door to complain about our two dogs and their incessant barking. And before our gracious neighbor left, she insisted that we do something about it. So obviously, there was no way Mary was going to let me keep a rooster in our backyard overnight. Then the interrogation began, "Why didn't you just leave the rooster at the slaughterhouse and pick him up in the morning?" When I tried to explain what I had just been through, Mary was in no mood to hear it. She then started nagging about how I should've just dropped Gregory Peck off at the farm since it was right up the street from where I discovered him. "Well, if the last bird was really eaten by a coyote that jumped a six-foot wall, why in the hell would I leave him there overnight?" I snapped back. I mean my reputation was on the line here for a movie that could catapult both of our careers.

As it turns out, art does imitate life. Just like the character of Uncle Ray in the movie, I was having trouble falling asleep due to the anticipation of a crowing rooster. What made matters worse was the fact that it was the middle of summer, and the coolest room in the house just so happened to be the bathroom next to my bedroom. And, of course, that's where the cackling co-star spent the night. I was petrified to fall asleep, knowing that at any second a cock-a-doodle-doo could come blaring out of the bathroom, waking me and the entire neighborhood up from our peaceful slumbers. And as I originally observed at the slaughterhouse, this bird was not normal.

I knew there was something wrong with that rooster the minute the axe man from the animal hatchery brought him over to me. For one, the majority of his feathers had been plucked out, which is something that happens when fowl go insane, especially when they are cooped up in such a tiny pen with so many other birds. Also, this bird was very sickly and was puking and pooping constantly, even though I had provided him with the best feed I could find. To make matters worse, when Mary placed Rooster's body-double inside the cat carrier, which temporarily housed him, the cat carrier was sitting upside down. This meant that the shallow tray was acting as the floor and the deep pan was acting as the ceiling instead of the other way around. I wouldn't realize this mistake until I tried to carry Rooster II out of the house the following morning at six a.m. with temperatures already reaching upwards of ninety-five degrees. As I staggered down the front steps towards Mary's Pathfinder, the bird started frantically shifting his weight around, causing the cat carrier to tip over, spilling rooster vomit and feces all over my pants. The only gratification I got out of this whole disgusting episode was the fact that I used Mary's car to shuttle Rooster to the set that day. She probably still hasn't gotten the smell out of the seats from the excrement that sloshed around the inside of her vehicle on our way to the location.

We worked with a skeleton crew that day, and the gentleman who replaced the initial director of photography was much more talented behind the camera than the original monkey who shot the first batch of material. The problem with this fat Elvis-meets-Bob's-Big-Boy DP was the heat was killing him. The fact that he smoked ten cigars per hour didn't help matters either. This, in turn, led to the near destruction of the owner's property when he threw one of his half-finished cigars onto a pile of hay in the sheep's den. Thank God an alert sound man saw the tiny flames shooting up from the ground and quickly stomped them out.

With everybody suffering from the blistering midday heat, it was decided that a nice air-conditioned restaurant would be an appropriate place for a lunch break. But due to the fact that I really needed the extra twenty bucks that was offered, I remained on set while the entire crew escaped the oppressive swelter to nourish their weary bodies. All that was required of me to earn my extra twenty bonus dollars was to move several hundred pounds of equipment from the first filming location to the second one, situated about two hundred yards away. As the relentless valley sun pounded down on me while I tenaciously transferred the entire movie set single-handedly to our next post, I began seeing mirages of beautiful woman in bikinis lying next to a swimming pool being served tall, cool piña coladas by … Bob's Big Boy??? I was in the process of moving the last c-stand when the gang arrived back from their lunch hiatus over an hour later. They were even gracious enough to bring me back a soda and a sandwich for my sacrifice.

The only actors we needed for that afternoon shoot were Manny and Rooster. Frank was a very funny fat man who had a ton of talent but at the time had a renowned reputation as a party animal. I don't know where he had been previous to the shoot on that scorching August day, but when he arrived on set, he was completely plastered. As we prepped the set for his big scene with Rooster, he slept on a lawn chair in a shaded area of the yard.

It was almost time to film, and there was only one remaining problem left to be solved: How were we going to keep the actors in the frame together? I mean we were talking about an untrained, if not completely insane, winged animal. And it's not Rooster that I'm referring to. I was already nominated to be the one to put the grip gloves on and to hold Rooster in place off camera while Manny poured his heart out to the only one who understood him, his pet rooster. The scene was to take place over dinner and a glass of wine. We shot a couple of takes and were close to moving on to a different camera angle when I noticed a change in Rooster's behavior at the end of a scene. He lifted up his rear end and, like something out of *The Matrix*, fired a stream of turds at me that I bent backwards to elude. I kept a firm grasp on Rooster's feet while hopping up to an upright position, which seemed to tick Rooster off even more. I don't know if Rooster was upset because Manny was eating chicken for dinner or because there were no red M&Ms in his trailer, but this temperamental co-star began throwing a hissy fit. Wings started flapping, and everything at the table, including Manny, got sprayed with fresh rooster droppings. And Frank, already overheated, drunk, and belligerent, just stared at the producer for a good ten seconds or so before he could finally muster the words, "I f@#$ing hate you!" It was a classic filmmaking moment.

Soon after the completion of the movie, Mary and I were completely out of money, and I was, once again, hard up for cash, the translation being that I was desperate enough to go crawling back to the deli with my tail between my legs, especially since Snuffy had re-opened the Studio City store. One of the new head servers, Kelly, was a good friend of mine and was instrumental in helping me overcome the obstacles that I had created for myself when I quit cold turkey from the Beverly Hills location. I was now a re-hiree with a fresh outlook on life.

Celebrity-ism

Well, if you are the type of person who just can't get enough of celebrity gossip, you may have skipped directly ahead to this chapter in order to tear into the largest portion of celebrity scuttlebutt contained in this book. I will attempt to satisfy your hunger for this frivolous blather as it relates to these larger-than-life tabloid media creations. I hope I don't shatter any pre-conceived notions that you may have of these self-centered superstars who, when out of the public spotlight, can, at times, conduct themselves in less than appealing ways. On the other hand, some of these attention-grabbing headliners may surprise you by their very gracious acts, which may, in turn, further endorse your wholehearted support for the good fortunes bestowed upon them. The distinctions are remarkably self-evident, as I am sure you will find when the stories are presented. But remember, there is something about a restaurant setting that tends to bring out the worst in people, especially individuals who are hungry and surrounded by bright red colors, so please don't judge too harshly.

It is my understanding that before I began my ten-year sentence in Matzatraz, the entire cast of Seinfeld dined there on a daily basis. The studio lot where they filmed was positioned only a few blocks away from the deli, which made for a convenient yet tasty feasting spot after a long day on set. By the time I started working in Matzo Land, their successful run on television had come to an end, but some of the cast members still occasionally garnished our deli with their presence, namely, Jason Alexander and Jerry Seinfeld. It was a well-known fact amongst me and me mates that Jason Alexander had formerly studied acting with one of my coaches before hitting it big. On many occasions, I could have gone up to Mr. Alexander and said something cheesy like, "Isn't so and so a great teacher?" but I never really felt the need. It wasn't until the end of my deli career that I actually got to wait on Mr. Alexander, even though he had made quite a few guest appearances over the years. And to be honest, the one time that I actually did wait on him, he really got on my nerves. He seemed to be a little burned out from playing the funny guy all of the time, and his "out in public routine" grew instantly tiresome. Adding to our strained dynamic was the fact that after ten years of dealing with all kinds of people, I certainly wasn't going to give him any courtesy laughs. At that point in my life, after being rejected by Hollywood for ten consecutive years, I actually hated celebrities more than the rude, ungrateful idiots that typically filled the space between our walls. So, maybe he just caught me in a bad year. He was polite and did acknowledge me as a living, breathing human being so I give him kudos for being a decent guy and a generous tipper. His buddy Jerry is another story.

Mr. Seinfeld was the one Hollywood hotshot that I encountered more in person than any other red-carpet royalty during my ten-year stint in Los Angeles. I don't know if it was his addiction to our Chinese chicken salad or the fact that his gigantic ego got a charge out of eating in a restaurant that was practically willing to name itself after him, but Jerry loved to frequent the joint. I don't want my introduction of the King of Prime Time to be misleading as he was a very lavish tipper. The problem with TV's funnyman was how uncomfortable he made you feel while you were waiting on him. I guess my downfall with the man who liked to talk about nothing was the fact that I treated him like every other paying customer who dined there and not like the big superstar he knew he was who just wanted to be left alone.

To start with, Mr. Seinfeld's arrival would always be preceded by that of his writer friend Barry, who served as head table scout. Barry looked like Chris Farley meets Fred Flintstone and came assembled with a pair of Henry Kissinger bifocals to boot. Barry never liked to be seated next to a bus cart or more specifically near a garbage can that was attached to a bus cart. He would either politely ask you to move the cart away from him or request to be seated elsewhere. Besides holding an open table for the Jerr-ster, Barry was sent out early to investigate the feng shui of the restaurant. Barry would walk around the room until he found a suitable table and then would ask if he could sit there. He would usually just yell over to one of us servers to ensure this was okay. Everyone knew Barry and also knew who would be joining him. Once Barry finally sat down, he would get up and move at least one more time. This was always for naught because once the prince of peculiarity actually did arrive he would want to move to yet another area anyway, especially if he realized they were sitting in my section. I never understood this bizarre ritual but I always found it quite amusing to watch.

I have to admit, I never liked the show, but I did look forward to waiting on Mr. Seinfeld the first time he landed in my section. Jerr-onimo seemed like someone whom I could have a good time waiting on while I bounced some impromptu material off him. His show featured a lot of oddball characters quite like myself, and I found our chance meeting to be somewhat divine. Instead of witty banter during our first couple of interactions, all I walked away with after parting from his table were images of him whining to his friend, "Can you believe that guy?" He sat in the back of the restaurant during my inaugural servitude of his majesty, and because of his snippy attitude, I was determined to go on the attack and cover the entire twenty points of service that we were required to follow for each table. Hey, what did I know? He ate there so much he could have been a secret shopper (wink, wink). What better disguise than that of a famous celebrity? Julia Child worked undercover with the OSS (Office of Strategic Services). Maybe Jerry Seinfeld, if that was his real name, was operating as an undercover agent for the celebrity shopper's network.

Anyway, I usually kicked off my routine with, "Hello, welcome to the home of the matzo ball soup. My name is Jozef. Can I bring you a beverage or a bar drink? A margarita or a glass of wine, perhaps?" I think I got as far as "Hello," when Jerry abruptly interrupted me with, "We're going to need a few minutes." When I came back after the allotted time, the man of a thousand laughs said they were ready to order and gave me no opportunity whatsoever to interject. He immediately ordered his Chinese chicken salad and beverage of choice and passed the matzo ball to Barry. Since TV's jokesmith cut me off before I even had a chance to offer them the second thing on my checklist, my next question was punching its way out of me like a baby alien stuck inside my colon. Once Barry finally finished stammering through his order, I went retroactive on their asses by asking them if they would like an appetizer such as mozzarella sticks or a quesadilla. Barry graciously declined and thanked me as I collected the menus. Mr. Seinfeld just stared intensively at the wall across from him.

When the food was ready, I immediately delivered it to their table and asked them if there was anything else I could get them. This was company policy and yet another item on my checklist, not me kissing Seinfeld's ass as he suspected. But by that point, I could tell the Good Jerr-man was getting very annoyed with my persistence. Barry spoke for the duo by calmly and politely stating something to the effect of "I think we're good." When I returned two minutes later to fulfill the next item on my checklist, which was to check back within two minutes to make sure their food was okay, Seinfeld was irate. He dropped his fork on his plate and leaned back in his seat. A bewildered Barry just nodded his head yes and continued to chew on the mouthful of food that he had recently crammed into his face. I'm not stupid. I can take a hint. Up until that stage of the meal, my checklist was complete so I only went back to the table every few minutes or so to refill their drinks, which also seem to vex the master of the one-liner.

After being assured that they were finished with their chow, I naturally felt compelled to collect their plates and whisk them away. I was nearing the end of my checklist and was gearing up for the grand finale. I strolled up to their table and in the most benevolent way possible asked, "Would you guys like something for dessert?" To which I got a surprising response from Mr. Seinfeld, "TEA!!!! I'd like some TEA!!!!" And did I mention the emphasis was on the word TEA? He put so much energy into the word TEA I thought his head was going to explode. We had a variety of teas to choose from so my next obvious question was, "What kind of TEA would you like?" He said, "I don't know. Just get me some TEA!!!!" I said, "Okay, I'll get you some TEA!!!!" Emphasis on the word TEA. At that point, we officially didn't like each other. I tried not to laugh when I returned back to his table with his TEA, which only seemed to infuriate him more. From that day onward, whenever the Jerr-inator stepped foot in our restaurant, he would purposely avoid my section, even if Barry picked out a booth in my jurisdiction. To Mister Crabby Ass's credit, he did tip me sixteen on thirty-four, but I cringed every time he walked into our restaurant, and I hoped and prayed to God that I would never have to wait on him again.

There was a bright spot in this bitter tale that involved a mammoth of a man named Big Joe, who at that time was a new manager on the floor. Big Joe was just that ... BIG. He tipped the scales at around 350 pounds and stood about six foot three. He also had the temperament of a charging rhinoceros. Just one week prior, Big Joe put his fist through a company computer screen after somebody lit his fuse. Big Joe, for the most part, liked the servers but had very little tolerance for the customers. He hated their nagging and disrespect for the rule of law inside HIS restaurant. After three weeks on the floor, Big Joe was a powder keg ready to explode, and Barry's timing couldn't have been any better.

It was a very slow evening during one of Big Joe's shifts when Barry reared his ugly head and entered the restaurant as the point man for Team Seinfeld. Barry nonchalantly strolled past the host stand in his casual yet preoccupied way. His goal ... to pick out the perfect table. Barry had done this so many other times before he was completely comfortable in his own skin while making himself feel at home. This did not go unnoticed by Big Joe, who watched the whole frontal assault from inside the perimeter. One very important thing that I forgot to mention about Big Joe was that Big Joe could move, especially when Big Joe had a purpose. Barry had just given Big Joe that purpose. Big Joe at breakneck speed verbally cut Barry off before Barry could strut past no more than three booths. "Sir. Excuse me, sir," Big Joe shouted. Barry continued on with his overall inspection of the facility while Big Joe's plea fell on deaf ears. Big Joe was being ignored, and Big Joe didn't like to be ignored, not when the perpetrator was disregarding restaurant policy and disobeying a direct order.

Big Joe quickly caught up to the trespassing table spotter as he entered the server station where he was about to greet us all. I was lucky enough to have a front row seat to the event.

"Excuse me, sir. You can't just walk in here like that," exclaimed Big Joe.

Barry cordially countered, "I'm sorry, I didn't—"

"Go back up to the host stand and wait to be seated. You can't just walk in here like that," Big Joe cut in.

"What are you talking about?" retaliated Barry.

"You heard me!" Big Joe snapped.

"Wait a minute," Barry replied. While looking at me for assistance, Barry emphatically stated, "Tell him who I am."

And wouldn't you know it, at that exact point in time, I suddenly felt the need to stretch my neck and look off in a completely different direction that just so happened to fall out of the direct eye line of Barry. Coincidentally, I also developed an itch on my head and noticed a blank spot on a faraway wall that piqued my interest. It was weird. It was as if I had suddenly lost control of my motor skills and completely forgot that Barry was addressing me. It didn't matter anyway. Big Joe had a point to make.

"Get back up there. I don't care who you are!" Barry was now insulted, which added fuel to his campfire.

"I will not go back up there!" he cried out.

"Then you can leave," Big Joe insisted.

"You can't kick me out!" whimpered back a shocked Barry.

"I just did. Now get out of here before I call the cops."

All right, I had let this go far enough. Jerry and Barry had been dining there for years and were good friends of Mr. Snuffleupagus. It was now my duty to stop this out-of-control freight train named Big Joe before he derailed from his tracks and lost his job.

When I tried to step in, Big Joe wanted no part of it.

"Go check your tables!" he hollered. "And you, get back up to the host stand!" In a fit of what appeared to be anger or what was maybe just a brisk power walk, Barry whisked past the host stand and right out through the front door. Barry was out of sight and out of mind for a good ten minutes or so before I saw his big dopey head pop back up like a Whack-A-Mole. He wanted to speak with Big Joe. In a shocking turn of events, Barry apologized to Big Joe and then promptly went over to the host stand to be seated. By then, Big Joe had calmed down enough to gather an ample supply of intelligence as to who it was he was belittling in front of the entire restaurant. This time, after they both cordially presented their cases to one another, they made up in what had to be the most awkward form of male bonding I had ever laid eyes upon. It was another major victory for the little guy, but it would be some time before my treasonous acts would allow me near Seinfeld's table again.

Then on a random day, a couple of years later, both Jerry and Barry came in and sat down in one of my booths. It was a very slow night, and they really didn't care where in the restaurant they sat. Did someone drug them? Anyway, they were parked in my section, and it didn't faze them in the least. I gave Mr. Seinfeld his space and had very little interaction with him throughout the course of his meal. In other words, I scrapped the whole twenty-point checklist for one of the few times in my deli career. I collected their plates and offered them nothing for dessert. They requested nothing but sat there and talked for another hour or so. Mr. Seinfeld once again tipped me around fifteen dollars on a thirty-something-dollar check, which was kind enough. Then on his way towards the side exit, he came up to me and said, "I know we were taking up your table for quite some time so here's a little something extra." I thanked him as he extended his hand and slipped me some skin. As he walked out through the side door, I inspected the bill he had placed in my hand. It was a twenty. This act of generosity immediately replaced any ill will I had towards the Good Humor Man as a result of our previous encounters. I don't know if I simply wanted to cherish this more pleasant experience with the master of observation or if I just didn't want to have to walk on eggshells in the name of the almighty dollar, but I never waited on him again. As a matter of fact, I purposely relinquished his table to another server on two ensuing occasions, which resulted in bypassing a guaranteed fifteen-dollar tip each time. Sometimes in life, money just isn't everything.

Since I am currently writing this section of the book a few days before Christmas, I am unfortunately reminded of a run-in on Christmas Day with a certain celebrity by the name of Sharon Stone. Christmas at the deli was typically the busiest day of the year. Those of us who stuck around for the holidays often worked double shifts to fill in for the more fortunate members of our staff who were able to return home to be with their families. The money at the restaurant was nice, but it involved a lot of stress and very long hours. Sometimes a simple act of kindness by a warmhearted soul could make all of the difference in the world. On this particular Christmas Day, the deli was only moderately busy when Ms. Stone and her family set up shop at the counter area where I was stationed. I was already exceptionally fast when it came to serving this section, but when I noticed a high profile celebrity sitting at my counter on Christmas Day, I bumped it up a few notches. I immediately greeted the Stone clan and removed the large plastic menus from the holders located directly in front of them. I dealt them out with the efficiency of a Las Vegas black jack dealer while the well-known diva and her family situated themselves.

I am not one who is easily starstruck, so I reassured myself that people of their affluence would appreciate a high level of service from someone who didn't drool all over them. Everything was going according to plan, that is, until I attempted to interact with these Hollywood dignitaries for the first time. "Hello my name is Jozef. I'll be your waiter today. Can I bring you something to drink?" I waited for a response only to stand in the midst of complete and utter silence. I know I was loud and clear when I addressed them so I gave them just a few more seconds to reply. By now, I am sure Ms. Stone Cold could at least feel me standing directly in front of her. But instead, she continued to read her menu as if I wasn't even there. After a good thirty seconds or so, I announced again, "Would anybody care for a beverage or a bar drink?" You could almost hear the echo of my words ricochet off the walls of the restaurant. I could feel a rush of emotion sweep over Ms. Heart of Stone as she skimmed through her menu, but she remained silent. I couldn't figure out what kind of game she was playing, nor did I want to, so I politely stated, "I'll give you a few more minutes."

I kept an eye on them from afar when I noticed that, lo and behold, they were actually able to speak, to each other anyway. When they finally appeared ready to order, I waited a few extra beats just to make sure that when I did re-appear before them they would be ready to do the largest amount of ordering in the least amount of time. I could already tell that Ms. Beaver Shot was not particularly fond of the fact that we would have to interact again so I just wanted to make this whole process as quick and painless as possible. Again, I approached the family, who I was now beginning to regret had sat down in my section, with a "Ready for those drinks?" Then Mrs. Stone and her husband began conversing with each other again about something totally unrelated. Okay, now they were really starting to piss me off, and a few cynical questions started entering my mind like, "Why did you sit at the counter anyway ... with a kid nonetheless?" "Don't you realize a booth would be much more comfortable?" And, "I am a pretty good waiter, but I am not a mind reader so you are going to have to tell me what you want if you want me to bring it to you. Otherwise, maybe your food will just appear in front of you ..."

"We want to order," she coldly demanded. "Well, halle-fricking-lujah," I laughed to myself as she rambled through her order. After they finished requesting the solid portion of their meals, I once again hit them with the age-old question of "Would you like something to drink?" to which I finally got an answer. I quickly learned that they would speak to me, but only on their terms.

Most of the orders that came out of our kitchen that day were a little off, but with the big fish that had just plopped down on my countertop, I was going to make sure everything went according to plan. I can't remember what the Wicked Bitch of the West ordered, but I do recall that she had quite a few requests, or should I say demands, once the food got there. I seamlessly carried out every command she threw at me. I also remember immediately cleaning up their area the second they were finished eating. I even went out of my way to fetch them a few pastries from the bake case for dessert. They weren't exactly jumping for joy, but I at least felt as if they were in a slightly better mood as their dining experience came to a close. After they were completely finished whipping me around like a used dishrag, I spotted their credit card on the tip tray. It didn't even occur to me that anything remotely less than a ten-dollar tip on a forty-something dollar check would appear on the signed copy of their receipt, especially on Christmas Day. But when I retrieved the credit card slip, I was shocked to see a measly six dollars scribbled across the tip line. Six dollars on a forty-something-dollar check wasn't even 15 percent. Well, so much for an A-list actress and her successful newspaperman husband giving to the less fortunate on a fine Christmas Day. Hopefully neither one of them yaks on a bone and/or ends up in divorce court. Oops, oh well, I guess I can still hope that nothing gets lodged in their airways.

The only thing worse than unwarranted rude behavior and a lousy tip from a celebrity on Christmas Day was unwarranted rude behavior and a lousy tip from a celebrity on a regular basis. This distinct honor was awarded to Mr. Steven Stills from the seventies' super group Crosby, Stills, Nash and Young. You know the precursor to today's boy bands. The only thing more insulting than unwarranted rude behavior and a lousy tip from a celebrity on a regular basis was when it was given to you on a paper receipt produced by a black American Express card. For those of you who don't know what a black American Express card is, it is a black, titanium credit card with an unlimited line of credit. And Mr. Stills was as cantankerous as they come. Maybe this old fuddy-duddy would be happier in life if Crosby, Stills, Nash and Young would have incorporated some super cool dance moves into their barbershop-quartet rock melodies. Thankfully for our sake and the sake of future generations, they didn't.

There was one celebrity, on the other hand, whom we would practically maul in order to land him in our section. Whenever you'd see a flurry of servers rushing towards the host stand to lead him to a table, almost to the point of fisticuffs, you knew none other than the gentle giant Shaquille O'Neal had entered the building. The height of this activity (no pun intended) came during his heyday with the Los Angeles Lakers. Shaq was one of the easiest people in the world to wait on and was also very funny and friendly. He had the appetite of a grizzly bear and told you to keep the change on a one-hundred-dollar bill if and only if you got his order right.

I am over six feet tall, and I felt like a little boy standing next to him. Shaq is huge. I can't even imagine trying to shoot a basketball over him. We had a pair of autographed sneakers of Shaq's on display in our arcade that I was told were a size 22. If you had a paddle, you could take one of them out on the lake canoeing.

It was a random evening when Shaq took a seat in my section during a very frustrating shift. My other tables were currently filled with a bunch of nags who I knew wouldn't tip me even if I brought them everything they wanted on a silver platter. After working in the restaurant business for quite a few years now, I could smell them a mile away. But upon winning the Shaquille O'Neal lottery for the first time in my deli career, Chester came over to inform me of Shaq's simple demands, which, when met, resulted in a very generous gratuity. And because I usually had to work so hard for my money, I decided it was in my best interest to take time away from my other fussy tables in order to devote my entire attention to Shaq. At least if I got his order right, it would make up for a whole night of slaving away for these other numbskulls. This was a much more appealing choice than receiving a proverbial kick in the nads from my other customers. This strategy not only allowed me the opportunity to get Shaq's order right but also provided me with the time to give Shaq the full custom-service upgrade package. And as Chester predicted, showing a little TLC towards an effortless two top resulted in an instruction to keep the change on a one-hundred-dollar bill, which resulted in a seventy-dollar tip. Shaq definitely gets two thumbs up in my book.

On the opposite end of the tape measure is the next celebrity whom I almost stepped on when he cut across my path on his way to the host stand. Yes, this renowned gentleman, commonly known to the world as Mini-Me, was non other the Mr. Vern Troyer. I had never seen Mr. Troyer in person before, that is, until I nearly squashed him under my shoe. When I saw him scamper out in front of me, I thought a baby had broken loose from its stroller and was about to wreak havoc on our restaurant. I had to do a double take when I witnessed Mr. Troyer trying to reach a menu located halfway up the host stand. After a moment of "Oh, you're that guy from the Austin Powers movie," I asked him if he needed any help as he stood on his tippy-toes, trying to pull a menu loose from the tightly packed holder. He just shook his head no as he fully extended his little arm up as far as it could go until he could finally wrestle one free. Once he retrieved the giant plastic food list, he waddled back over to the take-out area where he rescaled the bench he was sitting on. He climbed back up on that thing as if he was mounting a horse. All I could think of during my first encounter with Mini-Me was that if Katya was telling the truth, Mini-Me's willie must have doubled as a kick stand or a third leg because this guy was tiny.

After my first indelible impression of Mr. Troyer, I saw him around the restaurant a few more times. On one particular evening, he was accompanied by a fairly attractive and normal sized lady. He always asked for a couple of phone books to sit on as he hated the idea of hunkering down in a booster seat. My twisted half would get the better of me during this notable encounter. I flagged down Jose D. the first chance I got and told him, "*Mesa diez y seis necessita la silla del bambino* (table sixteen needs a booster seat)." As Jose D. hustled off to fulfill this request, I grabbed a spot in the entryway to the kitchen so I could watch the fireworks yet make a quick getaway if things got out of hand. As Jose D. approached Mr. Troyer's table with the booster seat, Mr. Troyer's eyes grew to the size of half dollars. I could see the bottling anger quickly brewing in Mr. Troyer's face as an unsuspecting Jose D., just trying to do a favor for a fellow co-worker, stood bewildered while holding a booster seat at the head of Mini-Me's table. I don't know exactly what was said as I'm sure Jose D. didn't either, but the instructions were pretty clear that Jose D. should get that f%@#ing booster seat away from his f%@#ing table as soon as f%@#ing possible. The puzzled look on Jose D.'s face was priceless. Just as Jose D. began looking around to find out exactly why I sent him over to this little man's table with a baby seat, I quickly made my escape to the back of the house for some cover. Later on, when Jose D. eventually caught up to me, his confusion coupled with my uncontrollable laughter painted a very clear picture of the goof that had been played on him. This was met by a hearty laugh from Jose D. as well.

Usually whenever a celebrity was in our presence, word would spread like wildfire. Hey, did you see so-and-so on table fourteen? When Will-I-Am from the Black Eyed Peas dined with us one evening, things were no different. Henry, who served as our black celebrity resource guide, promoted his discovery of Will-I-Am with the fervor of a TV evangelist. This was standard protocol for Henry, who felt it was his duty to inform all white people when a black celebrity was present as retribution for all of the years of black oppression in the cinema. With Henry and others on the case, the VIP alert spread through the deli's ranks like a staph infection. Not being one who recognizes celebrities, let alone pop music icons, I had no idea who I was looking for.

A younger, hipper server named Mike was standing at the counter when I shouted over to him from the soup station, "Hey Mike, have you seen Will-I-Am from the Black Eyed Peas?" Mike came back at me with a completely unexpected response that went something like this, "No I didn't. Honestly, I wouldn't know who he was if he was standing right in front of me." The problem with Mike's plot-thickening statement was that Will-I-Am was not really standing right in front of Mike, but was sitting right in front of him instead … with a date nonetheless. The only thing worse than what Mike and I had just done would have been for the two of us to slide into position in front of Will-I-Am and break into our rendition of "Let's Get It Started" while doing the running man. Mike originally suspected Will-I-Am was sitting right in front of him when Will-I-Am looked directly at Mike-I-Am after taking in his innocent response, which caused Mike-I-Am to have the reaction of "Oh shit, what if this is Will-I-Am sitting right in front of me?" After Henry confirmed Mike's worst fears, Mike, being the nervous Nellie he was, couldn't stop harping about how he couldn't believe what he had just said. Mike-I-Am continued to beat himself up for the remainder of the evening. A good time was had by all.

This one goes out to all of the ladies out there. The next chance meeting I am about to describe to you just so happened to be with none other than world renowned pop icon Justin Timbercake. Oh, excuse me, what I meant to say was Justin Timberlake. Although this teenage heartthrob feasted with us on a regular basis, he was always very soft spoken. Had it not been for a couple of co-workers pointing out to me who I was waiting on, I would have never even put two and two together. The only memorable thing that happened between me and Mr. Timberlake was the fact that he ordered a piece of German

Chocolate cake as an appetizer, which he inhaled as a precursor to his meal. I found this to be somewhat odd, especially given the former Mickey Mouse Club member's skinny frame and the fact that he also completely devoured a large entrée afterwards. Sorry girls, I wish there was more. Maybe you can fine-tune this story through your stargazed lenses to mean that he is sweet.

Eugene Levy was also a frequent flyer at the deli whom I had the distinct honor of waiting on. It took this troublemaker only two visits before I was chasing him down in the parking lot like the filthy animal he was. The problem with this rabble-rouser was that he thought he could get cute and pull the old grab the wrong credit card slip routine, which had him stuffing the receipt with my tip written on it in his pocket while he left the blank copy behind. I can still picture the surprised look on Mr. Levy's face as I converged on him at full speed in the dark section of our parking lot. He was probably mortified, thinking I was hunting him down for an autograph. When I informed him that I was on to his little scam, he started apologizing profusely with an "Oh my god, I am so sorry." Yeah right, pal. Save it for the authorities. As we traded slips, I watched his every move. He pulled out the signed ticket from his pocket that had my very generous gratuity written on it as I cautiously handed him back the receipt that boasted the blank tip line. He once again tried to give me the old "Oh my God, I am so sorry" act, but once again, I wasn't buying it. I came to the conclusion that this nice guy front along with the really great family he was posing with were all part of this psychopath's pleasure. I'm just glad I didn't buy into it. And I wouldn't be surprised if he rented out his alleged "family" from time to time just to continue the façade. I'm also sure he included a very generous gratuity on the ticket that he conveniently misplaced in his pocket just in case he was ever confronted by the likes of Jozef Rothstein who had the wits and the know-how to expose him as the very cool guy he was.

One celebrity that I never really cared for until I actually waited on him was Tom Arnold. Mr. Arnold came in one night during a very busy shift. He mentioned he was in a hurry and said that he would appreciate anything I could do to rush his order. I had already started five other tables, and his arrival just coincided with bad timing. Although it probably took a little longer for Mr. Arnold to get his meal than he would have liked, he was very patient, very gracious, and tipped really well. He was dining with a very attractive lady, and both were extremely pleasant to wait on. The couple also went out of their way to thank me on their way out of the restaurant. Two thumbs up for two very cool people.

The most friendly and gracious of all of the celebrities that frequented our joint had to be Adam Sandler and his sidekick Rob Schneider. Mr. Sandler came in often and was very courteous as well as very generous to our entire staff. Mr. Sandler hosted a Christmas party at our location one year and went out of his way to tip the entire wait and bar staff an extra one hundred dollars per worker. Rob Schneider was a very funny dude who decided to heckle me at that same party as I was returning from the storage area with a quart of cranberry juice. The room was packed, and as I tried to push my way through the crowd, Mr. Schneider announced, "Make room for the cranberry. Coming through. PLEASE, make room for the cranberry." I also had a brief conversation with him on a different night in the men's restroom that started with him asking me how my night was going. When I answered, "Busy," he responded by saying, "That's good. People gotta eat." I shot back with a "Yep."

I was constantly amazed by one of our servers, Samantha, and her ability to retain the most obscure Hollywood trivia. This hit a crescendo one night when Samantha asked me if Adam Sandler was in the restaurant. When I answered, "No, why do you ask?" Samantha responded by insisting that Mr. Sandler's baby was present. I laughed because I didn't think there was a person alive who could recognize a celebrity through his offspring and assumed she was kidding. But around fifteen minutes later when Adam Sandler entered the building and joined the very same table Samantha had pointed out to me, I began to question my disbelief. When it was later verified that Mr. Sandler's dinner guests included his nanny and his newborn toddler, I asked Samantha how she identified Adam Sandler's suckling without seeing Happy Gilmore first. She simply stated that she remembered seeing a picture of his little tyke in the tabloids. Talk about an obsession with celebrities!!!

Some uneventful celebrity sightings that I had at the restaurant, as well as in the general vicinity, included those of "Norm" (George Wendt) from *Cheers*, who was crossing Ventura Boulevard a few blocks away from the deli when I spotted him. He was serenaded with a few shouts of "Norm" from passing cars as he cut across the busy intersection. I imagined it would get pretty old living your life as a TV character instead of the individual whom God created you to be. I guess one could have just asked Fred Berry from *What's Happening!!*, who still wore his Rerun outfit on the golf course where he caddied twenty years after the cancellation of his show. Speaking of Rerun, I spotted Raj (Ernest Thomas) and Dwayne (Haywood Nelson), also from the *What's Happening!!* gang, on a business meeting one slow afternoon at the deli. While riding in an elevator at a local movie theatre, I was surprised to run into Vincent Schiavelli, who played the subway ghost in the movie, *Ghost*, when the door slid open to my floor. I have to be honest. He scared the freaking crap out of me. Was I still alive? Was he going to start yelling at me? Although he was a strange-looking man who usually played abnormal characters, I read in his obituary that he loved to cook. Who would've thought?

One of the strangest sightings that I ever experienced at the deli was that of Erik Estrada from the 1970's hit TV show *CHiPs*. What made this encounter so unusual was the fact that the day before I saw Mr. Estrada in person for the first and only time in my entire life, I received a random letter in the mail from my cousin, who lived almost three thousand miles away. Keep in mind that I rarely ever talked to my cousin, and it had been a couple of years since our last correspondence. But inside the envelope was a picture of Erik Estrada, with no shirt on, doing a "Hey, what's up, guy?" thing with his hands while delivering his patented, million-dollar Cheshire grin for the camera. And my cousin, being the jokester he was, wrote, "Erik Estrada Wants You" in bold marker across the top of the page. So you can imagine my surprise when Erik Estrada shuffled into our restaurant the following evening, and the hostess led him directly to one of my tables. I contemplated telling Mr. Estrada about this ironic twist of fate but decided to keep it to myself and a couple of trusted co-workers.

I was very lucky the next celebrity didn't drop me like a bad habit when I blindsided her with the world's cheesiest pick-up line. This well known vixen was none other than former female boxing champion Mia "The Knockout" St. John. If she didn't have such a sweet personality and an awesome sense of humor, I probably would've had a difficult time explaining to my co-workers why a former Playboy Playmate had dislodged a few of my front teeth. When this stunning bombshell walked past me for the first time ever, I just had to say hello. When she responded back with a very sexy hello, I quickly followed up with the pragmatic question of "Do you have a boyfriend?" She paused for a second and then deliberately answered, "No." From there I immediately asked her, "Do you want one?" At first, Ms. St. John was completely stunned by the frankness of my question, but after a couple of seconds, the absurdity of the situation hit her like a ton of bricks, and she began laughing hysterically. This didn't get me a date, but it did prompt her to come by and say hello to me every time she entered the restaurant. Those were the days.

Speaking of people who had the potential to knock me out, Mike Tyson and his entourage came in for dinner one evening. On a busy night, you seldom knew who you were about to wait on as you usually just spotted a random body part sticking out of an alcove that alerted you to the fact that you had a table. As I rounded the corner to address yet another booth, Mr. Tyson's snarling tattooed face just so happened to be pointing directly at me as I stepped into view. I couldn't help but make immediate eye contact with Mr. Tyson but quickly decided that my best chance for survival would be to look off in some other arbitrary direction. As with a male gorilla, staring firmly into his eyes is an unmistakable challenge to a physical confrontation and one that I was not ready to partake in. He and his male associate were accompanied by two stunning Euro trash babes, who looked as if they had just jumped out of a porno movie. Come to find out, they probably had just jumped out of a porno movie because Mr. Tyson, at that time, had been considering adult films as his latest endeavor. If you read this Mike—I mean Mr. Tyson—please don't kill me.

As we edge closer to the grand finale, I have to mention a Paris Hilton sighting that took place one dreary evening at the deli. Ms.

Hilton was incognito wearing a large black derby with giant sunglasses. It was so ridiculously obvious that she was a celebrity it was as if she went completely over the top so you would recognize her as a celebrity. I just so happened to be approaching the bathroom area where Ms. Hilton's male companion was standing guard as she powdered her nose or did whatever it is big time celebrities do whenever they're in a bathroom being guarded by their own personal henchman. As I neared the restroom, the door flung open, and before I knew it, I was face to face with what appeared to be Paris Hilton … in a wacky disguise. As I passed by her and into a nearby section, I chortled to myself as a few heads turned to catch a glimpse of her. It was at this time when I stopped, looked back, and not so subtlety asked the entire section, "Was that Michael Jackson?" to which there was a roar of laughter. My comment caused her to freeze in her tracks for a second until she hastily continued on her way.

As a lead up to my grand finale celebrity encounter, I'd like to take this opportunity to give a shout out to some of my fellow co-workers who have gone on to achieve a certain level of success and notoriety in the film and television industry. Chad Brannon became a star on *General Hospital* while Kiko Ellsworth became a popular character on *Port Charles* as well as a star and guest star on and in numerous television shows and feature films. John Stevenson built up a decent list of television credits while continuing to sling drinks at our popular hot spot. Lisa Guzman played a small part in the movie, *The Family Man*, with weasel Nick Cage and also played a part in *I ♥ Huckabees*, along with her boyfriend Ben Nurick, who played a more substantial role in the same film. Ben also moonlighted at the deli but worked as a personal assistant to David O. Russell as well, which I am sure didn't hurt his chances when auditioning for the gig. Coupled with the fact that Ben's surgeon dad had the ability to drop some serious coin into the production, and the next thing you know, you've got yourself a major movie credit. I am not saying any of this happened. I'm just saying that it wouldn't surprise me if it did. Regardless of the fact, Ben did a great job in the role.

On the musical side of things, one of our late-night regulars, who went by the name of Happenin' Harry, usually always arrived at the deli accompanied by some former rock and roll icon. I loved heavy metal music as a kid, and since Harry jammed with these guys on a weekly basis, he was always hanging out with some of the coolest 1980's metal gods. Harry palled around with CC Deville from Poison most often. CC was a hilarious guy, who was hugely popular with the LA crowd. The one encounter I wish I could have back occurred on a graveyard shift when Harry brought over his guest of honor for the evening and introduced him to me. "Hey Jozef, this is Joe," Harry casually announced. "Hey, what's up?" I nonchalantly replied. This dude didn't even strike me as a musician, and after Harry and Joe exchanged some small banter with me, they gracefully exited the restaurant. The next time I saw Harry, he hit me with a "Hey, Jozef, do you know who that was?" referring back to the mysterious Joe. "No," I said. "Who?" When he told me it was Joe Elliot from Def Leppard, I started screaming like a little school girl and nearly wet my pants. I contacted every one of my friends from high school who was into Def Leppard and told them the news. One girl in particular berated me for not recognizing this rock-and-roll legend and was ready to hang up the phone on me due to my pop culture ignorance.

I also got to work with the wife of Randy Guss, drummer for Toad the Wet Sprocket. Randy came through the restaurant with his son quite often, and I found Randy and his family to be top-notch people. As for me, I was wasting away like the leftover cabbage someone left in a remote area of the restaurant, and my time was passing by like the sands in an hourglass.

But for now, let's lighten the mood with our big hurrah, shall we? The celebrity sighting that stirred up the most interest, the most controversy, and the one that almost got me run over by a speeding car in our parking lot was none other than that of Brittany Spears. The first night I encountered Brittany, that is if I can be so bold as to call her Brittany, was on my way back from break. Previous to my being measured up for a hood ornament, I went out to my car to check my voice mail messages and to chitchat with my girlfriend. When it was time to get back to work, I got out of my car in the far parking area and crossed into the parking lot closest to the restaurant. As I walked across the paved surface towards the employee entrance, a black Mercedes whipped onto the property and came barreling towards me full speed. The car was being tailed by three other vehicles that were just as merciless. I was expecting the windows of the trailing cars to roll down and start releasing machine-gun fire. After jumping out of the way and screaming, "What the f@#? are you doing?" I heard a girl's voice ask, "Was that Brittany Spears?" By the way, I'm okay, thank you for asking. After changing my drawers and pulling myself together a bit, I returned to the floor to ask some of our staffers if Brittany Spears had indeed just passed through our parking lot at Mach 1. It was confirmed. I was also informed that she had been scouting out our restaurant over the past couple of days. Keep in mind, up until that point in time, I had never seen Brittany Spears nor even heard of her to be within close proximity of our establishment. On that magical night, however, I was nearly mowed down by her driver.

A few weeks later, as I was going about my business, I noticed customers lining up along the windows like little kids at the Shamu exhibit at Sea World. I thought to myself, "What the hell is going on out there?" After seeing nothing but a bunch of photographers and a mob of people outside the nail shop across the street, I figured maybe a foreign diplomat was visiting or a crime had been committed and the media was hot on the trail. It wasn't until I overheard a mother and her three kids gloating to a nearby table that Brittany Spears was next door getting her nails done that I realized what all of the fuss was about. And all of this attention to see her get a manicure? I can't imagine the stir she'd create if she was taking a crap. When she finally did exit the salon, her security team ushered her through the crowd and into her awaiting vehicle so quickly that I, maybe, saw the top of her head for, like, three seconds. Truth be known, I wanted to catch a glimpse of her so I could tell my niece in New York that I saw her. I know what you're thinking, "Sure, you have a niece in New York," but I really do. Anyway, shouldn't the fifty-thousand-dollar question really be, "What has Ms. Spears done for the good of society to garner all of this attention?"

And if that event wasn't silly enough, a few weeks later, out of nowhere, I was once again jarred from my doldrums when a fleet of vehicles quickly filled the parking spaces just outside our restaurant.

It was topped off by a van that jammed on its brakes and slid into the last remaining spot right in front of the window where I was standing. Then like something out of Willy Wonka's Chocolate Factory, people of all shapes and sizes, with cameras dangling around their necks, started darting across Ventura Boulevard to once again swarm that very same beauty parlor. A much more aggressive mob formed at the entrance to the shop this time, and it wasn't long until tempers were flaring. Two photographers who were jockeying for position on the sidewalk took their grievances out onto the middle of Ventura Boulevard where they broke into a fistfight during rush hour traffic. The way these folks were behaving you would think there was a hostage crisis and the SWAT team had been called in. But once again, it turns out that Brittany Spears was getting her nails done. Now this time I was curious. Not really curious as to what shade Brittany had decided to go with that day, but curious as to what in the hell drove these idiots to behave like that and curious as to why anyone would care that Brittany Spears was getting her nails done. Then I thought to myself, what has our society come to? This time I had a better view of her as she exited the salon. I could sense the tension she must experience every time she's confronted by these profiteers. And as much as she appeared to be disturbed by the circus act that followed her, I also got the sense that it was a part of her that she needed. Once again, like clockwork, she briskly got into her car and vanished from the scene.

The day finally came when Ms. Spears was able to shake her pursuers and actually dine in our restaurant. This occurred a good month or two after her last spectacular, and I wouldn't even have known she was there had a fellow staff member not leaked the information to me. Somehow, she had eluded the hordes of paparazzi that normally tracked her every move. She also managed to pick a time when the restaurant was almost empty. If any of our more business-minded clientele did notice her, I am sure they could have cared less. She ate on the patio, and to be quite honest, she was very beautiful to look at in person. The strange thing about that day was that it just so happened to be the exact same day and time, unbeknownst to her, that her ex, K-Fed (Kevin Federline), was in the adjoining arcade, playing video games. Only our staff knew this dirty little secret, which was not revealed to either party.

Infamy (The Dark Side of the Biz)

In the next few chapters, we will leave the glitz and glamour behind us to delve into the more nefarious side of Hollywood and into the more grim realities of the restaurant business. And who better with whom to start this plunge into decadence than the former mayor of Cincinnati, who admittedly paid for sex with a prostitute while in office and who makes a very favorable living bringing out the worst in humanity on his national television show, Jerry Springer.

I had seen Mr. Springer in our restaurant on a few different occasions, but I had the distinct honor of waiting on him only one time. And as much as I hate to admit this, his show was once a guilty pleasure of mine. I couldn't help but gloat to other members of our wait staff as to who just ordered a corn beef sandwich from me. I even chanted, "JERRY, JERRY, JERRY," as I picked up the sandwich from the deli window. Mr. Springer, as I am sure you can imagine, was very courteous and tipped quite nicely. But the most interesting part of this raunch show host's brief dining experience at our chophouse was when a young couple stopped Mr. Springer dead in his tracks on his way out of the building. What started out as an innocent "Hello, we're fans of your show" from two seemingly amicable followers disintegrated into an un-filmed episode at our local eatery. As accusations shot back and forth, I was waiting for chairs to start breaking and fists to start flying. I watched in awe as Mr. Springer, who was at first simply being courteous to his two admirers, found himself backed into a corner by a pair of scorned lovers looking to hash out their romantic differences in a public place through the insight of one very unprepared talk-show host. Mr. Springer finally dismissed himself from the quarrel with his trademark, "I gotta run, but good luck to you both." As he bolted out the front door like a flash of lightning, the conflicted duo gradually simmered down enough to return to their love nest on booth fourteen.

Conflict seemed to be this franchise's middle name. At the center of this strife was usually none other than our token crazy black man, Chester. Things came to a crescendo one night when Chester and one of our token crazy managers, Paul, went on a reign of unprofessional behavior during one very long and drawn-out evening. The fireworks began when Paul called one of Chester's friends, who visited the restaurant on a regular basis, a "no-good whore." To a more rational employee, this would have been a great piece of evidence to present to Mr. Snuffleupagus and his comrades to begin the removal process of at least one of the five tyrants ruling over us working-class serfs. But to Chester, it was a reason to threaten the life of our manager and to scare the bloody hell out of every patron who had made the unfortunate decision of dining with us that evening.

On any particular shift, typically, I hoped to report to work, do my job, and go home with as few headaches as possible. But as this conflict pressed on for more than two hours, I had no idea how much mental energy it would take to actually achieve this goal. As someone whom Chester would confide in, he immediately explained to me what had sent him over the edge. Since it was a weekend night, I calmly told Chester to settle down until Monday morning when the corporate office re-opened and I would serve as a witness to his mistreatment. But as I mentioned earlier, Chester was highly regarded by our entire wait staff as the co-worker most likely to go postal. And as he would prove during this self-induced crisis, he earned that distinct honor for a very valid reason. As allegations launched back and forth for over an hour, these two malcontents had to be physically separated on several occasions by customers and staff alike. The amazing thing about this whole debacle was that Chester was still able to provide service to his tables. Finally, as both parties reached their pain thresholds, Paul decided to send Chester home for the evening.

Messing with Chester's money would prove to be the proverbial straw that broke the camel's back. Chester made a threat on Paul's life, grabbed the remainder of his things, and then stormed out through the side exit. A nervous onlooker anxiously called 911, then rushed to settle up his tab so he could make a quick exodus. Chester, in the meantime, jumped in his Corvette and started doing doughnuts in the middle of Ventura Boulevard. If this act failed to capture anyone's attention, slamming on his brakes and bringing his car to a sudden stop didn't. When Chester popped open his trunk and sprung from his car, the ten or so customers sitting on the patio scattered in every possible direction. Chester then threw his apron in the trunk, slammed down the hatch, and re-entered the building. Shortly after, insults were once again firing back and forth across the restaurant like poison-tipped spears. In what had to be a record response time, LAPD arrived to diffuse the situation. Chester was then escorted from the premises to avoid any further complications.

On Monday morning, as I expected, I received a call from the corporate office, asking me for my testimony. By that point, Chester had dug himself into such a hole there wasn't much I could do for him, or in other words, I just told the plain truth. "They were both completely out of line," I asserted. I despised Paul because he continuously made Chester and me (the two hardest-working employees on his shift) complete the brunt of our crew's tedious side work. He did this because he was jealous of the fact that we were both making more money than he was. So, for our punishment, he would let all of the little suck ups go home early so that they could watch TV with their girlfriends or boyfriends while Chester and I got stuck with everybody's side work. So my confession involved a scathing attack on this bozo of a manager who engaged in a whirlwind of inappropriate behavior for the whole restaurant to see. In the next few weeks, Paul was let go.

Chester's fate, on the other hand, had a different outcome. About a week later, as I was preparing matzo ball soup in the soup station, who comes bustling out of the kitchen in his work uniform but Chester? My jaw hit the ground. As I greeted him, I tried to figure out how in the hell he could come back to work after threatening the life of a manager, which, in turn, left the witnesses of his rampage in trauma therapy for the rest of their lives and resulted in the LAPD removing him from the property. When I asked Chester how he was able to pull this little miracle off, he simply shushed me and insisted that he wasn't allowed to talk about it. What I came to conclude over time from this shocking re-emergence of Chester was that, as one of our store's top sellers (along with me), he was a very valuable asset to the team because he provided a nice sized bump to the company's bottom line. This fact alone made him nearly immune to all of the company's mundane policies and procedures. It also exonerated him from nearly all city and state laws as long as he could keep his illegal transgressions to himself.

Unfortunately for Chester, a few months later, he finally committed an act so despicable, so intolerable that he sealed his fate as a burden to the corporation. Chester was caught dipping into company profits. His technique entailed giving out personal markdowns to customers who paid him in cash. Chester got so careless with his method that he started quoting the actual cost of the meal to his tables but would immediately offer them up to half off if they paid him in cash. This strategy could only be employed if the customers ordered something that the servers prepared, like soup, beverages, and/or desserts, etc. What Chester didn't realize that fateful evening was that he was offering the "Dining with Chester Personal Discount" to members of the corporate office who, in turn, reported his actions to Mr. Snuffleupagus. When I heard why Chester was finally relieved of his matzo ball duties, I knew he would never be working at our restaurant again. It just goes to show you that there is honor among thieves.

Chester wasn't the only worker cutting into company proceeds. William, one of the only managers that I actually liked during my ten-year span at this clam bake, was caught skimming money right off the top and right out of the company's safe. He met a fate similar to Chester's. And Chester stood in a long line of servers who hung on to their closed out tickets so they could reuse them at a later date. The trick, like Chester's, was to present the already cashed out ticket to a guest if their item or items matched what was on a previously closed out check and could be made without the assistance of a cook or a deli worker. If the customer offered cash as payment one simply kept the money for the entire amount of the bill plus tip. If the client wanted to settle up with a credit card, the waiter would then have to ring in the order and charge the credit card. But, there were even more elaborate schemes that involved the collusion of managers and cooks. In these higher-level scams, the server would have the complicity of either a cook, who would make the food without a ticket and then split the cash with the server, or a manager, who would void the ticket after the guest *cashed* out and then split the profits with the server. I avoided all of these additional sources of revenue and just decided to grind it out and work hard for the money. Cue the *Flashdance* theme song. To me, it wasn't worth the consequences and was probably the only reason I was able to survive in that bright red environment for ten years while so many others failed.

Members of our staff weren't the only ones trying to pull a fast one on the company. As I mentioned earlier, many of our customers also loved to skip out on their bills, especially during the late shift. During my heyday on graveyard duty, these attempts at thieving the restaurant (or more important, stiffing me) resulted in a pack mentality amongst us servers. We all knew how much crap we had to put up with for the small amount of tips we received and how difficult our thankless jobs could be. When someone tried to rip us off, we now had justification to tell these assholes what we thought of them and, when required, gave them a nice little reminder to never do it again. After a few years of partaking in this street justice just to extract a five- or ten-dollar tip, these chases became pointless. I mean, it was Los Angeles where people have gotten killed for a whole lot less, Chester almost being one of them.

You had to give the guy credit. He was passionate about his money, so passionate, when a table walked out on him one evening and tried driving past him in the parking lot, he jumped on the hood of their car. They were finally able to shake him by jamming on their brakes. But Chester, being the resilient go-getter he was, jumped up from the macadam and stood in the middle of the only exit the car, now traveling in reverse, had as an option. When the car accumulated enough distance between them, it accelerated towards Chester. Surprisingly,

Chester dove out of the way at the last possible second and let the car escape. The car careened onto Ventura Boulevard, where it sped away with a piece of Chester's earnings for the evening. I am surprised that Chester didn't jump in his car and hunt the guys down like I did one night. Oops, did I say that?

Because we were all on edge to begin with due to the nature of our jobs, all we needed to hear was the buzzword "walkout" or "I have a walkout," and the calvary was set in motion. One night, a two top of mine tried to make a break for it but only had a slight head start when I noticed there was no payment on the table. As I ran after these infidels, it caught the attention of a few other servers on the floor. Mid-stride I screamed "WALKOUT," and the hunt was on. Before I knew it, I was leading almost the entire staff, and some of our regular customers, on a high-speed chase down a back alley to catch the culprits. Julio caught one of the guys a whole city block away. He and a couple of bus boys escorted the offender back to where our clan had assembled. A few others and I caught the bigger guy in a nearby parking lot where we MADE him pay the bill, PLUS tip. At first, he refused to provide the gratuity, but after some convincing, he graciously realized the error of his ways and felt that a 20-percent stipend was more than fair and appropriate for the excellent service he had received that evening. The five or so pissed off people that boxed him in had absolutely nothing to do with his very thoughtful decision … All right, well, maybe we did just a little.

On another walkout, I wasn't so lucky. These guys had executed this well-orchestrated plan so perfectly that I had never been more duped in my entire restaurant career. For starters, this gang of five Armenians sat in the back of our eatery, right next to the patio door. It was a busy night, and at that time, this little fact meant nothing to me. Early on in the meal, these gangster wannabes also requested a to-go menu. Again, not until a little later would it all add up. All five guys ordered the exact same thing, which included root beers to drink and one of the most expensive entrees on the menu, the chicken parmesan platter. Because I was swamped, I was spending a lot of time in the kitchen as I needed the additional time to assemble and prepare the entrees for my many tables.

These guys were only halfway finished with their meals when I hotfooted it to the kitchen to check on an order. When I returned to the floor, I heard my name being paged to the front of the restaurant. When I arrived at the cashier's station, I was told that I had a phone call. This was quite peculiar as I never received phone calls at work. But being that I was already pressed for time, I urgently grabbed the phone and prompted the caller with a "Hello?" There was no response, and then I suddenly heard a click. Again, weird, but my main concern was getting back to my section and attending to the matters at hand. It wasn't until I returned to my section and found five half-eaten meals sitting on a deserted table next to the patio door that it all started to register. These Armenian goons had dined and dashed and used me to make it all happen. They did this by having me fetch them a to-go menu, which contained the number to the restaurant. They then called me in order to distract me long enough to run out through the side door and jump in their awaiting getaway car. I learned many valuable lessons that evening, including how to recognize the signs of a walkout much more quickly.

One of my more satisfying rundown highlights came on a night when Henry had a walkout. Henry was always busting my balls that he could beat me in a footrace because he was black. When even big Bill got into the chase this one particular evening, we all knew it was on. My fellow co-workers had a huge jump on me right out of the gates. I was the last one to get the memo that Henry had a walkout, and therefore, I was the last one out the door. This chase had to be one of our longest on record, and it again broke one of our restaurant's sacred rules that we never leave company property to catch a perpetrator. My adrenaline was pumping due the thrill of the hunt. I quickly propelled from the back of the pack to the front. I blew past Henry for the lead as I zeroed in on our target in the near distance. I turned it up a notch and was the first one to stumble upon this out-of-breath swindler at a nearby strip mall, where he ran completely out of gas. Henry was the first backup to arrive and dropped anchor with his presentation of the check. It wasn't long before we had this out-of-shape shyster, whose posse had left him for dead, entirely surrounded. In general, all we had to do was catch one member of a clan, and even if that one scoundrel couldn't pay the bill, we could usually force him to rat out his buddies or simply detain him until the peace officers arrived. I hate to say it, but nine times out of ten, these perpetrators were dressed in velour sweat suits.

As this particular marathon came to a close, the suspect in question paid the bill, but as he was walking away from the disbursing crowd, he tried to tickle my balls as to say, "Screw you." For this, he received a swift kick in the ass and would have lost a few teeth had he engaged me further. Please never ever mess with a group of angry food service workers; we are ticking time bombs, especially when we are in predatory mode to catch you after you try to take advantage of us. And particularly when you are surrounded by five or ten of us who want a piece of you for all the crap we had to put up with all night and couldn't do anything about. So for your own safety, please take my advice. In this particular case, justice was served, and Henry got his money. But as a result, he also lost his bragging rights after he was handed a stunning defeat in a wide-open jaunt down Ventura Boulevard.

I often asked myself, "Self, is it any wonder these customers are stealing from us when Hollywood is most likely stealing from them?" And if Hollywood wasn't stealing from them, they sure as hell were stealing from me. Or maybe, I was just everybody's punching bag. I know this probably sounds like a sour-grapes story where an unaccomplished writer drums up some crazy story about how a recently released blockbuster Hollywood movie has a similar theme to a screenplay that he's working on, but this is anything but that. As a matter of fact, my script had been shopped around to many of the major players long before this movie was ever released, and I didn't even assemble all of the evidence until after I researched the particulars a few months after the movie's box-office debut. I won't mention the company's name, but its initials were Universal Studios. I was actually looking forward to seeing the copyright-infringed movie in question because I not only enjoyed this type of genre, but I also wrote about it. But as I watched the movie from my stadium seat inside of the Hollywood ArchLight Theatre, I found myself somewhat enjoying the film but also becoming increasingly disturbed as the narrative played out according to my story line. It wasn't until I was walking out of the movie theatre that night that I could finally admit to myself that the film that I had just paid over ten dollars to see was stolen from my original screenplay.

As more time passed by, the blatant facts surrounding this possibility moved to the front of my consciousness. So the first thing I did was buy a couple of different versions of their screenplay. Then I checked the registration dates. Their original draft was registered more than two months after my script had been received by the robber barons in question, and the original version of their script had even more similarities to my story than their final version. Their project was also initially called "Untitled," which was strange because their title also took on the characteristics of my title but was simply changed to another geographic location and named accordingly. Then, it dawned on me why the studio had called me immediately after I had pitched my first project to them and wanted to know if I had an agent. Of course, they asked me to sign a waiver stating that I couldn't sue them if they made a similar film. I was new to the business, and when I sent them my material, I was also very naïve.

In hindsight, I now realize that Universal Studios was in the planning stages of a project for a famous musical artist when I contacted them with my pitch, and it was in direct line with the type of story they were looking to produce. They obviously weren't opposed to receiving some free intellectual property to pass on to their writer for hire either. I, on the other hand, just wanted a Hollywood high roller to read my story and discover my talent. From there, in my mind's eye anyway, I'd receive a nice fat paycheck and would be sipping on margaritas poolside on top of a large building in downtown Los Angeles. And maybe, just maybe, I would even get to act in one of my movies. Looking back, I am sure they read the words "clueless sucker" stamped across my forehead when they spat me on me and threw me into their fermenting pile of undesirables who didn't have the connections or the resources to stop them. Their assessment turned out to be accurate.

During my first few years as a writer, I went on a creative flurry, sending out my best three scripts to every top Hollywood decision maker that I could think of. Unfortunately for me, every one of the power brokers on my mailing list had deep enough pockets to make any one of my projects become a reality. Again, another big mistake for someone with no legal or artistic representation or any clout whatsoever in the business. I would have been better off sending my scripts to someone who maybe wanted to rip me off but didn't have the resources or the distribution avenues to have my work seen by the public. Then again, I guess if you want your work to be seen by the public, you have to take the chance of sending it to the key decision makers. Hollywood is a crapshoot, and as I would regretfully learn after my follow-up script was also ripped off, it is all about the connections, baby. And if you don't have them or if you tick off the wrong member of the inner circle, they will pick the meat off your rotting carcass until there is nothing left but your decaying bones.

After my first intellectual property was stolen, I was slowly becoming aware of the inner machinations of Hollywood. But my biggest battle was with the good and decent side of myself. A little voice kept switching on inside my head, telling me, "They couldn't have just done that to you; it is probably just a coincidence. You wouldn't do that to someone." And as I was preparing for the role of the title character in my second and most passionate story to date, which I was ignorantly assuming I would get to star in, I was shocked to learn that a big-name Hollywood actor was also training for a similar role. I immediately went home and researched that actor and his new project online. Sure enough, my fingerprints were all over that piece as well. The thing about both of these occurrences is that I had a paper trial leading directly to the people responsible for the criminal act of copyright infringement. The first encounter I chalked up to experience. But by the second pirating, I was fuming mad. The second heisted script was an improved derivation of my first and was a much more personal betrayal. I had trouble falling asleep at night, and when I finally could drift off, I would shoot out of bed screaming at the top of my lungs. When I hear the expression, "You got burned," I now literally know exactly what that means because my insides felt as if they were on fire. I was also more edgy at work, especially when the ads for the movie that I created kept running on our restaurant's TVs. So, at the end of the day, I had to endure the promotional trailer that was being shoved in my face while I was conjointly stuck in Matzo Hell. It was nearly unbearable.

This time, I decided to do something about it and searched for a capable attorney to handle the case. I made it all the way to the final stage with one of Tinseltown's heavyweights, Manning and Marder, which was going to take my case on contingency. The final knock-out factor for me came when they told me that I would not be able to make my version of the film. I was adamant about making my movie as I still wanted to create my interpretation of my material. Thankfully, the pirates who had stolen my intellectual property damaged it so badly they still left me that option. The attorneys at Manning and Marder had warned me of another client of theirs who had been ripped off by Universal Studios. While their client was suing Universal for copyright infringement, that same client went on to make his movie as he had originally intended. Universal Studios, in response, turned around and sued their client for stealing his original story from them and shut down his production. I am traditionally a peaceful person, but had this happened to me after the blood, sweat, and tears that went into my work, there would have been a body count. What magnified this whole situation even more was the fact that I was trapped in a thankless, dead-end job while others were profiting and basking in the glory of my hard-earned work.

Then, I learned my second brutal lesson in Hollywood. It's all about the connections, baby. Oops, well, I guess there is only one lesson to be learned in Hollywood. One of the writers who got the credit for my now second plagiarized body of work was related to a head honcho at one of the big three talent agencies, CAA. When I looked up the high roller that I had originally sent my script to, there was only one picture of him online, and ironically, it was with that shark from CAA that I had just mentioned. His aspiring relative, who was thrown a bone from my decomposing cadaver, didn't even have a single movie credit to his name until he stole my work. And he still, until this day, has not had another script produced let alone had a box-office success, which I believe goes to show you that he succeeded on my dime. And a success it was. The movie grossed around eighty million dollars in the US box office alone. But, I decided to drop the suit before it even got started with the hope that I would someday get to direct and star in my avant-garde film.

Now that that is off my chest, let's talk about a more arousing part of the entertainment business, quite literally, that of the porn industry. Many of the BIG names in adult films loved to dine at our eatery. Ron Jeremy was a regular as was Mary Carey. Not only was Mary Carey endowed with a wonderful career in dirty movies; she also ran for governor during the 2003 recall election of Gray Davis. I am still trying to figure out which of the two professions is sleazier. Her platform consisted of such silly political promises as taxing breast implants to generate more revenue, hiring porn stars to negotiate better energy prices, and starting a "porn for pistols" program that would allow gun owners to turn in their weapons for porn material. Her political philosophy was so ridiculously idiotic that it's a wonder she didn't win. Her rationale was that if guys had more orgasms they'd be less violent. It sounds like she completely understands the purpose of the second amendment. With porno for pistols, you get to swap one right for another just like in her profession where they get to swap one partner for another. And her take on global warming is, "Just wear less clothes." Well, I just hope the globe isn't cooling as some thirty thousand scientists predict because, if it is, it could get a little nipply out there. I also realize why she never got elected. She needed a great running mate. And since she is also from the great state of Ohio, wouldn't the team of Carey/Springer make for a great presidential ticket? If you think about it, they really couldn't be much worse than Obama/Biden or McCain/Palin.

One of the highlights of my deli career occurred when porn star Tabitha Stevens (cool name by the way) came in to pick up a to-go order one night at the deli take-out counter. She was very friendly to my fellow co-workers and me, who gradually inched our way up to the front of the restaurant to inconspicuously ogle her. I used to watch *Bewitched* as a kid and often wondered how Tabitha Stevens would turn out as an adult. I had no idea it would be quite like this. Ms. Stevens (as if that were her real name) was very candid as she answered every one of our probing question, no matter how screwy the intercourse got. And I don't know if you've ever tried to have a heart-to-heart conversation with a porn star before, but the more serious the conversation grew, the more hilarious it became. Take for instance, when she told us what she did for a living was actually a hard job. She thought we were laughing because we assumed that having sex all day is easy. So she went on to defend her position with, "No, it really is." I responded with "Well, I am sure it is … hard," to which she shot back, "It is." "What is?" I retorted. This flew right over her head as she went on to tell us how some of the male actors she worked with were really big and that it hurt to have sex with them. And that it's not easy having sex in front of a camera crew who is watching you all day. This also drew laughs from our rapidly expanding congregation due to the sheer taboo of the subject matter. I asked her why she got into the porn industry to begin with, and she said that she loved having sex and that being a housewife was too boring. She also used the distance between her hands to measure out the size of the largest penis she'd ever had. All I can say is that I wouldn't want to get clubbed over the head with it.

Lost and Worn-out Soles

In both the restaurant and the entertainment business, I was meeting more and more people who could best be described as lost and worn-out souls, kind of like the title of this chapter. In many ways, I guess I was becoming one myself. I was also wearing out the soles on the bottoms of my Payless slip-resistant shoes that I trekked thousands of miles in each month to refill drinks and slosh through toxic kitchen debris with. I'll get into the latter topic shortly. But the one thing that I lost in all of my years of waiting tables that ended up becoming the biggest riddle to me was the half of roasted chicken that disappeared from an entrée that I was delivering to a table.

As I grabbed the popular dish from the window, I was certain that the chicken was actually on the plate, otherwise how would I know it was my order? As I exited the kitchen, I looked down to make sure the chicken was still on board. I only had two plates in my hands. One ceramic dish held the half of chicken in question and was accompanied by mashed potatoes and mixed vegetables while the other plate contained a tuna fish sandwich complemented with beans and coleslaw. There was no noticeable shift in weight or anything out of the ordinary that raised a red flag. But when I placed the platter on the table, the customer blatantly asked me, "Where's the chicken?" not unlike the ornery old lady from the 1980's Wendy's commercial asking, "Where's the beef?" After a few seconds of confusion, I quickly scanned the path that I had just traveled. I set the tuna fish sandwich down in front of the befuddled guests and immediately apologized. I then told them I'd be right back.

I quickly retraced my steps, grilled the bus boys, and even searched the garbage cans in the kitchen, all to no avail. The cook thought I was clowning with him when I told him that I'd lost the chicken on my way out to the table. He refused to make me another one. Great, now I had to get Sardine involved. She only took my side after a few of my stammering workmates pledged that I had truly lost it (the chicken that is). As word spread through the ranks of our staff, finding this missing rotisserie became a quest. We soon had every man, woman, and child on our deli team involved in the search-party efforts. We looked under tables, around people's belongings, and in bus tubs. As we snooped around, we had to explain to the growing number of disturbed and agitated customers what we were looking for. I think most of these befuddled guests thought we were trying to pull one over on them. I later joked with one of my colleagues that it must have landed in somebody's soup. A former co-worker of mine recently contacted me on Facebook and asked me, "Did you find that chicken yet?" If I was unable to find it back then, does she really think that I would be able to find it five years later? So my answer was obviously "No." Until this day, the case of the missing chicken still remains a mystery.

Now, back to our regularly scheduled program. I guess those of us who did venture out to Hollywood, for the most part, came from some sort of broken past. We wanted to be respected and admired and were in search of some sort of love that we didn't receive as a child. And man, we couldn't have picked a worse place to try to find it. Usually all of the people who said they were in LA for a change of scenery and swore up and down that they didn't move to LA to be in the movies were completely full of shit and had some sort of hidden agenda. Wes was one of those people. Wes relocated to Hollywood with big dreams, but after a year or so of barely trying to "make it," he completely gave up on his aspirations and just wanted to make it through the day without killing someone. Every little thing got to Wes, and it seemed as though he would have been much happier in a state with a few less people, like maybe, Alaska. And not in one of the major cities but maybe in a spot a little further north like a REMOTE SECTION OF THE ARCTIC CIRCLE!!!!!

Wes was my go-to guy. He was the mayor of Looney Ville, but I loved him for it. I also reaped the rewards because of it. The perks I'm talking about came in the form of additional tables. Since Wes really didn't care for people, a table of four or more had the potential to push him to the point of no return. Things would be going fine for Wes until someone in the group wanted to change the cheese on his burger from American to Swiss. At that time, Wes would get abruptly short with the customer and boil with so much anger his face would turn beet red. Then after he took the entire order, he'd stomp over to the computer station where he'd throw down his notepad, spouting expletives. This is where I came in and was solicited with the eloquently spoken words of "Hey, ya wanna take a table?" The first time I was presented with this dilemma, I have to admit I was a bit skeptical. The only reason a server in our restaurant gave up a table was because it entailed waiting on a real wing nut who was known for stiffing the waiter. I had fallen into this trap one too many times before to take Wes at face value, but Wes would ease my fears by assuring me that he had already taken the whole food order and delivered the drinks to boot. Those very words sent an instantaneous message to my brain of "That's over half of the work." So I quickly rang in the order as fast as Wes could recite it to me and then immediately hit send before he could renege on the deal. The first time I typically greeted Wes's victims was when I arrived with their food.

As soon as I'd make contact with the table, I'd jump into the good cop-bad cop routine that Wes, as the bad cop, had already established. The very first time we pulled this off, it paid dividends as I received a twenty-dollar tip on an eighty-dollar check. And because Wes had already worn the table down so much during their initial conflict, these people just, by and large, wanted to get their food, eat, and get the hell out of there. This usually made them maintenance free, and this happened almost every time. The only inconvenience for me was fielding a question like, "Man, what's up with that guy?" To which I'd respond with something like "Ah, he's just having a bad day. But I'll be your waiter now so if there's anything else you need just let me know and I'll be happy to get it for you." I now found my new deli best friend and would purposefully scout out the restaurant for any large parties making their way to Wes's section.

Wes obviously could be a real prick if you asked too much of him. He was usually placed on counter duty because it was the easiest station to handle and was the closest to the kitchen. Even at the counter area, I'd see Wes get into some real bloodbaths over such simple requests as the customer wanting a to-go container or requesting only certain fruits in his fruit salad, to which Wes would respond, "You're going to have to go to the deli to ask for that. I don't have time to pick that out for you," even though it was the kitchen staff that did the actual picking out. Wes just had to ring it in and then bring it to him.

The most classic Wes moment came when he was waiting on Gene Simmons from the legendary rock band KISS. I guess Mr. Simmons confused me with Wes as we were both tall with blond hair. Mr. Simmons asked me if he could have his sandwich to-go after waiting over fifteen minutes for Wes to bring it to him. I immediately told Dr. Love, "No problem." When I approached Wes, he was under a huge amount of stress while attempting to ring in an order for the one other table he was waiting on. When I told Wes of Mr. Simmons's request, which seemed like no big deal to me, Wes made a break for the bad boy of rock and roll. I couldn't think of any reason why Wes would be bee-lining for Mr. Simmons so I guess I just assumed Wes was hurrying back to the kitchen to alert them of a modification to his order.

I watched in utter amazement as Wes aggressively confronted Mr. Simmons while shaking his head no and pointing in the direction of the deli. Mr. Simmons, who is a big dude, immediately jumped up from his seat and just stared Wes down. Wes, paying no attention to his disgruntled customer, scurried out from behind the counter and quickly made his way back over to his unfinished work on the computer screen. As Mr. Simmons strutted towards the deli, he continually glared back at Wes. I asked Wes what he had said to him, and Wes said that he had told Mr. Simmons that he didn't have the time to change his sandwich to a to-go order and that he would have to re-order his sandwich at the deli. This meant that Mr. Simmons would now have to start the whole process all over again and wait even longer for a sandwich that had already taken over fifteen minutes to receive. I asked Wes if he knew who his latest whipping boy was and he said, "No … who?" When I told him it was Gene Simmons from KISS, I thought he was going to cry. Wes seemed to be a closet KISS fan, and when I told him how much he had tipped another waiter, Francesco (fifteen dollars on a thirty-dollar check), he immediately became very sullen. I also had waited on Mr. Simmons on a previous occasion, and to be quite honest, he was a bit of a dick to me, but he still tipped me eight on forty.

As with any good thing at the deli, good things never seemed to last. Just as Wes and I were getting into the swing of things and I was taking over all of his large parties after he dropped off their drinks and extracted their food orders, Wes was caught inhaling the propellant from a whip cream can and was relieved of his matzo ball duties. I begged Henry, who caught Wes in this desperate act, to allow Wes to remain on the job for such a minor violation. But this was all for naught as Henry didn't miss a beat and knew the motivation for my request, which is probably why Henry kept such a close eye on Wes to begin with. That, and every time you'd pull out a whip cream container to top off a dessert, the whipped cream ran out of the canister like a bad case of diarrhea.

I can't even begin to tell you how many pairs of shoes I ripped through while working in that restaurant, partly because, in order to use my tip money most sparingly, I would buy the most economical slip-resistant shoes Payless or K-Mart had to offer. These shoes would always show their first signs of wear and tear by fraying at the big toe within the first couple of months of purchase. I had one pair in which almost the entire sole was separated from the shoe. I don't know how I made it past Henry and Sardine's scathing critiques of our uniforms, but I guess I just knew how to walk and stand while they were around to properly hide the defects. The floor in the restaurant was like a sheet of ice when it got wet, and working without slip-resistant shoes was practically suicide. I'd watch a countless number of customers wipe out on the floor as this was a guilty pleasure of mine. My all-time personal favorite was a hot drunk girl in stiletto heels who came prancing in one night at four in the morning and quickly found herself sprawled out all over the wet and grimy floor. The worst incident came when an eighty-something-year-old man went to sit on his chair, which slid out from under him. He hit his head on the floor so hard I thought he was dead. He turned out to be a little disoriented but okay. He even went on to eat a half of a corn beef sandwich. Again, sometimes I think the only thing keeping some of those old timers alive was the grease and fat from our sandwiches. How the company prevented lawsuits from all of the hard spills and wipeouts that slippery-when-wet surface incited over the years is beyond me.

During Chester's glory days at the deli, he unfortunately developed a rash on his feet from the harsh chemicals being used to scrub the kitchen floor at night. He made such a stink about it that the upper management eventually changed the cleaning formula. Previous to that crisis, the restaurant was on red alert after failing a health inspection, and the restaurant was not about to compromise its quarterly profits in order to accommodate a worker who was standing in the way of a sanitary work environment without a very valid reason. I guess Chester and the ten other wage earners whose skin was melting off their feet provided the justification necessary to switch formulas.

While we all know Bert was offered free meals from passing guests because of the holes in his shoes, there was another vagabond well worth mentioning. His name was Gary, and in all honestly, he resembled a large ogre. A large ogre with green goop crusted into his eye sockets and who drooled from the side of his mouth when he talked. Gary was an artist whose paintings resembled those created by a mentally retarded six-year-old child. Once in a while, though, one of his pieces would actually catch your eye. His works were featured in a gallery back East, and he often brought in his most recent creations for all to see. He'd set up shop at the counter area and would stop any passersby who weren't incredibly horrified by the sight or smell of him. Once he roped them in, he'd proudly show off his display. If anyone actually made the mistake of liking one of his paintings, he'd start hustling them for whatever they were willing to pay for it. Some nights when he came in after painting, he looked as if he had just crawled out of a chimney. James Hetfield, the lead singer of Metallica, was seen buying a few of his works.

Gary would set some of our managers on fire when he'd bring in his oil colors and set up shop on our fake marble countertop to work on his demented portraits. Once in a while, depending on the type of night it was and who was on duty, he would get away with this crap. Gary also brought in a guitar every once in a while that he really didn't know how to play. Because Gary had a loud, boisterous speaking voice to begin with, whenever he belted out original tunes, like "Gefilte Fish Blues," his crackly baritone voice bellowed throughout the halls of our restaurant. I enjoyed talking with Gary, but whenever he turned twisted and mean on the turn of a dime, I would abruptly end our conversation. This happened more times than not. Gary was finally eighty-sixed from the restaurant just as his hygiene was hitting an all time low. Leading up to this brilliant management decision, Gary was also caught stealing food off other people's plates. And he was busted more than once. Some of these victims were completely finished with their platters and had already left for the evening while others were still consuming their meals but either stepped away to use the restroom or turned around to talk to a friend. So between Gary's pungent body odor and the gruesome sight of stolen food falling from his mouth, Gary was permanently shown the door, located just a few yards away from the freak magnet known as "the counter."

Now for the story of Angie. Angie was an older woman in her late fifties who was in the midst of an ongoing substance-abuse problem. She once dated actor Gregory Hines and had the pictures to prove it. This earned my immediate respect as I had been a Gregory Hines fan ever since I saw him in the Mel Brooks classic, *History of the World Part I*, where he performed the African shim-sham. Angie was immediately likeable and charmed many of our patrons, including members of the band "The Sticks" as she called them, to which I quickly translated back to her as "Styx." Angie's flighty work patterns became very noticeable shortly after she was hired. One day she would be at work two hours before her shift, and the next day, she'd show up an hour late, if she'd show up at all. There'd be times when she'd take the bus to work and other times when she'd be waiting on a ride. Angie's deli career came to a crashing halt one night when she decided to take a nap on the floor in an empty section of the restaurant. When we first discovered

Angie, we thought she was dead. She was having complications with her living situation and was taking certain pills to go to sleep and others to stay awake. Her unstable lifestyle eventually led to her downfall. Angie did, however, come in one night a couple of years after she was dismissed by the company. She had kicked her dependency on drugs and was doing very well for herself. She had started her own clothing line, which specialized in rehab themed apparel, inspired by her renewed commitment to beat her addictions. I wish her the best of luck, and it just goes to show you that it is never too late to turn your life around.

There were also other notable sad stories, like that of an attractive young lady named Meredith who worked with us and whose car broke down on the 101 Freeway. When she got out of her vehicle to relocate herself to the side of the road until help arrived, she was hit by an oncoming car. She didn't have health insurance and spent a month on life support. She ended up partially paralyzed and remained in very poor condition. She never worked with us again. Then there were lost souls like Chrissy and Ned who tried to convince everyone that they were going to be big stars one day but who just couldn't get anything off the ground, no matter how hard they tried. I shared their feelings of frustration, but I never tried to make people feel less than me because I thought I might be a big star one day. When you think about it, their situation must have been a lot harder to deal with if and when reality ever set in.

Then there was the old lady who came in every night and just stared into space as she perched at the counter. After a few hours of her indoor stargazing, she'd go out to her car, turn on the engine, and fall asleep … for hours. The first time I actually witnessed her in inaction, she scared the living daylights out of me. She was hunched over in the driver's seat with her face planted against the steering wheel while her car idled away. I immediately knocked on her window but got no response. I urgently ran back inside the restaurant to tell our manager, "I think the old lady who was sitting at the counter earlier is dead. Her car is running, and she's slumped over in the driver's seat with her head pressed against the steering wheel. I knocked on the window …" As I rattled off my horrific discovery to him, he just laughed and said, "She always sleeps in her car with the engine running." "Oh, how funny,"

I thought to myself. Her nightly routine went on for months. I got to see firsthand how silly I must have looked after witnessing dozens of people rushing through our front doors to report the same incident with what must have been the same ghastly look on their faces. Finally, the mighty LAPD intervened and warned her that she couldn't crash there anymore because they were getting way too many calls about a dead woman hunched over the steering wheel of a running automobile. So much for "We the People" being secure in our own property, even if it is driving up the price of gasoline.

Because Hollywood draws in all types of people from all walks of life arriving in town for all types of reasons, I am dedicating my next story to all of the guys out there. Never in a million years would I suspect that an opportunity, such as the one I am about to describe to you, would ever present itself to someone like me, but it did. I was plugging along on a typical weekday third shift when a beautiful young women and her gorgeous girlfriend entered the restaurant in their pajamas. This beautiful young woman, who I'll call Candy, was wearing a Playboy hat, and although she was dressed down in cotton PJs, she was simply stunning. They sat in one of my booths and were extremely fun and friendly to wait on. For one of the few times during my pathetic ten-year existence in Hollywood, I actually felt as if someone understood me, my humor, and the complexity of who I am (not really but I like to tell myself that anyway). Regardless, when these two bombshells stood up to leave, Candy, in the sexiest tone imaginable, asked me if I was married. When I told her no (I wasn't going to mention that I had a girlfriend out of sheer curiosity), she handed me a business card with her picture on it. Only in this business photo, she was wearing a tight little miniskirt and stiletto heels. She told me who she was and that she was the most downloaded Playboy playmate on the Internet at that particular time. She pleaded with me to call her because she and her girlfriend wanted to "hang out" with me. I thought she was going to kiss me, but she simply smiled and implored me, again, to please call her as she squeezed my hand. At first, I had to pinch myself to see if I was still alive. Then, after walking around the restaurant in a euphoric daze for the next few hours, I eventually returned to earth and began to think about how I was going to handle this indecent proposal.

On my one shoulder, was my loving and trusting confidante, Mary, who was actually lying next to me in bed asleep as I was rationalizing what to do. On my other shoulder was the sexy temptress and her beautiful Playboy bunny friend who I checked out online and can honestly say was well worth the few hours or so I spent studying her photographs. Each had her sound arguments for what kind of decision I should make, but when I did all of the math and weighed out all of my options, I am probably going to lose all of my male readers at this point in time and for that matter maybe even some of my female readers too, but I decided not to call her. Breaking free from my daily routine and covering up what the hell I was up to seemed like such an overwhelming and daunting task that I decided it would not be worth the effort. Plus, I really cared about Mary and would never want to hurt her like that. If I were single I would have shown up at their door with nothing on but the radio, but that just wasn't the case. Unless you are Hugh Hefner, opportunities like that maybe, and I emphasize the word "maybe," come around once in a lifetime. I guess I'll have to come back in another lifetime to try it all over again. Oh well, as they say, life goes on.

Playing the Role (and not the French Roll)

In Hollywood, it can be construed that perception, not substance, is king. Take for instance, Michael Ovitz, whose urban legend had him renting a fleet of Mercedes Benzes with his new startup agency's name "CAA" engraved on the license plates. The cars were allegedly then driven around town and parked in front of the fanciest restaurants in the city in an effort to woo some of Tinseltown's most reputable names. At the deli, the schemes weren't quite as elaborate, but they were schemes nonetheless. Anybody who was somebody or wanted to be somebody in Hollywood at one time or another passed through our deli.

One person who was already somebody and pretended not to be anybody was comedic legend Andy Kaufman. This was one of our restaurant's many claims to fame, especially after *Man on the Moon* with Jim Carey was released. Mr. Kaufman took a job as a bus boy for a week at our restaurant after he had already achieved a high level of notoriety. Because it was part of his bit to mess with people, he quietly went about his job for an entire week without breaking character. I'd overhear the stories of how he'd receive a lot of suspicious stares while he was busing a table, which prompted him just to eyeball people back. If anyone asked him if he was Andy Kaufman, he would react in a few different ways. Mainly, he would just abruptly answer, "No, but I get that a lot." Or he'd respond, "Who?" Other times, he would get rip-roaring mad and holler back at the person because he was tired of people asking him that. He played the part brilliantly and never let on to any of his inquisitive onlookers who he really was.

At the restaurant, I was also pretending not to be me. Like an exotic dancer at a strip club who plays the most enticing yet detached character she can come up with to maximize her profits yet get her through her day, I had one of my own. It was that of Happy Jozef. Everything Happy Jozef did was "no problem" and was done with a smile on his face. And if you did something to piss Happy Jozef off, he would belittle you in front of your friends and family until you had to laugh at your own stupidity. As the years went by, this character was perfected to a *T*. Happy Jozef also had a slew of Happy Jozef one-liners ready to rattle off for a variety of dining situations. Lines like, "Welcome to the home of the matzo ball soup. I am Jozef. I will be your waiter this evening." If Happy Jozef picked up a stack of plates from a table, he would enthusiastically advise, "Please do not try this at home. I am a trained professional." As a way of offering bagel chips, Happy Jozef would ask, "Would you like hubcaps?" to a customer who was order-ing soup. While placing the meals on the table, he would say to each recipient, "THE WORLD FAMOUS ...," and follow it with the name of the dish, "THE WORLD FAMOUS spaghetti and meatball ... THE WORLD FAMOUS pastrami sandwich ... THE WORLD FAMOUS mac and cheese." If one of Happy Jozef's co-workers asked Happy Jozef if he needed anything, Happy Jozef would respond with, "A week in Maui." If a customer was drinking a lot of soda, Happy Jozef would quip, "Is there a hole in your glass?" or "Do you have a hollow leg?" If someone accidentally went up to pay the cashier instead of paying Happy Jozef, Happy Jozef would rush up to the unsuspecting customer, crying out, "I thought you were making a break for it. Good thing I stopped you when I did." Usually the customer would respond with a "How come?" to which Happy Jozef would reply, "'Cause the snip-ers on the roof would have shot you." If a bill came out to the amount of $18.73, Happy Jozef would drop the check with a "Yep, 1873. That was a great year. Back when air was clean and sex was dirty." After butchering the "Happy Birthday" song, Happy Jozef would announce to the party, "You can also purchase our Christmas album at the front counter." The proof was in the profits that Happy Jozef, Inc. steadily accumulated throughout its ten-year span. It usually required around fifty cups of coffee to play the role effectively, but it allowed me to carry out my job as worry free and efficiently as possible.

And speaking of characters, I had the good fortune of working with one straight out of a television sitcom, a woman known to everyone as Flo. Of course, Flo wasn't her real name, but even late-night customers who saw her for the first time would instinctively blurt out, "Flo," as she passed by their table. From my experience, it seemed as though every restaurant and truck stop in America worth a grain of salt had a Flo-type waitress working in it. Our Flo had many unique qualities that set her apart from the thousands of other Flos across the country. One of these characteristics was her uncanny ability to break dishes. This skill set came about as a result of the chronic arthritis that plagued her aching, worn-out body. Flo was only fifty but looked like she was going on two hundred. Of course, she smoked like a chimney and drank a gallon of Maxwell House per hour. I often teased Flo by telling others in the area that she only operated if you poured a pot of coffee down a chute in the middle of her back. This would elicit one of her snappy rebuttals like, "I'm sorry; I don't speak stupid." Flo was a steely employee who worked longer and harder hours than any of our finest youths.

One thing you never did, and I don't care who you were, was touch Flo's hair. She spent hours in the mirror before work primping her 1950's throwback hairdo and would turn into a rabid animal anytime her fur was compromised. One night, I accidentally brushed up against her fro and found myself on the receiving end of a swift donkey kick to the thigh. This type of erratic behavior made me want to antagonize her even more, especially in front of a group of co-workers. I'd come out with things like, "Did you know that Flo sleeps on a shelf in the dry storage room where she also plugs into the wall to recharge at night?" And she'd respond with her usual comeback of "You're an asshole." Being that we were the restaurant's two top sellers, we were bitter rivals who were in a constant state of competition. We also frequently compared sales reports.

The way Flo prepared her coffee at the beginning and end of each shift was nothing short of nauseating. There were times when I was seriously waiting for her to go into a sugar coma. She would pour eighteen packets of sugar and five mini creamers into a ten-ounce cup of coffee, then stir. She also prepared this lethal concoction at the end of each shift just before she claimed to be going to bed. Yeah, right, she went to bed. She probably spent the rest of the morning redecorating her house. Her diet consisted of grilled cheese and bologna sandwiches, and her hairstyle resembled that of a sixteenth-century military helmet. I've never seen anyone more infuriated and on the verge of homicide as I did the night Flo accidentally tipped over an open can of orange soda while she was pulling down a pizza box from a high shelf. The orange beverage splashed all over her and drenched her perfectly molded dome and monkey suit, which by the way, was always sparkling clean and as crisp as a cucumber. After dousing herself with soda pop, Flo looked like a drowned rat in an orange shirt and refused to speak to anyone. Flo's inner conflict must have been killing her because she couldn't force herself to leave work, but she also couldn't stand the fact that her hair and her clothes had been soiled. But being the super server she was, Flo did have a back up uniform in her car. Of course, she blamed me for the whole incident because she claimed that I was the only one tall enough to place the open can that high up on the shelf. Fortunately for me, I don't drink orange soda.

Flo took her job way too seriously and even wore what we referred to as her "utility belt." It was made up of a pouch attached to a fake diamond-studded belt. The pouch contained such essential restaurant items as a stapler, a church key, pens, paperclips, and breath mints. You could easily recognize the amount of hours Flo spent preparing herself each night for work as her hair and makeup were always done to the nines. It was also very evident that Flo lived for her job as she was always completely stocked up with all of the latest supplies plus backups.

Not that I tried to, but I think there were times when I really got on Flo's nerves. Anytime a plate dropped or a glass broke anywhere in the restaurant, both staff and regulars alike would yell out, "Flo," whether she did it or not. This chapped her ass, and for some reason, she always blamed me for the remarks. Forget the fact that she took on an impossible number of tables that someone in her dilapidated condition should have never even thought about taking.

One night, a friend of mine and his three buddies came in for a late-night snack. After finishing my side work, I decided to join them. Of course, Flo was cranking out her usual double shift, and as fate would have it, she was ministering our table. When I joined my friends, the first thing out of Flo's mouth was, "What are you doing over here, you asshole?" I said, "Sitting here. Can I get a drink please?" "Yeah, right," she shot back as she briskly walked away. Five minutes later, she returned and asked me if I was really sitting there, to which I responded, "What does it look like to you?" She reluctantly brought me my drink and announced to the table that their food would be right out. She again busily hurried away without taking my order.

The guys were getting a charge out of our dynamic so they asked me if they could videotape me giving them the lowdown on our love-hate relationship. Right in the middle of my telling them how Flo was always dropping and breaking things, she glided up to our table from behind. Coincidentally, at that exact point in time, my friend decided to stand up to use the restroom, and before I could utter the words, "Watch out," he plowed right into Flo, spilling the tray of food everywhere. Their timing was impeccable. While the guys were fighting to catch their breath from laughter, Flo was cursing me up and down and sideways and blaming me for the whole incident. She told me she would never wait on me again. For a good two weeks, Flo refused to even speak to me. This did, however, make my friends' visit worth the price of admission, especially since they caught the whole thing on video. They kept rewinding the tape and playing the unfortunate incident over and over again until it was embedded into our psyches like a piece of mainstream media propaganda, constantly repeating itself over the major networks.

Flo didn't have to pretend she was the smoky-hole character that she came off to be; she actually lived and breathed it (barely). Others had to work a little harder at their persona. Take Bob and Ted, for instance. If I would have been cast in just 1 percent of the roles these two wannabe producers offered me, they would need a supercomputer to store my IMDB credits. These two were always working on their next big script, and I was always going to get a part in it. They would enter the establishment as boisterous as can be while shaking hands with just about everybody in their path. When they finally got situated at a table in the most visible part of the restaurant, they would each order a cup of coffee and a glass of water and then tie up the table for hours. About a half an hour into their grand façade, we would receive a call from the water department asking us if we had a leak in one of our pipes as these two blubber brains were single-handedly consuming the city's water supply. When and if they did order, it was always something small and cheap, like an order of mozzarella sticks, which they'd split between them. Of course, their bill would only come out to around ten dollars, and from there they'd only leave you a one-dollar tip. That was on top of the fact that they'd talk your ear off whenever you weren't in the process of refilling their drinks every two minutes. We'd all head for the hills when we saw these two legends in their own mind entering our eatery. There were even times when I went as far as placing standing menus on my empty tables in order to say to the hostess that "these spots are reserved for anybody but them."

One day, Bob's mother was celebrating what had to be her ninetieth birthday. She was sitting in a wheelchair, and when I first spotted her from just a few yards away, I had to do a double take. I thought she was the Crypt Keeper. She did move from time to time in order to nibble on a thin slice of tongue sandwich that Bob cut off for her. But because Bob was too cheap to buy her a dessert for her birthday and she was too senile to notice, Bob asked me to bring her a small side of potato salad with a birthday candle in it. Bob also requested that we sing happy birthday to her in order to make this one birthday she would never forget (not in the next five minutes anyway). As I prepared the potato-based dessert back in the kitchen, I gathered as many co-workers as I could, if for nothing else, the pure absurdity of the situation. As we approached the table with her illuminated picnic favorite, we began delivering a birthday hymnal in the key of "what the hell is going on here?" And to be quite honest, I never heard nor saw a more solemn group of yodelers in all of my life. As we ended the song, we were met with a few scattered claps throughout the restaurant and by a few chuckles from within our merry band of misfits. We laughed about that episode for weeks.

Ted, on the other hand would bring in what I used to call his "wacky sticks," which were almost as bad as Bob's "wacky birthday dishes." The purpose of these two oscillating metal wands was to gauge whether or not you were lying to him. He'd ask you some random asinine question, and then, depending on how these rods lined up, they'd indicate to him whether you were being honest or not. He also based a lot of his life decisions on what these shafts told him to do, not unlike the Son of Sam carrying out the murders suggested by his neighbor's black lab. Apparently, these beanpoles also provided financial advice and good legal counsel. This erection set was comprised of two thin, eight-inch metal scepters that were bent on the ends so he could twirl them between his fingers. They would flippantly swing around until they arrived in a rest position where Sideshow Ted would make his reading. Until this day, I still have no idea how Ted reached his conclusions even though he explained the whole process to me over a thousand times.

Another waiter named Vince and I did impressions of just about everybody who traipsed through our front doors and seemed to do so for the sole purpose of getting on our very last nerve. Making fun of these annoying sphincter brains was a good way to laugh off the misery we were subjected to, and our Bob and Ted impressions were our favorite. Bob was very animated and spoke in a very gruff voice. "Ah, that's great, Jozef. Thank you so much. Just put a candle in the potato salad. She won't know the difference. She's got one foot in the grave anyway (laugh). Don't tell her I said that, though (even though she's sitting right there). Yeah, that's fine. Thank you so much, Jozef."

Of course, no staff member was safe from our ridicule either, especially a complete d-bag like Henry. Our impersonations of Henry immediately wiped the fear and disdain from any member of our crew who had been trapped under Henry's iron fist. We would highlight Henry's bullying tactics along with his annoying lisp in order to make it plainly obvious how ridiculous and innocuous his tough-guy bravado really was. And we would even crack Henry up with our parody of the old Jewish couple Al and Margie who visited our facility on a nightly basis.

Al was the spokesman for the relationship who hyperventilated between syllables when he spoke. He would also consistently call you by the wrong name, even though you'd been waiting on him for the past five years. "Ah, Mike," he'd say. "No, it's Vince," Vince would reply. "Ah, okay Spence. Can I get a corn beef sandwich? And make sure there are no chotskies, you know, fillers. And she'll have a baked potato." They were nice and tipped well, but for some reason they drew a lot of ire from our entire wait staff, who avoided them like the plague. I often found myself most grateful whenever Al and Marge entered the restaurant and my section was completely full.

There was one person who I loved every time she popped into our restaurant, whether it was busy or not, and that was Kira. Kira was sexy. And Kira was crazy. One of my first introductions to Kira was on a packed graveyard shift when she, in a short miniskirt, walked the entire length of the floor on her hands. When she arrived at the front door, she kicked the portal open with her foot (while in a handstand) and continued towards the parking lot while remaining in a handstand. This drew a thunderous applause from the dining crowd, who I'm sure also loved the free show. Once she hit the parking lot, she sprung back to her feet, ran over to the large plate glass window, and banged on it to incite the crowd even more.

To give you an idea as to what kind of physical specimen Kira was, first, just let me say, "Wow!!!" and that Kira was also a Ms. Reebok competition finalist. You know, not one of those manly women who look like they can lift your car, but one of those incredibly athletic, flexible, and toned babes who has just the right amount of muscle to make a man lick his chops. After talking with Kira a few times, I also learned that she had once worked as an exotic dancer. This sent light bulbs flashing off in my brain as I was looking for a way to market my first movie script to Hollywood execs. The screenplay I had in mind just so happened to feature a character who worked as an exotic dancer. It only seemed natural for me to ask Kira to present a copy of this script to these babbling misanthropes. I thought to myself, "Self, what better way to get the attention of some crusty old Tinseltown executive sitting around in his stuffy office than to send in this gorgeous super babe who would drop the script in his lap and then give him a lap dance?" Kira entertained the thought, but I wasn't making nearly enough tip money in my measly waiting job to employ this knockout of a woman who was now getting paid ridiculous sums of money to work as a legitimate model and dance teacher.

One of my last experiences with Kira unfortunately ended on a sour note. Kira was being incredibly loud one evening towards the end of my matzo ball tenure. She was smashed out of her mind, and her brazen personality wouldn't allow her to quit entertaining the clients that she brought in from a dating service that she owned and operated. For the past few weeks, Kira had been bringing in these potential couplings after occupying them with cocktails and video games in the adjoining arcade. When it was time to get down to business and find out if there was any compatibility between these lovebirds, they all came over to the restaurant for a bite to eat and some chitchat.

On this particular evening, it was probably not their best move. Kira liked to drink, and when she did, she would undergo this metamorphosis that transformed her from a sweet and charming person into a raging lunatic. I had already witnessed this about-face one too many times before, but never quite like this. I began to notice her enormous mood swing as profanities spewed from her mouth by the bucketful while she obnoxiously approached every occupied table in the restaurant in an effort to bring them into her disoriented world. This eventually set off one of the male customers in the back of the restaurant who simply wanted to enjoy a night out with his buddies. From across the room, this recluse yelled for her to "shut the f#@k up," which of course drew an immediate response from Kira, who stomped directly over to his table and confronted him. Because this guy was trying to establish himself as somewhat of a gentleman, he again warned her to "shut the f#@k up and get the f#@k away from his table." That was just prior to this mountain of a man marching over to where Kira's traumatized mingles sat in horror.

The group, now feeling that they were involved in something that wasn't advertised on the website, obediently sat motionless in their chairs as the behemoth hovering over them delivered his ultimatum, "Either you shut her up, or I'm going to start hitting one of you." Not exactly my idea of a great first date, especially for a group of metrosexuals looking to impress their dates with their new iPods. As Gadzooks's patience was about to expire, the petrified singles group remained frozen solid. But one thing you never do, and I don't care who you are, is pick a fight with a singles group, especially if you are in between the organizer and her offspring. Suddenly, from across the bully's blind side, came Kira, roaring back with a solid punch to the head and karate kick that just missed his face. At that point, we, the staff, had decided it was time to override our manager's inability to resolve the situation amicably and elected to jump into the middle of David vs. Goliath.

As we separated these two adversaries, the half hillbilly-half aristocrat lashed out and accused us all of negligence for allowing the conflict to reach that point. As this browbeater belly-ached to anyone who pretended to care, Kira continued to taunt him with a "Come on, I'll kick your ass. I know karate." I couldn't believe she came out with that one. If he would have hit her, it would have been lights out for him, but fortunately for him, he didn't. It may have had something to do with the fact that my elbow was jammed into his larynx. While our manager was explaining to Kira that she needed to leave the premises immediately, Sea Bass went back over to his feeding trough to round up his posse. I strongly encouraged them to exit through the front door as Kira left through the side door. They eventually complied. Kira was the instigator behind this whole ugly incident, but I wasn't about to forward any of that information to the police when they arrived.

One would think that with the police bearing down on our location, Kira would have been well on her way to anywhere but a place where law enforcement agents were about to swarm all over her in order to interrogate her. But as I looked through one of the side windows, who do you think I saw on the patio joking with a group of Armenians, but Kira? So I quickly made my way out to her latest comedy tour stop and urged her to get out of Dodge. She didn't seem to care that the LAPD was about to descend on our premises by the way she flatly exhorted, "I'm not worried. I dated most of them, anyway." This comment split the sides of some of the Armenian gangsters Kira was fearlessly entertaining on our outdoor patio. Sure enough, when the police arrived and began their investigation, she nearly had them pissing their pants from laughter with her re-enactment of the ruckus.

It's still a mystery to me as to how she got them to take her side so quickly, but after a good ten minutes of hilarity and high jinks, one of the officers politely asked a member of the Armenian mafia to "make sure she gets home safely," to which he responded, "No problem, sir." One of the more honorable members of the gang drove her home that night and admirably returned to the group soon after.

Kira then contacted me a few days later in a desperate attempt to patch things up with the deli. She had been a long-time customer of our local hot spot and a friend to many of us there. Apparently, Kira also found it to be a romantic enchantment zone for her courting Romeos as well. But her outcry to mend the wound she had inflicted was all for naught as I had already given the deli a zero-day notice of my resignation, which did not sit well with Gus and company and which gave me zero negotiating power. I unfortunately left California a week after this ill-fated episode and never saw Kira again. Regardless of the fact, I am still left with the very fond memories that Kira provided during my ten-year stretch at Matzo Ball Incorporated.

Land of the Fruits, Nuts, and Flakes

It's time to break out your pink tutus and your purple boas because we are about to take a walk on the wild side and delve into the very dark and twisted world of the gay mafia. Members of this sleek organization are immediately recognizable to each other, but as for me, sometimes it took a little while. I guess, when people's sexual preferences came into question, I really could not have cared less. Don't get me wrong. With co-workers like Gus, Sardine, or Ricky (who I haven't mentioned yet), you'd have to be delusional or suffering from a head injury not to realize they were gay. But with someone as private and as straight acting as the likes of Ned, sometimes it took a little longer. Ned's case took me some two years to figure out. Once I was in the know, it seemed as though I had just entered the ranks of a secret society that had known this little tidbit of information since day one. This conclusion became even more pronounced as I received snippy little comments like, "What? You didn't know he was gay?" Of course, nobody goes out of his way to tell you these minor details when you are not a member of the gay and lesbian cartel. My gaydar must have been out of batteries when I turned it towards Ned because he just seemed like every other annoying wannabe artist in LA who was always trying to get attention. But in hindsight, shouldn't that have been the dead giveaway clue?

Looking back, I think it was Ned's lack of self-esteem that sealed his secret from me for so long. But Ricky, on the other hand, was a completely different story. From the second I saw him, I just knew. My normally unreliable gaydar was registering off the charts. If George Michael had a long-lost faggier brother, it was Ricky. It was like my comedian co-worker friend Jeremy used to say, "Ricky gets his hair done more often than my grandmother." And it was true. There wasn't a day that went by where Ricky didn't drastically change something about his appearance. Usually he'd switch up his hair, but other times, he would add or subtract something flashy from his uniform, completely overhaul his accessories, or start a new facial hair pattern. It's not that you tried to notice. He just made it impossible for you not to. And talk about a whiney little fag. This guy would whine so much you'd have to stuff a block of cheese in his mouth to shut him up. And right from the horse's mouth, the one thing that he loved to do was perform. Perform what you may ask? That's not what I meant. What I meant was perform as a female impersonator.

Yep, I said it, and I wouldn't have believed it if he hadn't whipped out the pictures from his purse to prove it. His favorite celebrity to impersonate was Marilyn Monroe. Now, if he didn't walk as if he had a broomstick up his ass, didn't talk with an annoying lisp, and you saw him from a few hundred yards away, you might think he was a college football player or something because he was a fairly tall and stout individual. But imagine forcing this manly frame into a Marilyn Monroe, Cher, or Judy Garland costume, and you have a very frightening image on your hands. If memory serves me correctly, I believe Ricky stumbled onto the job at the deli because he was hamming it up a few doors down.

The tranny bar in our neighborhood was called the Queen Mary, for obvious reasons, and it was a real hit on the weekends. For years, people tried to get me to go in to see a show, talking about what a great time it was, but they were wasting their breath. I'd rather watch paint dry. At around two thirty or so on a weekend morning, some of these performers would start trickling in for some post-show cuisine, drawing hoots and hollers from the rambunctious party crowd who loved to watch the freak show parade through our store. The grand prize of the transgender scene was Janae who in reality was a really big black dude who unleashed a viscous temper when pushed far enough. This unfortunately occurred on almost a weekly basis. Janae would walk in with these loud costumes that looked like something out of a Mummers Parade. One evening he/she came in with a large white hat that was so humongous and had so many things dangling from it, it looked like a chandelier. If light would have emanated from it, it would have blinded the entire restaurant. And what a royal pain in the ass Janae was to wait on. He/she was very fussy and tipped very little in relation to the hoops you had to jump through to fulfill his/her every request. He/she wanted the world to know he/she was a prima donna, and I took every precaution necessary to avoid serving this endless pit of confusion.

Other trannies came in not only from the Queen Mary but from the general public as well. Some of these dudes were, from what you could tell, ugly enough as men that they certainly didn't need to go traipsing around as women. Many seemed to be in some sort of mid-life crisis. They came in all shapes and sizes. And as much as I hate to admit it, there were a select few that made you second-guess your sexuality. You really had to scrutinize these imposters to make a positive identification. With that being said, every once in a great while, you could kind of understand how Eddie Murphy, who occasionally appeared at our deli, maybe fell into this trap. I'm not going Crying Game on you here; I'm just trying to provide a little heads up to my brothers out there whose new love interest has a lower voice than he does and is also overly obsessed with Marilyn Monroe.

At first, I was weirded out, if not completely petrified of these human oddities. But as time wore on, I began to loosen up and even played along with these fruitcakes in order to help perpetuate their fraud. Towards the end of my matzo ball career, I saw dollar signs on everybody's forehead and was willing to say almost anything to anybody in order to receive a good tip, even if it meant regurgitating in my mouth. I was even able to restrain my laughter when a cross-dressing male placed an order in the most feminine way possible while straining his vocal chords to do it. Of course, I, being Happy Jozef, would make him blush by saying, "Will there be anything else ma'am?" at the end of his order. Or if they came in as a group, I would compliment them with a "Don't you all look pretty tonight," even though you could see the hair underneath one of the dude's stockings. Every once in a while, I would even greet him/her with a "Good evening, ma'am." And you'd be surprised at how many seemingly straight and athletic guys would come in on dates with them. Maybe that's what short-circuited my gaydar because I still can't for the life of me figure any of it out. But hey, what do I know?

I had already learned at the deli how strong the ties of the gay mafia were, but it wasn't until I got my biggest agent meeting to date that I uncovered how deep their slimy claws really reached. The agent I was scheduled to meet with was named J. Michael Bloom and he was the founder of a small boutique agency named Meridian Artists. Mr. Bloom had an excellent reputation around town as an agent and had represented many A-list actors and writers throughout the years. One of his many claims to fame was serving as Alec Baldwin's first handler. And here it was right in front of me, a real agent meeting. And it only took me six years to get it. I wanted to be at my best, so I walked into Mr. Bloom's office as if I owned the town. I introduced myself, and as I went to sit down, one of the first things out of Mr. Bloom's mouth was, "I could really use a blowjob." "What?" I thought to myself as I just stared at him like, "What the hell did you just say?" He quickly covered up his comment by jokingly stating that he was "only kidding." At that point in my Hollywood struggle, I had an insatiable appetite for success, but I was now wondering what it would cost me to achieve it.

One thing was for sure, Mr. Bloom owned the conversation. The more I talked about what my goals were and the types of characters I wanted to play, the more he came out with things like, "I could really use a neck rub" or "I had a trainer who looked a lot like you. I used to like the way he worked me out." These statements caught me completely off guard. I now felt as if I was brought into his office for more than just an interview. I could suddenly empathize with every woman in town who ever felt pressured to jump on the Hollywood casting couch in order to advance her career. As a side note, there were a few rumors circulating around town that many of the big name celebs who weren't blue bloods or direct descendents of Hollywood royalty had to let go of their sexual inhibitions to make their way through the Hollywood maze. This was a price that I wasn't willing to pay. Call me a prude, but the interview ended with my butt cheeks still intact. That minor detail was overshadowed by the fact that my chances of acquiring a real Hollywood agent had just flown out the window, the same window I wanted to chuck Mr. Bloom through. Oh well, such is life.

Mr. Bloom died on February 21, 2008. I remember during our interview that he commented about not feeling well because of some health issues. When I followed up with Mr. Bloom by phone to thank him for taking the time out of his day to try and seduce me, I mean to meet with me, his assistant informed me that he was out of the office due to an illness. His obituary in *Variety* read that he died of complications from pneumonia following surgery. I can't say for sure, but it sounds like the HIV to me.

And if J. Michael Bloom didn't have HIV, I can say with absolute certainly that two notorious offshoots of the deli's gay community did; a black gentleman by the name of Larry and a flamboyant Mexican named Enrique. Larry was yet another gay man who slipped past my gaydar. Larry was a very friendly and likeable guy who, right from the get go, was very up front about his disease and his sexuality. Had he not been so candid, I probably would have never even figured out which side of the stream he swam on. Larry was a real guy's guy who could talk sports, music, and politics with the best of us. The problem with Larry was that his meds disoriented him and left the poor guy dazed and confused most of the time. It was, however, pretty hilarious to watch him bumble into the kitchen and forget why he was there or have him show up an hour late for work because he couldn't remember what time his shift started. All of that was fine and dandy until the day he hit his head on the bread rack and began bleeding.

Being the germaphobe that I am, I was on the verge of packing it in for the evening. Making an extra seventy bucks wasn't worth becoming infected with HIV to me. But the analytical (and more rational) side of my brain took over and reminded me that I needed that night's earnings to make rent for the month, so I simply decided to wear plastic kitchen gloves for the remainder of my shift. It also became a common practice of mine to spit into the sink and rinse my mouth out if Larry, or anyone for that matter, ever coughed or sneezed in my direction. This ritual was not isolated to the night Larry was bleeding in the kitchen. It was also standard operating procedure to wash my hands whenever I came into contact with him. I would scrub them just enough to remove any microscopic pathogens but not so hard as to create a lesion that the virus could slip into. I also followed this hand-washing protocol whenever I touched things like money, a dirty plate, a ketchup bottle, an empty glass, or whatever else I came into contact with. The spitting into the sink and scrubbing my face only transpired when someone coughed or sneezed within a certain radius of me, especially if he/she had HIV. The radius extended a little wider under that condition.

Enrique, on the other hand, was not quite as likeable as Larry. Enrique was another platinum member of the gay mafia with self-esteem problems equivalent to Ned's but with a temporary downward smirk imprinted on his cranium. This man not only chased after every, what he called, "cute guy" who entered our facility, but he also monopolized all of the good looking women on our staff as well. I don't really know why these hot female laborers were drawn to this drama queen other than the fact that he provided them with an alibi not to interact with the small number of us sex-starved straights who toiled there. I almost fell out of my chair the day Enrique told me he had sex with a woman. I responded with, "What was his name?" to which Enrique gave me a long whiney "Joozeefff." And as much as Enrique got under my skin with his "screw yous" and "shutups," I felt terrible when I found out that he contracted HIV. Because we were all part of one big, happy, dysfunctional family, who went through all the same ridicule and all the same torment day in and day out, I really did have a sense of camaraderie and compassion for those whom I had served with on the deli front lines.

Don't get me wrong. I am not getting soft here. I still did express my views when it came time to. One of these issues happened to be over gay marriage, which came in the form of a California proposition widely known as Prop 8. Because I was (and still am) against asking the state for any kind of permission, whether it be to bear arms or to marry (regardless of sexual orientation), I had to vote no on this proposition based on principle. But imagine trying to tell that to a group of people who tried to overturn a city bus in downtown Hollywood the day Prop 8 failed, and you have a potential bloody mess on your hands. The sifting-out process began with members of the rainbow cartel smugly yet privately asking each one of us how we voted on Prop 8. I don't think my response of "You don't want to know" was as unrevealing as I had hoped.

As word spread through the restaurant like wildfire, the gates of hell swung open. Shouts were coming at me from so many different directions I just wanted to duck my head and run for cover. I finally made up my mind to simply holler back at anyone who was willing to listen to the basis for my decision. This only seemed to incite more outrage. The accusations were flying at me so ferociously and so viciously that it caused me to tip over a vanilla milk shake that I was carrying on a tray. As a result, the creamy beverage splattered onto the floor and all over the bottom of my pant leg. In addition to all of the nasty insults being slung at me, I also now looked as if I had just jumped out of a porno movie. When the fruit pie syndicate was finally finished dog piling on me and after a little time had elapsed, I felt obliged to make a very vocal apology to the same-sex advocates on our staff and their supporters by more calmly providing the rationale for my vote. I went on to explain how my stance on the issue wasn't really a reflection of how I felt about what they were doing in the privacy of their own homes but that it was more of a decision that was in line with my own conscience and morals. This explanation still drew some hems and haws from the apple-butter gang, but at least I figured I was being honest with them.

The one person I felt no empathy for, especially after she said to me, "Oh I guess you think you would make a better parent than me," was Sardine. I felt no remorse for her and thought to myself, if you treat a child even remotely as badly as you treat other grown adults, I wouldn't want you parenting a Tasmanian devil. Later on, when the smoke finally cleared, a few shy conservatives emerged from the woodwork to tell me they had voted the way I had. Great, guys. Thanks for your support! They also begged me not to tell anybody which lever they had pulled. Could you blame them? One of these closet traditional-marriage employees named Steve actually made a comment to me a little later that evening to the effect of "that was really brave what you did back there," to which I responded, "Yeah, it was brave … and stupid."

Not only did I have gay co-workers jumping down my throat, but I also had gay customers ruffling my feathers as well. The situation I am about to describe to you happened at the center of the universe for all of the mentally ill people in Los Angeles … the counter area. On almost a weekly basis, a new crackpot of the week would set up shop at our imitation marble counter. For the first few days or so, things would appear to be going somewhat normal. But by week's end, our nutty flavor of the week would usually be taking a poke at whatever manager was struggling to remove him from the restaurant. If I had a nickel for every time this happened … Anyway, the fruiter tooter in this next example fit the mold perfectly. Physically, he was a short, balding man who instantly gave off the vibe of a child predator. I would sit back and watch him try to seduce all of the young bloods who were new to town by telling them that he was a producer and that they should come over to his place for an audition. I watched in horror as some of these aspiring thespians actually gave out their digits to this sociopath. Finally, my number was up, and it was my turn to wait on our resident pedophile.

He went through his usual routine of how he worked in the film business and yada yada yada, but when he saw that I was disinterested in his "achievements," he came at me from a different angle. He claimed he was a famous singer. "Oh brother," I thought to myself as I played along with his fairy tale by asking him what songs he sang that I would recognize. Until this day, I wish I could eat those words as I had no idea what they would unleash upon me. In a matter of seconds and what seemed like a bad dream, Mr. McGoo shot up out of his stool and began serenading me in front of the entire restaurant. And not at some discreet volume that only a few nearby patrons could hear but at a deafening decibel level that transformed this exceedingly noisy restaurant into deadpan silence. Everything went quiet except for the earsplitting operatic performance that was playing out directly in front of me. And there was no mistaking whom he was singing his love ballad to as he glared right at me, no matter which way I turned. He honed in on me like a shark hunting a wounded fish, and I have to admit I was completely stunned. I was frozen stiff and prayed to God that he would just go away. As he kept positioning himself to look directly in to my eyes, I couldn't decide whether I wanted to punch him in the face or just burst out laughing. But by this time, you could hear a fork drop, which I did; probably because the person who dropped it was so stupefied by what he was witnessing, he lost all muscle control in his body. When Enrique Palazzo finally reached his climax (in a non-sexual way, God, I hope), it can be said that he didn't exactly electrify the crowd. A long period of serenity elapsed before a few murmurs eventually led to a gradual return to business as usual. I remained catatonic as my life flashed before my eyes. I was in the midst of an all-time low, and there wasn't a hole deep enough to throw myself in. Of course, within a few days this crackpot of the week also went bananas and took a swing at our manager, William, as he was escorting the Phantom of the Deli from the premises. Another week, another nut, another dollar.

On a completely separate occasion, one particular weirdo of the week accused me of trying to kill him. This guy sat at the end of the counter and apparently felt he was temporarily hired to question everything I did. At first, I thought he was just another annoying jackass trying to tell me how to do my job. But when his meal didn't immediately appear in front of him just a couple of minutes after he ordered it, this loon went berserk. I was in the middle of taking another order when mad stork jumped out of his seat with his arms flailing. Apparently, the insults he was screaming at the top of his lungs were directed at me. Why he wasn't shown the door at that point in time, I will never know.

Obviously, our manager at the time also spoke crazy and instantaneously clamored that I bring out his order. But when Koo Koo for Cocoa Puffs got his evening slop a couple of minutes later, he refused to eat it because he accused me of poisoning it. It was as if this guy wanted me to kill him with the amount of hatred he was spewing at me. His level of inappropriate behavior was beyond anything I was equipped to deal with or better yet, had the patience to tolerate. This was now out of my hands and escalating to the level of management intervention. In other words, I was tired of putting up with this ass wipe. Someone needed to soothe this lunatic and collect the money he owed us for the food he never ate before I choked him with his own tongue. This was just one more reason why I never wanted to become a manager. Our managers were underpaid, overworked, and underappreciated, and they constantly had to diffuse situations like the one just mentioned, which seemed to occur on an hourly basis. Plus, I never spent time in a mental facility, so I lacked the necessary qualifications.

If you haven't had your fill of fruits, nuts, and flakes yet, then I have one last story for you that I hope will finally curb your appetite for these delicious morsels. You know, I never even got her name but this incredibly sexy woman in booth twenty-three caught my eye one evening. It was probably the way she smiled at me and then bashfully looked down into her salad bowl after making eye contact that I found so incredibly erotic. My body temperature started to rise from this simple interaction, and I felt myself drawn to her table like a moth to a flame. I don't think I got much past hello when she asked me, "What time are you finished?" I thought to myself, "What? It can't be this easy. Something is way too good to be true here." But, she did arouse my curiosity, so I decided to investigate a little further to see where this would lead. Keep in mind I was single at the time.

As I was banging out my side work, this alluring temptress told me that she would wait out on the patio for me to finish up. Because it was a slow night and the manager was most likely in the back office sleeping, I decided to slip out early and first talk with this gorgeous gal before getting swept up in a night of ecstasy.

Good thing for rational thinking. After sitting down and engaging this stunning beauty in some casual discourse, she decided that she was going to bring a few more people into our conversation. This would have been fine and dandy if not for one thing … We were the only two people sitting on the patio. She would say something to me. Then, suddenly, she'd begin speaking to the empty space next to her. Then she'd answer a question from the figment of her imagination seated across from her. The response from that hallucination must have been unsettling because it triggered a very heated argument between them. Then she had to deal with an idiotic question from the apparition located next to her while she handled the imaginary party across from her. I was having trouble keeping track of who was saying what to whom, but it was really something to watch. And because I felt as if (a) I was being left out of the conversation and/or (b) I simply wanted to wake up the next morning alive, or at least without a rabbit boiling on my stove, I decided I was going to try and slip out the back door without her noticing. I waited until I finally had the attention of the moderator of crazy fest to explain to her that I forgot to take care of something very important inside the restaurant (like myself). At that point in time, I made a quick exodus from the table.

I had a few remaining tasks to take care of before I could make my getaway so I knocked them out as fast as humanely possible. I then made an immediate beeline for my car. When I looked over my shoulder to make sure "they" weren't following me, I was in for yet another surprise. Crazy Jane was already in the parking lot with her tongue jammed down some random black guy's throat. I couldn't help but stare at this intriguing scenario as I continued on in the direction of my vehicle. From what I could ascertain, this gentleman had just pulled into the parking lot in order to grab a late-night treat. Man did he get one. And if the knife from my drawer didn't kill me, I am sure the STD she'd give me eventually would, so thank God for the ability to reason.

Hey, It's Just a Damn Sandwich!

As more and more of these ravenous animals called customers marched through our front doors, I began to notice the behavioral changes in these beasts from the moment they threw themselves down into one of my cushy vinyl booths up until the completion of their meals. I was constantly reminded of a big-cat park that I visited just outside of Phoenix, Arizona, called "Out of Africa," where I got to witness, first hand, a giant lioness scarfing down the hind end of a steer. As I approached the cage of this majestic creature, she hovered over her food and roared at me, as if to say, "Back up, Jack. This is my meal." This was a warning signal and the kind of urgent notice that immediately prompted a zookeeper to emerge from behind the pen to insist that I move back to a safe distance. A riled up lion could be a real problem for the staff who had to physically interact with these large felines. I quickly complied as I tried to discern who was the bigger threat to me, the lion devouring her meal or the enraged zookeeper. You could hear the bones crunch as this beautiful beast chewed through the carcass she was feasting on. When finished, this magnificent mammal licked her paws and drifted into a more relaxed and playful mood. Let's return to the deli, shall we? It's not that a full stomach always had a sedating effect on these cranks, but for the most part, padding their bellies calmed them down enough to reduce some of their tongue-lashings.

My first of many major blowouts with these clove-footed hellions came on my first and insanely busy Christmas Day. I know the holidays are supposed to be a time of goodwill and cheer, but not at this popular stomping ground where every narcissist in LA is forced to interact with the very same people he or she spent years in therapy trying to recover from. The holidays always seemed to bring out the worst in people for one of two reasons. Either (a) these mental cases had to deal with family members, usually in from out of town, that caused them an unnecessary amount of stress during the holidays or (b) they were away from those very same family members who normally caused them an unnecessary amount of stress during the holidays and were experiencing withdrawal anxiety. And all of this took place inside a jam-packed, bright red delicatessen where the ones with family gazed in admiration at the ones without and vice versa. The place was a powder keg ready to explode. The wait times were abnormally long, and there was hardly any room to move let alone breathe inside these crammed quarters. Because we were only one of a small handful of restaurants open on Christmas Day, it seemed as though everyone and his cousin Lupe who stayed in town and wanted to get out of the house for a few hours traipsed through our continually revolving front doors.

My double shift began in the large party area of our eatery. This section contained three large booths that could hold up to six large adults or twelve little people. It also consisted of movable tables that could be joined together for large parties. Things actually went quite well during my first shift, but the bar was abruptly raised when I was switched to a nearby section for my second shift. In essence, I was juggling two very busy areas at the peak of our rush hour, and I soon found myself hitting the panic button. The crowd was relentlessly streaming in that day, and after waiting over an hour in a line that wrapped around the building, fast service was expected. But with the kitchen staff already in over their heads and the servers scrambling for their lives just to keep people from walking out, making it through this Christmas nightmare would be nothing short of a miracle. Unfortunately for me, I was moved from the large party area of our chophouse over to the fastest turning and quickest paced station known to mankind. And because I was still in the early stages of my deli career, I was literally on the verge of a nervous breakdown. I shuffled between sections in an attempt to wrap up old business in my previous section while trying to satisfy all of the latest demands in my most recent assignment. With my head barely above water, a five top was crammed into one of my small booths. This would prove to be the crack in the dam that unleashed the reservoir.

Although these savages were warned upon entering the establishment that there would be a slight delay in their service, this friendly piece of advice would fall on deaf ears. From the second they sat down, the patriarch of the family was riding me like a rodeo cowboy. When his sandwich arrived twenty minutes after he ordered it, you would think I had lit the old timer's ass on fire and tried to put it out by kicking it, the reason being, the fiery senior soon realized that his triple-meat, triple-club sandwich was made with corn beef instead of pastrami. Now, there was going to be hell to pay, and I was the first one in his line of fire. As he cursed me up and down and sideways, I did everything I could to assure him that I would do whatever was necessary to correct the problem. I also let him know how busy the kitchen was and that rectifying this simple mistake would not be an easy task. But because he demanded pastrami over corn beef, I had to honor his request. In an attempt to keep him occupied, I let him gnaw on his potato salad and baked beans while I attempted to switch out his meats back in the deli. I begged and pleaded with the deli guy to move my request to the front of the line to ward off a void on this provocateur's check, but by that point, the deli guy couldn't have cared less. I went back at least three separate times to look for the crusty senior's remake while also juggling fifty thousand other requests thrown on me like a cheap suit. Just as I was about to go back one last time and either strangle the deli guy or pick up my sandwich, I was cut off by none other than the burning fossil from table eighteen who stormed towards me like a force of nature.

I'll give it to the old coot. He had a temper and a way with words. As he belittled me in front of the entire restaurant, which had ceased all conversation in order to enjoy my public lashing, I begged and pleaded for the old buzzard to return to his seat while I got him his sandwich. But he enjoyed holding the floor way too much to discontinue his relentless avalanche of insults. Had I not already reached my boiling point about three hours prior, I probably would have been able to handle this situation in a much more rationale manner. But after being poked and prodded for what seemed like an eternity, on a day when I was removed from my own family who usually caused me an unnecessary amount of stress during the holidays, I had reached my breaking point. Suddenly the old man went from being a customer who was always in the right to a customer who was about to receive a serious can of whoop ass. In the middle of his vulgar jeers, the only way I could keep this attack dog off me was by asking him the brazen question of "Wanna take it outside?" Had he said yes, I probably would have followed him to the door and then dead bolted it shut once he stepped outside of it, but it never got to that point. He immediately took this new infraction to the highest possible level in order to make his case for my earlier point in this book, which states that these ungrateful idiots will do whatever it takes to ruin your life just because it makes them feel better about themselves. As fate or just dumb luck would have it, who would coincidentally be present on this disaster of an evening other the man who just happened to be on site whenever things were spiraling out of control? None other than the man who would fire you for looking at him wrong, Sal.

When Sal caught wind of my actions, he hunted me down like a bear chasing a picnic basket and pulled me into the isolated sally port that led to the patio. He immediately badgered me with a "Did you ask that guy to step outside?" I quickly responded with a "yes." But because I needed that crappy job, I abruptly justified my actions by replying, "I just did it to get him off me. He was screaming at me in front of everybody." This seemed to strike a chord with Sal, who just stared at me inquisitively as he contemplated my fate. "You can't say things like that to the customers. Don't ever do it again. If you do, I'll fire you. Where's he sitting?" he continued. I pointed over to my nemesis's table and said, "Over there." All right, I'm going to get him another server. Just stay away from him." I thought I was going to cry. For the first and only time in my life, I wanted to give Sal a big fat kiss on his big bald forehead.

As I watched from afar, Gramps finally got his meal and seemed to have let bygones be bygones. He could finally enjoy the company of his family now that he was stuffing his face full of pastrami. The restaurant had slowed down enough to give everyone a little breathing room. I still had to walk by Grandpa Monster's table while serving the remainder of my customers so I decided to be the bigger man and apologize for my actions. The check was still in my name and because my replacement only had to go over to their table one time and then drop off the check, she allowed me to keep the tip, which I had suffered an immeasurable amount of public humiliation to receive. I remember it was generous, and the old geezer was probably just grateful that he didn't go into a coronary while showing his family that he could still take care of business. When I bumped into Sal a little later on that evening, he told me I was lucky that the deli guys had called him over to report Old Country when he went ballistic on them. At that time, they had warned Sal that the server of a grown man in an adult diaper was about to be next. It turns out the fate of my job and, hence, my survival in Hollywood came down to the fact that Mr. Bananas had chastised the entire deli department in much the same manner he did me during my public thrashing.

Some of these people loved to push you to the edge just to see what they could get away with. I remember one middle-aged chap who dined alone with us one evening. This particular gentleman kept getting more and more irritable every time I returned to check back on him. Then out of nowhere and for no apparent reason, he came out with "You know, you're a real freaking asshole." I wasted no time in snapping back with "Well, you're a real f&%*ing jerk off!" and walked away. I kept my distance from this loner for the rest of his meal, and he left me five bucks on twenty. This was one of the few times during my ten-year tenure while caught in this rat trap that a difficult customer actually handled our differences like a man and dealt with me directly, rather than running to our manager like a little crybaby. There was one other notable time when this happened.

The subject in question was a loose cannon from the second he plopped his crabby ass down in my section. This remained the case until we were physically separated and the subject was escorted from the premises by our manager on duty. The story of how we got there was a typical deli love story where a short, bald Jewish man jumps into a booth, aggressively grabs his menu, and starts scratching his head out of frustration because the server is not there to immediately greet him. When the server does arrive, the agitated man baby insists to the server, "You're going to get me …," and the server responds, "Okay I'm going to get you … Will there be anything else that I can get you?" The waiter, knowing that he has a ticking time bomb on his hands, makes every effort to enter the food into the computer as quickly as possible and then goes out of his way to be in the kitchen to pick up the entrée as soon as it is completed. The server then drops off the fresh-as-can-be dish to the unruly customer and asks him if there is anything else he can get him. When the completely out-of-line patron barks back with a sudden "No!!!" the waiter then goes about his other business until he sees another waiter flagged down by the same grumbling crackpot shortly thereafter. When the original server checks back with the recluse to see how his meal is going after the assisting server fulfills the man's request, the primary server receives a sharp and hostile "I'm fine!" The server then decides to give the upset diner his space until his meal is over. When another secondary server tells the lucky server responsible for keeping this stick of dynamite from spewing his anger all over the walls that confine them that this impatient agitator is ready for his check, the principal server hastily prints the check and immediately drops it off to him.

When up until this point, the fairly patient server politely informs the inexplicably irate customer, "I'll take that when you're ready," the indignant singleton replies, "No you won't. You're not taking anything!" The server then decides to get to the bottom of the situation because (a) it's his job to collect the payment for the bill and (b) maybe it will push the ungrateful prick to take a swing at him so he'll be forced to defend himself. So the fired-up server chases down the raving lunatic who is racing towards the register to settle up his tab and asks him, "Is there a problem?" When the combustible misanthrope responds with a "Yeah, there's a problem; you're the problem," the server attempts to very clearly and concisely explain his position to this off-the-wall sociopath but instead receives an escalating "Wanna take it outside, bitch?" Spontaneously, the towering server steadily and calmly works his way into the mug of the sniveling mad man that is getting on his very last nerve, as if to say, "Go ahead. Hit me, and I will knock that bad attitude right out of you and beat you with it." Finally, a couple of co-workers save both parties from the embarrassment of a mid-restaurant scuffle in which the physically dominant server looks bad for beating someone so defenseless into a bloody pulp and the instigator looks bad because ... well, actually under all of that blood, it's really hard to tell how he looks. Then the manager finally intervenes and receives payment for the bill. The manager then points the still grumbling mental unit towards the door, which this nut job promptly exits through just before he vanishes into the night. But unlike most real-life love stories, this one actually has a happy ending.

Because I was off for the next couple of days, I missed the bawdy customer's return to the deli. I shuddered when Vince, who was one of the servers on duty that night, told me that Nusty the Clown came back and wanted to speak with me. Vince also informed me that he gave the Jewish Jostler my entire work schedule for the week so that he knew when he could find me there. I wanted to strangle Vince. Sure enough, no more than an hour into my first shift back, the little ingrate who had chastised me in front of a packed house had something more to say to me. When I reluctantly arrived at the front of the restaurant where he was waiting for me, he began with an apology. He welled up as he confessed to me that he was in a bad mood the night of our altercation because his wife had filed for a divorce, and he was sorry that he had taken it out on me. He also went out of his way to tell me that he knew he had me in a position where I couldn't retaliate and that he thanked God later that night that I didn't hit him. He then asked me to get him a cup of coffee. He didn't tip me on the night of his tirade, but when I circled back around with his take-out coffee, he handed me a twenty dollar bill and told me to keep the change. I was speechless. "Did someone just offer me a random act of kindness? In this place, nonetheless?" I thought to myself. In all my years of dealing with the rudest people on earth and also some of the nicest, I never had anyone who had treated me so badly come back and ask for forgiveness. This still stands out in my mind as the greatest redemption story of my life. I actually became somewhat friendly with this gentleman and always went out of my way to help him whenever he came in to dine with us.

I was really beginning to enjoy the job that only a few years ago I had only pretended to like. I loved showing people a good time and wanted them to have a first-rate dining experience, even if it went unnoticed by hollow heads like Sardine. To me, it didn't matter. But in another rare instance of random kindness, a very friendly black man and his wife, who were extremely pleasant to wait on, came into our bistro one evening. Honestly, I wanted to tip them for being so cool and for making me laugh so much during our brief time together. When the meal was over, the gentleman asked me how much I wanted him to tip me. This caught me completely off guard, so I responded politely with "I really don't like doing this, so just put down whatever you think is good. Anything is fine." He just stared at me and said, "No, really. How much?" As I later found out and what I also sensed from the challenging nature of this gentleman was that he was a very successful businessman who loved the thrill of a good negotiation. As I pondered his question, I bought some time with "Whatever you want." He insisted again with "Tell me how much you want me to tip you." I, then, not so subtly, shot back, "A hundred bucks." Without hesitation, he scribbled down one hundred dollars on the tip line, signed the bottom of the receipt, and handed it to me.

Now this dilemma later weighed on me in two ways, the first being, should I have requested a higher amount? I mean, I was doing okay at the deli, but I had a ton of overdue bills, and the tires on my car were about to fall off. The other side of the coin was that a hundred bucks was a decent night of earnings for a whole shift, let alone for just one table. Was I being too presumptuous and greedy for just bringing him a couple of sandwiches? Then my partner, Mary, in her very soothing and spiritual nature, assured me that people who have done well for themselves like to give back to people they think could use a helping hand. Boy, was she right. And because we had established this rapport from the onset, every time this gentleman dined in my section from that day onward, he tipped me one hundred dollars. Talk about counting your lucky stars.

Now in another twist of fate, I often fantasized about running into manager Phyllis Carlyle in our restaurant because I felt that her management style would be an excellent fit for the type of career that

I wanted. I also convinced myself that she was one of the few Hollywood dignitaries who could take me to the top. As I discussed earlier, I continued this daydream even after I destroyed any chance whatsoever of forming a business relationship with her and her company. Even though our correspondence traveled south for the winter, I still attended a panel discussion at the Barry Finn Acting Studio that featured Ms. Carlyle. That was the first and only time I ever got a visual on her. Because I directed an intense question at Ms. Carlyle regarding representation that she fielded nicely, I was able to keep a fresh mental image of her somewhat current in my mind. No matter how hard I worked at reversing the damage that I had caused with my pestering persistence, there was no recovering from the initial bad impression that I had left on Ms. Carlyle and her agency.

This minor detail became completely obvious to me after I directed a few phone calls and mailings to Ms. Carlyle's office as a follow up to that seminar. When my extension of the proverbial olive branch went completely ignored, I gave up hope entirely. But as I have experienced many other times in my life, the thoughts that are most dominant in my mind always seem to find a way to come to fruition in my life. Ms. Carlyle sitting in my section and ordering a scoop of tuna and a bowl of mushroom barley soup a few years later was no exception. When she sat down at my table, I was almost positive it was she, but I didn't want to embarrass myself by coming off as unsure, and I certainly didn't want to make an ass out of myself by asking some random stranger if her name was Phyllis Carlyle. At that point in time, I really didn't know how I felt about her or what I should do. I mean she was pretty friendly and even joked with me when I brought her the mushroom barley soup by observing that "You could swim in the bowl," to which I responded, "Please … only when the lifeguard is on duty." This drew a slight smirk from Mrs. C., but I could feel her detachment as she also seemed to place who I was. My suspicions about her identity were confirmed when she was ready to settle up her bill, and I read the name Phyllis Carlyle at the bottom of her credit card. I ran the card and dropped it off at her table with her receipt and some to-go containers. "Thank you very much Ms. Carlyle. Have a wonderful evening," I graciously insisted.

By that time, I am sure something very strange started to dawn on Ms. Carlyle, especially after I had firmly positioned myself in the only escape route from her section. I doubt she immediately recognized who I was, even though I probably had sent her over one hundred headshots. I wanted to offer her one special, final farewell. I am sure she could feel my gaze as I studied her every move. Finally, as she made her way past where I was standing, I hit her with a very deep and demonic "See ya in the movies" that only she could hear. She turned her head slightly to make sure that it was I who was addressing her. She then slowly and cautiously focused her eyes back towards the front of the restaurant and briskly picked up her pace. Ms. Carlyle appeared to be very tense and seemed to be holding her breath as she created some distance between us. When I went back to her table to pick up the credit card slip, I discovered that she had left me a nice 20-percent gratuity but that she had also forgotten her doggy bag, containing her mushroom barley soup and scoop of tuna. I immediately grabbed the items and raced towards the front door. When I finally reached the parking lot, her black Mercedes went rocketing past me even though I was waving her doggy bag and signaling for her to stop. As her car prematurely peeled out from the parking lot and darted onto Ventura Boulevard, it was nearly T-boned by an oncoming car. Her luxury vehicle then briskly sliced through traffic and, in no time, built up enough speed to make a quick getaway.

When I called her office the following day, not even her receptionist answered the phone. I left my name and number in the event that she wanted me to hand-deliver her packed-up items to the office. This final attempt to reach her was honestly just one last laugh for me. It also marked the last time I would ever try to contact her or her office goons again. Hollywood had a way of making you feel less than by dismissing you as a person of little or no value, so if I creeped her out or knocked her off her high pedestal for even just a few hours, it was well worth the effort. Hopefully, I left an impression on her she will never forget.

I never seemed to have much luck in the section Ms. Carlyle dined in either. Maybe it was cursed. The area in question was located right next to the bar, which also seemed to bring out the worst in people. An isolated Saturday night will serve as the perfect example.

The worst part of working the graveyard shift was dealing with all of the drunken imbeciles who came in at all hours of the morning. The majority of them were loud, stupid, and incoherent. The four prizes that trickled in during this one particular late shift set up shop across the aisle from where the great Ms. Carlyle had once sat. These guys obviously consumed more liquor than they could handle and were escalating to the level of belligerent assholes. The most buffed and self-assured member of the group ordered a skirt steak. I graciously worked with these guys to patiently extract their orders, even though they were hammered out of their skulls and were busting my balls throughout the entire process. After just a couple of minutes of ultimately punching in their requests, I was summoned to the kitchen. When I arrived back at the line, the lead cook had some bad news for me "We're out of skirt steak." With no time to lose, I hustled back over to the table so I could inform the lush who had ordered that specific cut of beef that we were out of his selection. I was also going to let him know that if he had a backup plan I could quickly submit his new order to catch it up to the others. That's how I drew it up, but the second I formed the words, "We're out of skirt steak," on my lips, this ignoramus immediately accused me of lying to him. He then huffed and puffed about how I was messing with him. But because I was used to dealing with quite a long list of irrational alcoholics just like him on this wretched shift, I was able to steer him in the direction of another item. I mean, there was a tip on the line, and if these boozers decided to leave at any point during this whole ridiculous process, all of my efforts would have been for naught. Finally, this bozo decided on a pastrami sandwich.

After ringing in his order for a second time, I was once again hailed to the kitchen a couple of minutes later to speak to the deli. This time they were out of pastrami. This was the only time during my entire ten-year stint at Camp Matzo Ball that we ever ran out of pastrami, and I was convinced that the deli guys were messing with me. To play it safe I double-checked with the manager on duty to make sure we were out of this popular item. I dreaded going back to the table. Not because I feared the guy whose parade was about to get rained on but because I was no longer in the mood for his bullshit. But unfortunately, for me, at some point during the course of his meal, he would have to find out the truth, so away I went.

Of course, when I arrived with this latest newsflash, he was absolutely convinced that I was doing this on purpose. Now it was full on. I reluctantly took his verbal abuse for a good twenty seconds or so before he made the mistake of standing up and grabbing my shoulder. In my ten years of waiting tables, I never took a swing at a customer, but in this case I don't know how I refrained. The one thing that I hated more than anything in the entire world was when people touched me. Whether they were pulling on me to get my attention, touching me in order to be cute in front of their friends, or in this case, physically threatening me, I had a zero tolerance policy. Hell, I didn't even like my co-workers touching me. I exploded on this guy by dishing out everything he had dumped on me and some. Security then pounced on this idiot just before I was about to remove his head from his body. To my credit, I didn't lay a hand on him. But I did have to run a few miles after work to calm myself down a bit. I truly believe that if someone would have assaulted me on that job I would've killed him simply as a result of all of the pent-up frustration I had accumulated over the years. I often joked that if my Hollywood career didn't work out, my next job would be that of a hit man. Who knows, if this book doesn't sell, maybe I'll give Katya a call.

The last notable event that developed back in the section of the damned came on a very busy night while we were entertaining our usual share of misfits who expected everything five minutes ago. Alas, sometimes the pure timing of when you sit down determines how quickly your order comes out. And with so many other extenuating circumstances involved in each order, I'm surprised any food came out of that kitchen at all. Anyway, after years of endlessly whizzing around like a fly in a jar, along with the stress of not being able to get ahead in life and the despair of being rejected on a daily basis in my acting career, that job was starting to take a real toll on me. And excuse me if I had to earn every single dime I'd ever made and had the audacity to realize that people are emotional beings who liked to be treated with a little respect from time to time. The guy I was waiting on probably never worked an honest day in his life and must have been born in a manger. He ridiculed everything I did, which included placing his soupspoon on the side of his soup bowl. This harebrain was upset because some of the soup spilled onto his spoon before HE got a chance to put it in the bowl. What a pussy! I have an idea for a new law in California. How about we place a firing squad outside of each restaurant? Every time a customer complains about something so trivial … so retarded … he is immediately escorted outside, blindfolded, and given his last words. A lit cigar is then stuffed in his mouth, and his guts are splattered all over the outside of the building via machine-gun fire. As a result, the blanketing of his blown-out innards now provides aesthetic appeal as our new exterior suitably matches the bright red décor found inside. Now, back to our story!

When I eventually picked up numb nut's meal from the window, I was so tripped out by his whole spoon on the side of the bowl thing that I forgot to bring him his horseradish. Well, God forbid someone dare make a mistake in his presence. Besides this horse's ass going off on an endless rant throughout the duration of his meal, when he received his credit card slip at the culmination of his bitch fest, he engraved a giant zero across the tip line. If that wasn't enough, he also scribbled, "You're a real airhead!" across the top of the receipt in bold ink. I still have fantasies about what I would have done to him if I would have caught him out in the parking lot. For one, I would have fenced in an entire ten-block area. From there I would have dressed him in a Disney costume that didn't unzip. Then he'd get a thirty-second head start to take off running while I mounted a fifty caliber machine gun to the top of a dune buggy. If he managed to escape over the tall barbed wire fence on the far end of the perimeter without being mowed down first, he would be deemed the victor and would walk away a free man. But if I caught him, well, let's just say I would definitely have some fun with him first. After a few hours of shooting off his knee caps, boredom would set in, and I would probably want to figure out how many bullet holes I could pierce him with. After finally finishing him off, I'd leave him out to rot under the hot burning sun until he, in his now rancid polyester suit, completely biodegraded. I know I may seem like a real loon at certain times in this book, but I believe all of the credit can be given to these irrational yo-yos who flipped my switches on a daily basis and made it impossible for me to rein myself back in from these sadistic thoughts.

Politics of American Food/Idols

If I had to create a billboard for the political career I was about to embark on, it would've read "Jozef Rothstein: Serving our country, one table at a time." I don't know if it was from the many years of absorbing Chester's ramblings or it was the political awakening I was having as a struggling artist in Hollywood, but I was developing a strong urge to run for public office. I was on the deli payroll throughout the Y2K scare, the 9/11 attacks, and the bursting of the housing bubble, and I also spent what was now over eight years aggressively pursuing a career in an entertainment industry that seemed to have shut me out from the beginning. It wasn't the American dream I had grown up believing in, and the more I learned about the corruption in our government along with my first-hand experience of the corruption in Hollywood, the more I wanted to do something about it. I didn't want much, just a level playing field, but how would I get it? Then, believe it or not, a Washington politician entered my periphery by the name of Ron Paul. In my humble opinion, most politicians speak in circles and in jargon that makes little sense to anybody, including themselves. It's as if they are trying to confuse you on purpose. But Dr. Paul's philosophy was clear, concise, and really resonated with me. He spoke to the common man and endorsed liberty and equality for all. The first time I watched him on YouTube, he honestly sounded too good to be true. But then

I went to his website, checked out his voting record, and realized this guy really practiced what he preached.

I also got turned on to certain truth films referred to me by fellow actors and activists. Movies about 9/11, the GMOs in our food, the new world order, propaganda in the news media and in Hollywood. These films all created an insatiable thirst in me for the truth. The more I learned, the more outraged I became. I was also realizing that my success and happiness in life were dependent on correcting the problems associated with too much government. I didn't immediately consider representing the people from my assembly district, but my participation in the Ron Paul campaign changed all of that.

I initially decided to volunteer as a precinct captain for the Ron Paul campaign, which involved knocking on doors to discuss the ideas of freedom and liberty and to promote the Founding Fathers' original intent for our country, which is that of limited government. Bringing myself up to speed was no small feat, but I was an avid researcher, and I loved to debate, so this new side of me was very second nature. I don't know how I found the time for canvassing while slinging matzo ball soups six nights a week and while also pursuing an acting career full time, but where there is a will, there is a way.

The state of California was already very oppressive and was becoming even more so. Traffic tickets had a 200 percent tax on them, parking fines were going through the roof, as was the price of electricity and water. I also received a ticket at an intersection where I was photographed by a red-light camera, and I fought back vehemently, only to lose to a judge who didn't understand or pretended not to understand our Constitution. We have the right to challenge our accuser in a court of law so I decided to call my accuser to the stand, which by the way, was a red-light camera. The judge said that the paid goon speaking on behalf of the manufacturer would have to suffice so I ended up with nearly a four-hundred-dollar fine. I was now a rat on a wheel, working ridiculously long hours just to pay ransom to a government who was supposed to be protecting my rights, not taking them away.

I once read a quote by Jim Bishop that states, "The truth which makes men free is for the most part the truth which men prefer not to hear." Many of my co-workers were now labeling me as the crazy guy, which was the exact same label I used to pin on Chester. Call it karma if you will. I can't tell you the opposition I faced while trying to explain to some of my co-workers that the red-light cameras were cash cows that actually caused more accidents than they prevented, the reason being most people jam on their brakes to avoid a ticket, which in turn results in many more rear-end collisions. One of our servers, Mike, insisted that I shouldn't have run the light to begin with and that I clearly broke the law. What Mike didn't realize was the company who installed the cameras, ATS, was accused of breaking all kinds of laws to get the contracts to provide and maintain these devices. And some cities were shortening the length of the yellow light in order to increase the number of infractions and hence the amount of revenue the *scam*eras brought in. Besides, studies have shown that if you simply delay the yellow light by just one second, not only does traffic flow much better but you cut down on 90 percent of the infractions. But the weakest and most pathetic aspect of Mike's point of view was his blatant disregard for his own rights. The camera violations don't allow you the right to challenge your accuser in a court of law, and they force you to become a witness against yourself. They also fail to protect you equally under the law as over one million judges, politicians, and even museum guards throughout the state of California were given specially coated license plates to exempt them from a ticket if their picture was taken. When I filed my appeal to challenge the unlawful decision made by my judge, who only handled red-light camera cases and was most likely on the Lockheed Martin/ATS payroll, I didn't send in one of the many necessary forms to the right place at the right time, and so, I lost my right to dispute the decision. Talk about a scam.

There were also other big scams that I was waking up to. The Federal Reserve was one of them. This con involves a private international banking cartel controlling the United States currency and in turn, most of the world's reserve money. While making calls at the Los Angeles Ron Paul headquarters, I got to meet the founder of the "End the Fed" movement, who encouraged me to become an active participant in their protests. It was a very eye-opening experience to learn of the other two central banks that existed in our nation's history and how they both deprived the people of their wealth and freedom, not unlike today. I was also learning from the many brilliant minds that I was coming into contact with that we were sold into slavery by FDR in 1933 when he agreed to use U.S. citizens as collateral for the newly established Federal Reserve Bank Note. This new Federal Reserve Bank Note replaced the former Federal Reserve Note that a person used to be able to exchange for an equivalent amount of gold or silver that backed the note's worth. The Federal Reserve Bank Note is currently backed by nothing other than "We the People" and our promise to pay the debt with everything we have, including ourselves.

Another bunch of fraudulent undertakings by our wonderful federal government were the Patriot Act, the Iraq War, the new FISA bill, the Real ID Act, and many other similar transgressions, which were a direct consequence of the biggest deception of the decade, 9/11. I would get into heated debates with customers and employees alike who backed the "official story" of the events that took place on 9/11, especially one regular who hung out at the bar every night named Big Jim. It didn't matter what the occasion was, Big Jim always made sure he was wearing one of his cheesy redneck t-shirts that boasted such phrases as "Gas is so expensive I can't afford to fart" or "Being stupid is not a crime, so you are free to go." His all-time favorite and the one that he paraded around in most often read, "It's better to have loved and lost than to live with the psycho the rest of your life." This guy refused to look at the most common-sense arguments in regards to the murdering of over three thousand people. Then again, is it really a surprise?

For instance, it wasn't just one building that collapsed into its own footprint at freefall speed (that, I'll maybe give you) or two buildings that collapsed into their own footprint at freefall speed (now you're pushing it), but three buildings (also Building 7) that collapsed into their own footprint at freefall speed. To top it off, Building 7 was not even struck by an aircraft. Add to the fact that independent scientists, like Dr. Niels H. Harrit from the University of Copenhagen in Denmark and Dr. Steven E. Jones from BYU, found nano-thermite in the pulverized rubble that created the white powder we all witnessed on TV, and you have a very elaborate conspiracy on your hands. Big Jim backed the "official story" more passionately than Johnny Cochran defending OJ. This was common with most people who just couldn't think of a world where everything they believed in was a lie. Also, a good portion of the naysayers never read the PNAC report that came out in September of 2000, which boldly concluded that America needed "a new Pearl Harbor" to justify going into the Middle East. Some of these doubters would avoid the conversation altogether by simply asserting, "I don't get involved in politics." My quote to them is from Desmond Tutu which declares, "If you are neutral in situations of injustice, you have chosen the side of the oppressor."

As I brought in all kinds of forms for people to sign at the workplace, such as the "Audit the Fed" and the "Stop Real ID" petitions, I was also pushing the boundaries of my job description. When Henry announced at a small pre-shift server meeting that "Yeah, the corporate office doesn't want us forcing our political views on our customers or other employees," we all knew who he was talking to. So I decided it might be a good time to lay off the solicitations. But just as I made a commitment to stop gathering signatures at the jobsite, what does the corporate office do but implement a finger-scanning device to read and collect our fingerprints. THE OUTRAGE!!!! I now had to go underground to find a few other brave employees who were willing to back me in opposition to these new devices, which to me and others in the freedom movement were all part of a conditioning phase into the new big brother surveillance society. Of course, the company didn't view it that way, especially when they boasted that they weren't even linked up to the Internet or sharing our information with other stores. They also tried to say that these thingamabobs were not actually recording our biological data because the computer made a computer-generated map of our fingerprints based on numerical data. This was a weak argument, to which I retorted, "Just because a digital image is captured instead of our actual physical fingerprint does not mean our very own unique patterns are not stored in the database." The computer tech that they brought in to address my concerns was dumbfounded with this rebuttal. I was disgusted with their rationale and warned them if they allowed any more biological reading instruments such as iris scanners or facial recognition technology onto our store premises we would take a much more aggressive stand.

Because my eyes were now opening to the new world being forced upon us, I felt as if it was my duty and in the best interest of my own self-preservation to alert others. This didn't come without consequences. Most important, I was driving Mary away. She couldn't understand what caused me to take such a radical turn and warned me on several occasions not to discuss any of my views with her. She wanted life to be as unrealistic as possible and didn't want me raining on her parade. She was enrolled in a spiritual psychology school and was surrounded by a bunch of manipulating psycho analysts who were trying to convince her that I was no good for her. Many of them were indoctrinated socialists who saw my views as extreme.

At work, I was also gaining a reputation. While attending a going-away party for a popular co-worker, someone got the creative idea to change the names of a few of our menu items to include the first names of various staff members. The idea of this farewell memento was to take the name or personality of a co-worker and fit it with an appropriate dish. I thought this was great idea until I glanced at my selection of choice, "Jozef in a Pot," which was named after our "Chicken in the Pot" platter. I believe the translation for that particular menu item turned out to be "crackpot." Now a quote from Mark Twain: "In the beginning of change, the Patriot is a scarce man; brave, hated and scorned. When his cause succeeds, however, the timid join him, for then it costs nothing to be a Patriot."

As things continued to deteriorate in our country, even before the collapse of the housing market, I found myself sharpening my knowledge of the Constitution and revisiting the original intent of the Founding Fathers. Henry was an avid shooter and took me out to the range on occasion to shoot his .357. I really enjoyed firing a gun and the feeling of power that came with it. Henry was a good teacher and was actually pretty cool outside of work. It wouldn't be long until I owned my first firearm and was practicing whenever time permitted. I was now exercising my second amendment privilege so kindly granted to me by the state of California (sarcasm intended). I also started recognizing the dangers imposed by criminal enterprises like the FDA on our food supply, and even though Mary and I were renting our home, I took it upon myself to plant and nurture twenty-three different types of heirloom fruits and vegetables in our spacious backyard. I now had a new hobby that kept me out of Mary's hair while she shuffled through her fairy cards and watched the boob tube from her favorite spot on the couch.

I think the final straw that beyond any doubt pushed Mary over the edge and broke the proverbial camel's back was the night that I went out hanging "End the Fed" and "Gold is Money" signs. These were to be fastened to two consecutive footbridges that hovered over the highly traveled 101 Freeway. I needed an accomplice, but I knew better than to ask Mary. As a matter of fact, I didn't even want her to know what I was up to. I bought the supplies at Michael's Craft Store while Mary was at work and promptly rushed home to complete these humongous posters before she walked through the front door. I quickly loaded up my car just short of her arrival and scurried off to work before she could stumble upon my revolutionary activities. When I arrived at the deli that evening, I kept the number of people I asked for help to a minimum as I didn't want to stir up any more sentiment to fire me than was already present. When I came across Miguel, an eighteen-year-old, five-feet-four-inches Hispanic kid who was more into the thrill of the adventure then he was the cause for liberty, we hatched our plan.

After work, we drove my car to the footbridge farthest from the deli and parked in the cul-de-sac near the entrance. We brazenly approached the overpass with determination as we were excited to start our mission. But just a few steps into our walk of death, we began to second guess our decision. Tractor trailers were whipping below our feet at breakneck speed, forcing the whole structure to shake. As we finally inched our way to the center of the catwalk, we first had to stop our knees from knocking so we could carry out our objective. As we eventually adapted to our new environment, a fresh rush of adrenaline swept over us. We hurriedly decided that we should fasten the top ends of the banner first. We agreed that in order for this to happen I, being six feet five inches, would have to drape the sign over the tall wire fence extending up from the guardrail. From there, we would fasten the top corners to temporarily hold the streamer in place while we secured the rest of the homemade billboard. Trust me, this was trickier than it sounds. I held onto the sign for dear life as I reached over the tall chain-link fence that was the only thing keeping me from splattering all over the concrete interstate below. I prayed to God that the mesh wire barrier that was gently separating me from the highway underneath me had met all of the safety requirements necessary to hold a large man in place, who just so happened to be dangling from an overpass. As I clutched the material with one hand, I poked two fingers from my free hand through one of the holes in the chain link fence to attach the first top corner. After briskly duplicating this task, we successfully hung up the first sign and, in a race against time, moved on to the second bridge.

We were well on our way to completing our objective on the second bridge when we started laughing hysterically at the insanity of our operation. I mean, what would happen if we dropped a sign onto an oncoming tractor trailer that, as a result of our actions, went veering off the freeway at eighty miles per hour? My body was shaking, and even though there was a slight thrill involved in our adventure, I couldn't wait to return to the safety of my car. We were nearly finished tying the last bottom corner of the second sign to the fence when we felt a strong illuminating presence from behind us. We turned around to discover the source, but the glare was so blinding that we could not make out what it was. Then we suddenly heard, "Get down off the footbridge now. Wait at the bottom of the ramp, and one of our cruisers will meet you there." When the tractor beam finally dimmed down enough to see who was behind it, we realized it was the California Highway Patrol, who had pulled off to the side of the road to catch us in the act with their floodlight.

Because my car was parked on the same side of the road as the cruiser, I got the bright idea to walk in the opposite direction of both. Completely ignoring the fact that if they inspected the vehicles in the cul-de-sac where I had left my car they would have found more than enough sign-hanging paraphernalia to link me to the crime. But it was too late as Miguel had already taken my lead and was following me in the direction that got us down off the footbridge in the least amount of time and as far away from the Highway Patrol as possible. I kept expecting a police helicopter to come swooping down from the sky to prevent us from disappearing into the night. All that I knew was that they were not going to take me in alive.

The second we hit the dark part on the ramp, we took off running. I had a feeling that Miguel's rotund shape would not suit him well in the long-distance sprinting we were about to embark on. These kinds of thoughts raced through my mind as I shot out to an early lead. I was hitting full stride when, all of a sudden, at the bottom of the ramp, I found myself in mid air. I caught my fall with my hands and forearms and skidded on the concrete pavement until I came to a complete stop. As I lay there, trying to figure out what in the hell had just happened, I could feel the multitude of burns on my skin and noticed that I was bleeding profusely. As I felt my way through the dark like Helen Keller in a wax museum, I discovered a pole that was sticking out of the center of the walkway that I guess I overlooked while travelling at full speed in 1-percent visibility. My leg was a little banged up from smacking into the pole, but I was determined to keep going. As I attempted to pick myself up off the ground, I could hear the pitter-patter of Miguel's feet rapidly approaching. I yelled, "Pole!" to prevent Miguel from meeting the same fate. He was able to decelerate just inches before striking the metal intrusion. Had he not come to a screeching halt at that exact point in time, he would've knocked his family jewels up into his esophagus. He helped me up to my feet and checked in with me to make sure I was okay. Before long, we were two fugitives on the lam, once again fleeing through a wealthy Encino neighborhood.

We alertly hid behind parked cars or jumped behind a row of bushes anytime we thought we heard an oncoming car. After about thirty minutes of bobbing and weaving through suburbia, we finally made it to White Oak Avenue, which was the same street that I lived on. Unfortunately for us, we emerged about two miles away from my car and even further away from my house. Miguel, being the street punk that he was, figured that the cops would probably be waiting for us by my car so we agreed to continue traveling in the opposite direction. We were only a few blocks away from Ventura Boulevard where there was a supermarket and a bus stop.

Making it to the supermarket would provide us with some cover and allow us to remove ourselves from broad view, so we made it our priority. We walked fast when there was no traffic and slowed up the pace when we felt heavier flow. This was already a two-hour plus ordeal, and it was well after three in the morning. Miguel had the foresight to remove the shirt he was wearing when we were spotted by the highway patrol, and he stashed it in some bushes. This was to avoid the police description given to any black and white in the vicinity. I can imagine the dispatch that came over the radio. "We have a six-foot-five, approximately thirty-five-year-old white male with blonde hair, possibly a history professor, and his accomplice, a five-foot-four Hispanic eighteen-year-old male, most likely a disgruntled student, heading off the 101 overpass towards Encino Avenue," to which there is a brief pause and a burst of laughter.

Anyway, we also separated ourselves so we weren't easily spotted as the duo in question. As I closed in on Ventura Boulevard, a police patrolman was rapidly approaching and gently hit his brakes to take me in. The officer slowed down but did not stop which made it obvious that he had more important matters to attend to. He sped up again and raced out of view. I let out a sigh of relief, and when the coast was clear, I made a mad dash for the grocery store across the street. When Miguel eventually caught up to me, we entered the store together. I tucked my arm away so as to not raise any suspicion. I actually shopped at this location and didn't want to run into anybody who could identify me until I at least cleaned myself up a little. We bee-lined for the bathroom, and I promptly stuck my arm under the cold water pouring from the spigot. A bloody water solution permeated the sink and circled the drain. I patted the open burns with a dry paper towel to soak up the rest of the blood. As we approached the night clerk for information on the busing schedule, I did my best to conceal my abrasions.

The checkout clerk told us that the bus came by once every hour and the next one wasn't scheduled to arrive for another fifty minutes. So we marched down to the bus stop to wait for the first bus out of Dodge. Because Ventura Boulevard seemed to be a hotbed for police action that night, we weren't so sure we wanted to take the chance of standing out in plain view. So we sat behind the covered terminal for another five minutes or so before scrambling back to the safety of the super. On our way back, we decided that we didn't want to take the risk of waiting for the bus so we summoned the first cab company the 411 operator could provide. The cab company told us they'd be there in ten minutes. A cruiser passed by on the main drag as we blended into the break area near the front entrance of the store. Of course, we weren't dressed like regular store employees but from the distant boulevard, I'm sure it was hard to tell. We started growing antsy when ten minutes turned into a half-hour. Miguel called the cab company back, only to find out for some reason they had decided not to come. Freaking great! So now we were forced to go back into the store to pump the teller for more information. When we approached him for the second time, we requested the number of the most local cab company he could think of and within seconds we were placing another call. The arrival of this cab was now going to closely coincide with the arrival of the bus. The million-dollar question that night would now be whether or not we were going to blow off the cab and simply jump on the bus if the bus came first or if we would play it safe and maintain our cover by skipping out on the bus no matter which one came first.

In the old adage of "Which came first, the bus or the cab?" the answer on this night would prove to be the bus. But only after we decided that we were going to play it safe and wait for the cab. Another interesting element was also thrown into the mix. As the bus was pulling out, a cop car was pulling onto the side street that led to the parking lot of the store. As I sat in complete shock, Miguel assured me that the police officer was not going to turn into the lot. Well of course, Miguel was wrong, and the squad car entered the property. Both Miguel and I decided that we were going to play it cool and casually act as if we always sat there at four-something in the morning with no other signs of life around. We could have made a break for the bus stop, but the next bus wasn't due for another hour. So, we agreed to stay put because getting up and walking away would have made us look even more suspicious than we already were.

As we sat at our little table, we could hear the officer's boots crushing the gravel on the pavement beneath him. His route of choice led him directly past our table. My arm was still bleeding slightly so I tried to keep it out of visual range the best I could while trying to look completely natural. We were now talking about the most idiotic thing known to mankind just to pretend that we were having a normal conversation. As the officer passed by, he inspected us suspiciously while continuing onward towards the empty market. Just as he passed through the sliding glass doors, we could see our salvation on the horizon in the form of a bright yellow cab. As the cab pulled up to the curb, the officer was exiting the store. He wasn't really in there long enough to purchase anything, but maybe he was inside the store just long enough to ask a few questions if you catch my drift. We were already inside the mother ship and giving the command of "Go" while also barking out the address of where we were heading. The cab rolled in that direction. I waited for the stereotypical movie line of "Freeze … Police," but it never came. I did, however, suspect that this cop was going to jump in his cruiser and follow us. But because he probably didn't have enough to go on and since we were already well on our way, I assume he just let us go, that is, if he was even on to us to begin with.

The thought of my leaving my car at the scene of the crime overnight was really starting to eat at me. Any little extra expense, like getting my car released from the pound, would have buried me alive, and I really didn't want to leave that possibility up to fate. Miguel's car was back at the deli where the cabbie dropped us off. From there, Miguel would drive me home. Somewhere around the midway point back to my house, I made the executive decision that I wanted to go back for my car. Miguel disagreed and thought that I should wait until the following morning to pick up my car so that things could blow over, but due to my adamant insistence, Miguel reluctantly complied. We drove around the neighborhood to make sure there were no officers on patrol in the surrounding area. When the threat of being spotted appeared minimal, Miguel quickly turned down the side street that my car was parked on. As we slammed to a sudden halt, I was already halfway out the door. We said our goodbyes as I jumped into the driver's seat of my vehicle. By the time I fired up my engine, Miguel was already at the end of the block. Of course, wouldn't you know it? As soon as I pulled out onto the main drag, a police car was approaching from the opposite direction.

I cool-headedly drove down the boulevard until I hit the first side street that I could turn onto. Cutting down this back alley would put me out of the officer's visual range. It would also lead me down a matrix of side streets that would allow me to shake this smoky from my tail if need be yet still reach my house. Once I slipped out of view, I put the pedal to the metal and gunned it. I made the first left I could make. I made a few more quick turns and flew down some straightaways, and voilà, I was home. I quickly gathered my materials from the back seat of my car and raced through the front door, which I softly pulled shut behind me.

I was stashing and destroying evidence as quietly as possible when Mary awoke from her slumber in the front room. She was now sleeping in the front room with our two dogs on a full-time basis because it was the furthest point in the house away from me and the bedroom I slept in. It was after five in the morning when Mary glided up to me and noticed the dried blood on my arm, the rip in my pants, and the remainder of my banner-hanging paraphernalia. She now wanted to know what the hell I was up to and where the hell I'd been all night. My response was, "All you need to know is that what I did was for our country and that you should be very proud." I don't think those were the exact words Mary was looking for. And I am pretty sure she didn't use any of them when describing the incident the next day to her trusted friend, who already knew me as crazy man. In Mary's eyes, I was skating on very thin ice.

As I got more and more active in the freedom movement, I found myself having a harder and harder time putting up with tyrants like Sardine, who would purposely set me up for failure or try to bait me into an argument so she could turn around and send me home for insubordination. She also suspended me for a week, to which I followed in Chester's footsteps and fought like bloody hell not to lose my shifts. A whole week with no cash flow would have sent me into dire straights, as I always seemed to be living from paycheck to paycheck just to make ends meet. I was also appearing at more and more protests that were being completely ignored by the mainstream media, even though hundreds, if not thousands, of people were rising up. The one anti-war march I participated in paraded right past CNN (the Communist News Network) with over twenty-five thousand strong in attendance, yet CNN refused to air the proceedings. This demonstration was on the anniversary of the Iraq War, and I wanted to puke when the Screen Actors Guild booked a time slot to speak regarding the union's goals in television and film, which they unsuccessfully tried to tie into the anti-war effort.

Because I believe the welfare state is just as harmful to individual freedom and prosperity as the warfare state, I formed a knot in my stomach while reading the many "Healthcare not Warfare" signs that littered the blocked-off streets. In short, I believe the free market is the most fair and prosperous economic system the world has ever known. It benefits the greatest number of people and is a far better regulator than the government because it puts the power of all economic decisions in the hands of the people and not some corrupted politician or bureaucrat with only his self-interest at heart. If we can return to a free market backed by sound money, as encouraged by Austrian economists and as explicitly instructed in our Constitution, we could once again have the greatest system ever devised by man. But it would require ending the current reign of the illegal banking cartel known as the Federal Reserve.

Another duo I caught trying to capitalize on large, frustrated citizens' movements to advance their own agenda was Bob and Ted. I couldn't believe it when I ran into them at a Tea Party rally and was even more shocked when they started whining to me about how they weren't allowed to speak to the crowd, even though they made it known to the organizer that they could get some real Hollywood players behind the cause. Why did they feel the need to tell everybody that their wonderful production company could bring these bona fide Hollywood power brokers to the Tea Party crusade? If that were the case, why didn't they just bring them? I don't know what planet they were from, but most elites in Hollywood are what many would call L I B E R A L S or what can be more appropriately defined as C O L L E C T I V I S T S. And when I say Tea Party, I don't mean the mainstream-media portrayal of the Tea Party that boasts Sarah Palin as its leader. I am talking about the group of patriots who were out during the Bush administration's reign of terror, throwing empty wooden crates off the Santa Monica Pier that read Department of Homeland Security, Iraq War, IRS, Federal Reserve, and every other form of government oppression you can think of. But even Hollywood Republicans, like Jon Voight, who would usually come in by himself and sit for hours while eating a bowl of chicken noodle soup with steamed broccoli added, was more about his party's platform than he was about returning to the true American principles that this country was founded on. Mr. Voight was an odd bird whom the upper management team insisted we give first class treatment to. I really liked a few of his movies, including *Deliverance* and *Coming Home*, so I had no problem honoring this request and rolling out the red carpet, so to speak, for him. I couldn't, for the life of me, connect with the man, which led to a very awkward exchange with him one day.

This happened when Mr. Voight came in through the side door one late afternoon and stood underneath a television set that was broadcasting extreme motorcycling. The area Mr. Voight decided to blend into was receiving heavy glare from the setting sun that day so I didn't even see him standing there as I was extremely fixated on the television. When I caught his silhouette out of the corner of my eye, I assumed it was my worker pal Ronnie who had just wandered off in that very same direction a minute ago. As the cycler completed an amazing stunt, I screamed out in awe, "Oh, my God, did you see that?" When I looked over to be sure Ronnie was taking in this jaw-dropping feat, I was taken aback when I saw Mr. Voight looking up at the screen with great interest. I'm sure everything would have been fine and dandy if I would have just kept the dialogue going and included him in on the fun. But instead, I retreated back into the same old distant and uncomfortable relationship we had already established from our previous encounters by saying, "Oh, I'm sorry I thought you were ..." I couldn't even finish the sentence. He immediately looked away from the screen like a hurt child as we shared a moment of uncomfortable silence. He then took a quick stroll through the restaurant and split. I felt like a heel for not treating him like an everyday human being, and he just plain left. You gotta love those sticky situations.

And I'll tell you what else was sticky, trying to gather twenty petition signatures in order to be eligible as a write-in candidate during the hottest month of the year (August) in the San Fernando Valley. Yes, that's right I finally decided to run for office and right in the middle of a heat wave. What made this feat so sweltering was the temperatures at that time of the year and in that section of LA County could and did reach upwards of 110 degrees. One very smart and dedicated patriot named James had gathered a long list of names and email addresses of activists associated with the various freedom movements throughout LA County. He then sent out a memo encouraging each and every one of us to run as a write-in candidate for the Republican Central County Committee of Los Angeles. We ran as Republicans mainly because the Republicans were in power at the time and were the party most responsible for destroying our rights and our country. Also, true Republican principles of limited government, limited taxes, peaceful non-interventionism, and personal responsibility resonated with us strongly. Those of us who made the decision to run did not like the neo-con agenda that engaged our country in perpetual war. In the past, I had been approached by various liberty-minded groups to run for this seat, but there was something in James's passionate plea that made me jump at the opportunity.

Not only did I have to get twenty hard-earned signatures to be eligible for the upcoming election, but I had to get quite a few more than the twenty mandatory John Hancocks required because the county registrar's office would eliminate any petitioner who did not fall in line with their strict guidelines. For instance, someone might spell a street name wrong or be considered an invalid member of my constituency simply because he/she had moved from another assembly district. And even though this person may have been in the process of updating his/her information, he/she would be voided off my list and considered "ineligible" if not officially re-registered at his/her new address. I think I got a total of twenty-seven signatures, and after submitting my form, I barely made the cutoff with twenty "legitimate" petitioners. Not really knowing any of my neighbors, I had to break out my "Ron Paul" registered-voters walk list in order to target the Republican voters in my district.

Despite the fact that I had made my rounds before, this effort took almost the entire two weeks that I had remaining until the deadline. In addition to the oppressive heat, I had to overcome lectures, return several times to catch up with people who never seemed to be home, discover people listed as Republicans were now registered as

Democrats, and my personal favorite, deal with asinine statements like, "This isn't the way you go about doing this." Thank you, Einstein. Would you mind sharing with me what the right way of going about doing this is? Let's see, I need to get over twenty petition signatures from Republican voters living in my neighborhood, and I have a list that includes the names and addresses of each and every one of them, yet you don't want me to go door-to-door to get the signatures? Brilliant, I wish I had thought of that. I guess I should have hosted a carnival at a nearby school and set up a booth next to the Ferris wheel. What a jackass! I told him I was trying to make a difference in our country, which was going down the tubes, and he told me to get off his property. And being the strong property rights advocate that I am, I immediately conceded to his request, although I didn't want to tell him that one of the reasons I was running was because we no longer had any property rights. But, that might have escalated the situation to the next right that we no longer have, which is the RIGHT to bear arms. I concluded that a quick no is better than a long maybe so away I went to the next address on my computer-generated printout.

Because LA County had never dealt with such a large-scale write-in campaign before, there was a lot of confusion as to what was required and what wasn't. Beating the first signature deadline allows office seekers the opportunity to have their names listed on the ballot. This is usually when the more seasoned contenders submit their paperwork. The second and much later cutoff gives lesser-known candidates, who don't have the backing or who maybe need a little more time drumming up signatures and support, access to the ballot as write-ins. It also affords contestants like me who trickle in at the last possible moment the opportunity to be included in the election. Being on the ballot provides a huge advantage, especially in today's world, because uninformed voters don't even have to know anything about your political philosophy. They may simply vote for you because your name is right in front of them and you belong to their party. There is a list of write-ins available at the polling place, but most people don't want to be inconvenienced to that degree to cast a vote for someone. Even if they did, they most likely wouldn't know what a write-in's views were on the issues anyway.

As with the ballot entry deadline, we all knew that we needed at least twenty "legitimate" petition signatures to be eligible as a write-in candidate. But we were also told that we needed at least twenty votes to hold a seat even if there were fewer candidates than openings. My district had four candidates running for seven available seats, which meant it was an uncontested district. This scenario served as a glaring example as to what kind of shape the Republican Party was in at that time. But all in the old guard throughout LA County who turned in their twenty signatures before the ballot deadline and were out kissing babies in uncontested districts thought they would be automatically appointed to their seats without actually having to go on the ballot on Election Day. But thanks to us rabble-rousers who threw a monkey wrench into their whole operation, everyone had to go on the ballot because we argued that if the write-ins needed twenty votes to hold a seat everyone should need twenty votes to hold a seat. And theoretically, although nearly statistically impossible, a write-in could get more votes than a candidate listed on the ballot whether he/she was running in an uncontested district or not.

So again, I had to go out stumping the whole weekend before judgment day to remind people to vote Jozef Rothstein in the upcoming election. I can't tell you the amount of apathy I received. I could have offered each registered Republican voter two hundred dollars to vote for me, and most of them still wouldn't have shown up at the polls. Even Mary refused to change parties in order to put a check next to my name. Leaders like Bernie, who was the Los Angeles County Coordinator for the Ron Paul campaign, didn't even get the twenty petition signatures necessary to be eligible as a candidate. When it was all said and done, I received a total of thirteen votes, hardly the results I was looking for, especially after returning home every night drenched in sweat after braving the hot valley sun. A few weeks later, I got an email from one of my fellow patriots stating that he had received his certificate of election in the mail even though he did not receive the mandatory twenty votes that we all thought were necessary. A few days later, I received my certificate. The emails were buzzing. It turns out about seventeen of us who did not get the previously assumed twenty votes were awarded our certificates anyway. I called the registrar's office to validate my achievement, which, to my pleasant surprise, was indeed authenticated by Dean Logan's office.

There was so much tyranny in our country and so little time that all of us newly elected freedom candidates started meeting as a group to discuss what we were going to do once we took our elected seats in order to make a real difference in the political system. We had national and state coordinators from the Ron Paul campaign come in and explain things like the Robert's Rules of parliamentary procedure to all of us first-time representatives. We also examined the current state of the party, both locally and nationally. It was decided that one of the major problems facing our committee was the current chair and her husband who were deep in the pockets of special interest. And because LA County was and still is the largest county in the country, we started getting very serious about actualizing a plan to take back our government, starting on the local level.

At our first meeting, we all took turns standing up, introducing ourselves and sharing what it was that motivated us to get involved in the freedom movement. We were a diverse bunch of citizens, not unlike the Founding Fathers and early patriots who sought independence from British oppression. Those whom I was now standing shoulder to shoulder with were common, everyday, good people who were tired of the corruption in our political system and who wanted to do something about it. Our group, like many others igniting around the country, was part of a grassroots movement, based entirely on principle, which also meant very little funding and even less media coverage.

We had around two to three months from the day we were officially notified by mail to the day we'd be sworn into our positions to hatch our plan, and that window of time quickly evaporated. The more experienced members of our group, who had been battling establishment insiders for years, estimated it would take a good two to three years to take over the committee and oust the current chair and her cronies. As our moment of truth drew nearer, we were very excited to become part of some real change. The night before the reorganization meeting, an email was sent out to all of us unseasoned mavericks, warning us to expect problems with our participation in the meeting.

That email was sent out by James, the very same person who had encouraged all of us modern-day Thomas Jeffersons to run. James had been in contact with the chair of the committee, who was essentially telling us to back off. He was also picking up on the nasty rumors that were swirling around amongst the disgruntled sitting members, who were warning each other to watch out for us troublemakers who were looking to take over "their" party and force our crazy ideas on them. It should also be noted that these "good Republicans" had lots of ties to big government proponents and special interest groups, which kept the committee's coffers full. Because one of our duties as committee members was to raise money for the party, we would have to work ten times as hard if we wanted to fund the committee with smaller but more personal contributions in order to break free from the chains that bound us.

It was decided that we would show up at the inaugural meeting as a group. There would be safety in numbers, which would also prevent any stragglers from being singled out and harassed with no backup. I was also advised to remove the Ron Paul bumper sticker from my vehicle because any member who was caught supporting any other candidate than the anointed establishment darling, John McCain, would be immediately removed from the committee. This new policy was written into the LA RCCC's bylaws in anticipation of our arrival and was just one more weapon in their arsenal to root all of us freedom-loving Americans out of their little club.

When we arrived at the main entrance to the large downtown building hosting the event, we were greeted by the Los Angeles Sheriff's Department. We were all dressed professionally, and by arriving in a cluster, it enabled us to overwhelm the two officers designated to screen the attendees. This cultural center was usually open to the public year round, but not on this particular day with each and every one of us major threats, who believed in liberty and justice for all, lurking around the premises. The two deputies on duty were actually very friendly and seemed to let us pass through their checkpoint almost in spite of any orders they may have received from the higher ups to shut us out. We leaped over one hurdle and were now one step closer to confronting the enemy. As we waited in line for our badges and to be sworn in, the established members who recognized us as outsiders began badgering us as we slowly inched our way towards the assembly room. We stood our ground and found ourselves getting more and more determined as the resistance mounted around us.

Of course, when we finally reached the gargoyle at the check-in table, we were met by the chair and her totalitarian husband, who had been anticipating our arrival. The mister had a photographed copy of a partial section of a statute from the California Elections Code that he claimed required us to have the twenty votes that we originally thought were necessary to hold a seat on the committee. This randomly chosen weak argument allegedly gave him the legal justification he needed to prevent us from entering the conference room. Then, in an effort to shoe us away, he nonchalantly told us that if we, instead, went to the first assembly district meeting in a few weeks an "elected" member could possibly appoint us to any remaining seats that were still available. I personally believe he thought that he could simply intimidate us into walking away and coming back after the re-organization meeting took place. Well, not in my house and not around my kids. That's when our leader, James, went toe to toe with this criminal trying to deprive us of our right to hold our duly-elected positions. James threatened to sue, and wife and hubby threatened to have us forcibly removed. We simply encouraged them to try it. Stalin Junior finally buckled and said that they would make a motion that, if approved by a majority of the committee, would allow us to sit in on the meeting but under no circumstances would we be allowed to vote for the committee's officers. This, of course, stunk to high heaven as not only unethical but highly illegal.

As the doors shut to the meeting, we began our work on the outside. One member fired up his laptop and started scouring the state elections code. I began calling local media outlets to bring attention to this injustice. James was on the phone with an attorney, and our parliamentarian was advising us on what our next step should be. Part of our action plan was already being put to the test inside the meeting. The goal of our supporters already inside the chamber was to vote for a predetermined temporary chair to head this special session. We handpicked a person who was well liked by everybody and who was considered to be fair by all. From there, we would at least have a chance of getting some of our people into important temporary positions. The plan had worked, and not only did we get our temporary neutral chair, we were also voted into the meeting. Another important event that transpired while we were preparing our case on the outside was that an actual committee would be chosen to hear our plea. This was made possible through a very concentrated effort by our allies within. If this committee within the committee found our evidence and testimony to be convincing enough, it would finally give us the standing we needed to vote in this very important initial gathering.

After the first break, we entered the assembly room to many grunts, groans, and stares. As the session reassembled, we patiently observed while "official" members nominated themselves to various temporary subcommittees. Finally, we were asked to leave the room with the committee that was going to decide our fate. The head of this group was a loyalist to the chair and her husband. The chair's husband, by the way, wasn't even a member of the RCCC but was allowed into the meeting while we officially elected members had to wait outside. The troll-looking man, who earlier served as the gatekeeper to the room, sat next to the temporary committee head. But to our great surprise there were two familiar faces on the seven-member panel that had attended our pre-meetings who we knew to be friendly to our cause.

The spokesman of the hearing rambled on for quite sometime as to why we weren't allowed to participate in the meeting that day, but he again emphasized how we could possibly be nominated to the committee at a later time by officially "elected" members. Conveniently, this would all take place after all of the key positions on the committee had been filled. We had come too far to back down now and were becoming unwavering as this nonsense went on. We respectfully allowed the gentleman to finish his circular argument until we collectively pummeled him with the information that we had accrued while waiting in the hallway. Thomas, who had read through the state elections code, discovered that not only did we not need the twenty votes that Dick Dastardly said were required, we didn't even need one vote in an uncontested district. It turns out that the twenty petition signatures were enough, which was why we were sent our certificates of election to begin with.

Our parliamentarian served as an example as to why she was not allowed onto the committee. She ran in a contested district where there were more candidates than seats, and only the top vote-getters filled the positions. Hence, she did not receive a certificate of election. In a contested district there is almost no way a write-in candidate can receive more votes than someone listed on the ballot unless a ton of money is spent. This is mainly because today's voter takes very little time to understand the issues let alone seek out candidates who will act in his or her best interest. God forbid if American citizens actually did something a little out of their way to ensure that their freedoms and prosperity are protected.

So we finished presenting our evidence, which came directly from the state elections code, to the tribunal who was about to determine our political destinies. As they mulled over the evidence, we sat firm and confident in our convictions. It was now up to the seven-person jury.

With two of their people and two of ours casting their vote, the decision would come down to three members who had no known allegiance to either side. All I can say is that our case must have been somewhat convincing because we were voted onto the committee by a narrow margin of four votes to three. Our hearing adjourned, and we re-entered the room with a sense of pride and accomplishment. When the announcement was made to the entire assembly that we were now official members of the RCCC, I could have never in a million years predicted what happened next. Before the temporary chair even had a chance to finish congratulating us, the opposition's side began dismissing themselves from the meeting. As they filed out of the room one by one, the auditorium grew emptier and emptier. It then became completely obvious that their intention was to put us under quorum so that anything we voted on that day would be null and void. We needed seventy members to legitimize our actions that day so we promptly started a headcount in the back of the room. With everybody standing, each member vocally added him or herself to the tally before sitting back down. As we zigzagged through the room it appeared as if the final number would be too close to call.

Our fingers were crossed as the roll call swept through the front two rows where all of us write-ins were sitting. This was the last stop for our make-or-break moment in replacing the crusty cronies who had been stinking up the committee for years. We hit the number seventy just a few seats from the end. The room held its applause until the very last number was called out, but you could feel the elation building. As the final member counted out "seventy-two," the celebration for all of the hard work and effort climaxed. Cheers erupted and congratulations were exchanged. But we immediately realized that we still had some serious work to do, especially since the chair had set one last trap that we would have to circumvent in order to accomplish our objective.

She had rented the room for only a certain amount of time, and our meeting hall was about to turn into a pumpkin. All of the previous theatrics served as divisive techniques to implode in our faces if things didn't go according to her schedule. We moved as fast as we could to elect the new officers. Knowing in advance who we wanted to take over the key positions served us well and facilitated our effort. We staffed all of the top positions, minus the treasurer, with all freedom candidates. What quite a few of the more experienced members of the LA freedom movement thought would take two to three years to accomplish transpired in one day. It was a huge victory for the little guy and renewed my faith that good people who care really can make a difference. As I reflected back on the day, I couldn't help but compare the embedded establishment committee members who were scurrying from the room to cockroaches scrambling for cover when exposed to a bright light. In this case, it was the brilliant radiance of truth and liberty that had them running for the doors.

When I arrived at work later that night still riding high from our victory, I made the grave mistake of mentioning to Henry what had happened. He couldn't help but have fun at my expense. He kept announcing to my fellow co-workers that "Today, the political world was shocked when newcomer and underdog Jozef Rothstein became a sworn-in member of … what was the name of that committee again? … the Republican Central County Committee." Many laughs were had at my expense, and not even Mary understood the importance of what had happened that day. Hopefully, these types of actions will be encouraged one day rather than ridiculed so that we can, once again, reemerge as the constitutional republic our Founding Fathers so graciously risked their lives, their fortunes, and their sacred honor to bestow upon us.

The Last Call/Curtain Call

I could now completely empathize with the woman from Chapter 2, labeled exhibit C, who grew incredibly hostile over the frivolous rules and regulations that the restaurant lived and died by because these silly corporate policies were really starting to weigh on me as well. I was now making the full connection between the restrictive corporate policies practiced at the deli and the oppressive codes and statutes infiltrating every area of American life, from having to wear a seatbelt to asking for permission to carry a firearm. I was hoping for a miracle. Would we be able to reverse the direction of our country and the way we were treated while slinging matzo ball soups to free ourselves, or would we continue to become further enslaved to the whims of the fat cats and their desires for us?

With that question now burning in my soul, I began recalculating my priorities in life, and it just so happened that walking down the red carpet with Brad Pitt was not one of them. In fact, I couldn't even stomach the charade called the Academy Awards, which were broadcast on our restaurant's TVs year after year, especially when I knew that I'd be slaving away for those who attended at the conclusion of the show. Many signs started steering me back towards small-town Pennsylvania where I was born and raised as well. As I looked around at young servers like Kevin, my own mortality was staring me in the face. Kevin left work early one night when he found himself having difficulty breathing. I just assumed he was suffering from the same anxiety that I felt every night when I had to restrain myself from choking the living shit out of some idiot at the restaurant who desperately deserved it. It turns out his situation was much different. Kevin was rushed to the emergency room where it was discovered that he had a bad heart valve. He was having a heart attack at age twenty-five.

Kevin, like so many of us living in LA-LA land, lived and died by the sword. Like the rest of us, Kevin moved to Hollywood with little family support and a jar full of change. He had big dreams and was even willing to pay the ultimate price to achieve them. Kevin reminded me of a younger me ten years prior. He often rationalized that ninety-nine out of every one hundred Hollywood scripts sucked and that his was great. Besides being a tad egotistical, Kevin believed that because of this his chances of getting his movie made were better than most. I agreed with Kevin's numbers, but since at that time I had been through almost ten years of some fierce battles vs. the Hollywood machine, I was either bitter or had a little insight into the way the town worked. It immediately occurred to me that even if Kevin's claims were true and his script was great and the other ninety-nine out of one hundred of them sucked, the deck was actually stacked against him. I explained it to him like this, "If a really good script has only a 1-percent chance of being made and a sucky one has a 99-percent chance of being made, then the odds are actually against you. You need to write one that sucks because ninety-nine out of every one hundred of those get made." Kevin looked at me as if I had three heads, but I think he knew deep down inside that I was right. And because I was a little more evolved than when I had first arrived in Hollywood ten years prior, I rationalized that I no longer had the ability to write the kind of trivial tripe that the Hollywood industrial complex devours. Our little Jozef was all grown up and didn't fit into the corporate entertainment empire anymore.

Another wake-up call came from my friend Rick. Rick and I met at a hockey clinic in LA, and we immediately bonded because of our insane workout habits. I took up the sport of ice hockey after I had written a screenplay that featured the game. I was convinced that even though I was a no name in the industry my project would be strong enough to warrant a Sly Stallone-type scenario, which would allow me the opportunity to star in and direct the very same project that I had also written. Yeah right, try explaining that one to a modern-day Hollywood agent. Rick and I worked out together twice a week without fail. We often wore down others who joined us or would often show up to an empty sheet of ice when those same victims realized they wanted no part of what we were doing. Since I was fairly new to the game, Rick's years of experience, coupled with the drills he learned at the many hockey camps he attended, helped elevate my game. One of Rick's best experiences in life was attending a hockey camp called Can/Am. It took place in the summer at the home of the "Miracle on Ice" Lake Placid, New York.

Rick had an interesting life story and was one of the most intelligent people I had ever met. He was a Cornell graduate and was once offered a career with the CIA. He spoke at least six different languages fluently and was a member of Cornell's version of Skull and Bones. He also was a Freemason, which I didn't hold against him. Because he worked in distribution, he was always traveling oversees. I often wondered if he actually was a CIA agent and just couldn't tell me. Regardless, we often had some heated political debates in the locker room that sometimes resulted in all-out shouting matches. He seemed to purposefully utter the most ridiculous government propaganda that I had ever heard in my life, which was at great odds with someone as intelligent as himself.

Rick also had his share of problems. He was one of only a small handful of male anorexics throughout the country, and he had entertained the thought of writing a book and appearing on Oprah to talk about it. When he undressed in the locker room, he looked like an Ethiopian because of his 2- to 3-percent body fat content. This low amount of body fat was almost unsustainable. He was also a fitness fanatic. A typical day in the life of Rick had him waking up at 3 a.m. to run on the treadmill for two hours. Then he'd show up at the rink from 11:45 a.m. to 1:15 p.m. to put himself through a grueling hockey workout. After that, he'd go to the gym and work out for another couple of hours. Our hockey coach used to confess to me in confidence that he felt Rick would probably die on the ice as he appeared to have some sort of death wish. With all of this working out, one would think that

Rick would have built up some sort of appetite. Nope. Not Rick. Every once in a while, Rick would go out to lunch with the guys from hockey but would refuse to let anyone watch him eat. Instead he would order a glass of ice and chew on the cubes or would smuggle a protein bar into the restaurant, which he would hide under the table. Then, when no one was looking, he would bend down and sneak a bite. I was told that he loved ice cream and that he ate that more than any other food. Chicken and beef were certainly out of the question as Rick was a strict vegetarian. Rick loved animals, which prompted him to tell me about the time he got into a fist fight at the gym when he overheard a Florida redneck bragging about the time he shot an alligator in the head. This accidental eavesdropping sent Rick into a frenzy, which resulted in a midday scuffle next to the nautilus equipment.

Rick was also very crotchety in a hilarious kind of way. If Rick liked you, he was one of the most generous, thoughtful, and up-front people you'd ever want to meet. If he didn't … well, let's just say he was ruthless. One of our fellow skaters nicknamed Duda annoyed Rick to no end. Duda acquired his nickname simply because it was the name, not his by the way, that was printed on the back of the hockey jersey that he wore week in and week out. Duda was a great skater but had the attention span of a grapefruit. He constantly screwed up the drills, which threw everybody out of sync and, as a result, drove Rick nuts. This wouldn't have been so bad if Duda wasn't always blaming his mistakes on other people and hollering at them in front of everybody. Rick had a zero tolerance policy for this kind of behavior.

One day prior to the main skate, Rick was doing his usual warm-up laps around the rink. Rick was always the first one on the ice and was well into his pre-skate ritual when Duda showed up to perform his usual lackadaisical routine of firing hockey pucks at the goal and skating around aimlessly. As Rick was rounding the corner, one of Duda's shots hit the top of the crossbar, flipped up into the air, and ricocheted off a pipe along the ceiling. As the puck bounced off the pipe, the aqueduct that Rick was skating under exploded. And like something out of a Nickelodeon skit, a grayish black water came dumping down on top of Rick. I was still in the locker room when all of this went down, but I have to admit I was a bit startled when the fire alarm began buzzing loudly and a voice recording came over the loudspeaker, urging everyone to immediately exit the building. My curiosity finally got the best of me, and I had to go see what the hell was going on out there. When I stepped outside the locker room, I noticed the gushing flow of water that was pouring out of the pipe like Niagara Falls and then spotted a drenched Rick who was covered from head to toe in a black liquid soot. One of the rink workers was trying to wrap a giant towel around the leak, and some of the guys were sweeping away the water in a desperate attempt to prevent the skate from being cancelled.

When I returned to the locker room, Duda was almost finished dressing and was doing everything in his power to exit the premises. He was acting like a teenager who had just thrown a rock through his neighbor's window, and I guess he thought he'd get stuck paying for the damage if the rink management could only catch up to him. He stuffed the remainder of his things in his hockey bag and then hightailed it out the back door. Rick, in the meantime, was furious. He got changed and left without saying a word to anybody. After the fire department arrived to shut off the water, we were told that we could still have our skate. Because of the heads-up move by some of our hockey cohorts, the ice just needed a little more sweeping, and we'd be good to go. I am sure Rick was even more pissed when he learned that he had missed a skate due to his bitter rival Duda's antics. Rick probably would have even skated in his soiled gear had he known we'd be given the green light. Then again, in this case, he probably would've been way too upset to enjoy the ice time.

Although Rick was about five feet eight inches and maybe 110 pounds soaking wet (no pun intended), he was one tough son of a bitch. He was a black belt in karate and once trained students at the Billy Blanks Studio. He would tell me stories of certain celebrities like Shaquille O'Neal, whom he trained. His only comment about Shaq was that he was lazy. If Rick would stop counting or would turn around to talk to someone for even a second, Shaq would stop the exercise. Shaq had to be constantly pushed by someone because, according to Rick, he lacked self-motivation. In hindsight, I tend to think it was Shaq just messing with Rick. Rick was also brought in to spar with Jean-Claude

Van Damme because of his quick fists, which provided a good look for Mr. Van Damme while he was in training.

Rick also made a movie down in Mexico with "Rowdy" Roddy Piper, who was a very cool customer at the deli as well. Mr. Piper always went out of his way to say hello to me, especially after I asked him about his incredible fight scene in the cult classic movie, *They Live*. It is considered by many to be the greatest fight scene in motion picture history. The scene, which also featured Keith David, ran over eight minutes in length. I rarely asked celebrities anything about themselves because, mainly, I didn't want to bother them or because, frankly, I didn't care. But Mr. Piper was someone whom I really admired and someone who immediately opened up to me in a very gracious and humble way. He went on to inform me that his fight-scene partner, Keith David, who was a very large and imposing black man, was also a professional dancer, which I would have never guessed in a million years. Mr. Piper also explained to me that they couldn't get the camera angle right on one of the fight scene shots because it kept coming out too fake. So Mr. Piper simply encouraged Mr. David to really punch him in the face, just to get it over with. Mr. Piper said he regretted that one for quite some time.

This story seemed to fall in line with the character of Mr. Piper that Rick experienced while filming with him down in Mexico. Mr. Piper was born in Canada and lived on the streets as a kid. He had been stabbed during that time and was shot at as an adult. He took to wrestling as an escape from his rough start in life, and he excelled in it. Mr. Piper also confessed to Rick about his wild days in wrestling and their life-on-the-edge shenanigans, like the time one of the guys parked a car on the railroad tracks so they could watch a train demolish it. Rick also mentioned that Mr. Piper married a little person. Although she stands at only four feet eleven inches, I am certain, after casually getting to know Mr. Piper, that he married her because of the size of her heart, not her body. This was a man who could look right through you and see what you were made of. Mr. Piper also earned Rick's respect because of the fact that he owned a business that was established for the sole purpose of providing jobs for working-class families and wasn't driven by profit and bottom line. This all falls in line with the "Rowdy" Roddy Piper I got to loosely know.

So now that Rick and I seemed to be kindred spirits in our love for hockey and for working out, it was decided that we would attend the Can/Am Hockey Camp in Lake Placid together. He told me it would be the best experience of my life and that it was the most awesome vacation he's ever had. As the time for my first camp neared, I found myself in a very precarious situation. I was low on funds, even after borrowing money from Rick to pay the admission fee, and I didn't have enough cash saved up to cover my expenses. Rick also planned to leave a few days before me, which would make me responsible for my own way to the camp from the airport, which was about a two-hour drive. To top it all off, there were no buses or trains that ran into or out of Lake Placid. I would either have to rent a car, hail a taxi, or take my chances hitchhiking, none of which I was prepared to do. So as my departure date approached, I started to panic. This also seemed to strike a chord with Rick, who was in a similar bind. His cat was sick, and the company he was working for wasn't doing well, which affected his sales salary. Rick would also fall behind financially if we went on the trip, so he devised a plan.

It was the worse plan I'd ever heard of, but Rick was determined to salvage our entry fee and postpone our trip until the following year, which would allow us to save up enough spending money. So he called the camp and told them we had a collision in a hockey game that left us both injured. I supposedly hurt my ankle and he his knee. The camp had a no refund policy but Rick pleaded our case, and our teammate doctor friends wrote us some very convincing doctor's notes. We were both grilled by camp officials who didn't quite believe our outlandish story, but once they received our authentic doctor's notes, they finally gave us credit for the following year.

During our whole next 365 days of working out together, Rick and I spent that time cementing our plans for the trip. We were to land in Vermont and then rent a car. From there we'd piggyback the car on a ferry across Lake Champlain and then drive the rest of the way to Lake Placid. Because it was a two-hour drive no matter where we landed, Rick pushed for the flight into Vermont because he loved the drive. Once in Lake Placid, Rick planned for us to hike the Adirondacks, which he knew like the back of his hand. After two long years, we were finally going to get to live out our pro-hockey fantasies (in a non-gay way, of course) and attend the camp. The week we were supposed to leave for Lake Placid, Rick and I were squabbling in a nasty email exchange, regarding our political philosophies. The nastiness was more on his end as he attacked me personally, but not only did I not mind the passionate debates, I actually looked forward to them.

Rick was also very anti-social when it came to people he didn't like. This included a group of pompous Armenians we sometimes had to share the ice with. The Tuesday before our Friday trip was no different. When I got to the locker room a few minutes late for our usual skate, Rick was already packing up his gear. He was upset because there were too many people on the ice, which, in turn would prevent us from getting a killer workout. He stated that he was just going to the gym. Then he surprised me when, out of the blue, he hit me with, "You know what I said in that email?" I had already brushed it off so I had to think for a moment about what he was referring to. Once I remembered, I responded with, "Oh yeah. Why?" He shot back, "Well, I wish I would have never said it." I told him, "Aagh, don't worry about it. I don't take any of our disagreements personally." I reassured him that it didn't bother me, and I told him that I appreciated the fact that he was so adamant about his position.

So now that we kissed and made up, it was time to plan the logistics of our trip. Rick suggested that we meet at his living quarters and then take a town car to the airport to avoid parking fees. This sounded good to me, other than the fact that I had never been to his pad before and I didn't know where he lived. He never gave me his address, but that was okay as we would probably be harassing each other through emails later on anyway. Because I needed to earn some extra dough for the trip, I had to pick up some additional shifts at the restaurant, which meant long hours for the rest of the week.

Around Wednesday, Mary offered to give us a ride to the airport rather than have us pay for a town car. That seemed good to me as I was looking to pinch every penny I could. I put a call in to Rick and left a message regarding this slight change in plans. When I showed up at our usual hockey clinic on Thursday, Rick was not there. Rick hardly ever missed a session, especially when it came to our beloved Thursday skate when we actually got to work with a bona fide hockey coach. But because Rick had been rehabilitating a very serious hamstring injury, I guess I just assumed he was resting up for the camp. I sent him an email later that day before I went to work, asking him for his address so I could, indeed, go over to his place to take a town car as Mary was now unavailable to give us a ride to the airport. When I arrived home later that evening, there was still no response from Rick. It was very unlike him not to respond, and I was getting a very funny feeling about our excursion. As a matter of fact, the night before our trip, I decided that if Rick backed out again, I was not going to go. Something felt very wrong about getting on that plane, and it was strong, like a premonition.

Rick had just lost his job in distribution and got screwed over badly in the deal. Even before that, Rick was barely making ends meet and was falling behind on his debt. Getting fired now made it ten times worse. The day we were supposed to leave, I thought Rick was simply blowing off the camp for a second time and just didn't have the heart to tell me, but again that just wasn't like him. When I called our hockey coach to ask him if he had heard from Rick since I hadn't, our coach immediately thought something was up. He instructed me to call the rink because he knew that they would have Rick's address at their disposal. Rick was a team captain and a long-standing member of the hockey community so all of his contact info was on file at the facility. Of course, when I called, all of the administrative people who had access to Rick's information were out of the office. As I pondered as to whether or not I should show up for my flight later on that evening, my intuition was telling me to "just forget it." Finally, right after Mary got home and coincidentally right after I drifted off into a little catnap, someone from the rink called with Rick's address. Mary insisted that I get up and get dressed so we could head over to Rick's place to find out what was going on.

Rick lived in a secluded and quaint little apartment complex in Sherman Oaks, California. When Mary and I arrived at Rick's crib, we pulled right up next to his recently purchased, brand new Volvo. On our way to Rick's apartment, I knocked on a neighbor's door to see if anyone had spotted Rick coming or going within the past few days. Liz, a very attractive woman in her mid-thirties answered her door and told us the last time that she saw Rick was on Sunday. It was now Friday. Liz then pointed out Rick's apartment, which was just a couple of doors down. When we arrived at the downstairs entrance, there were quite a few letters stuffed in Rick's mailbox, which, again, seemed very unusual for someone as anal as Rick. We made our way up to the second floor where we looked in through a window and found no signs of life. I then knocked on the upstairs door a few times, which drew no response. We revisited Liz's apartment on the ground floor only after she took the liberty of calling the landlord while we were snooping around. She informed us that the landlord, Helen, would be out for a few more hours and that we would have to come back if we wanted her to open up the apartment.

Mary also suggested that we head home and stop back later, but something just wasn't sitting right with me. So, I decided to call 911. After explaining the situation to the operator, she suggested that we have the police come over to do a walk-through. Ironically, as the police arrived ten minutes after the 911 call, so did Helen. Helen told us that a friend of Rick's had stopped by a few days prior to ask her if Rick had already left for the trip since he hadn't seen or heard from him. The friend was supposed to pick up a spare apartment key so he could feed Rick's cats while he was away. I believe when Liz called and said that we were also looking for Rick, Helen had a strong hunch something was wrong. That's what I believe drew Helen back to the premises much sooner than expected. The landlord was now severely concerned, as was I.

We all walked up the stairs to Rick's apartment together. As we encircled the door, Helen's hands were shaking so badly that she could not fit the key in the lock. The peace officer politely grabbed the key from Helen's grasp and gently opened the door. The two officers assigned to the scene ordered us to wait outside while they conducted their search of the apartment. When they returned, they informed us that Rick was in his bed, dead, and had been for what appeared to be about three days. That would take us back to Tuesday, when I was the last person from our hockey circle to see him alive. When Rick's wife,

Diane, arrived, from whom he was separated for over two years, the scene grew deeply emotional. Diane broke down, pleading and crying, and there was not a dry eye amongst us. But in Rick's death, there was also something very ethereal happening to all of us there that night. As the police performed their investigation, they could not have been more supportive. People from the rink were calling my cell phone as were fellow teammates, who were also offering their full support and understanding. Rick was only forty-six years old, and his cause of death was from thrombosis coupled with atherosclerosis. In laymen's terms, it was a hardening of the arteries in conjunction with a blood clot.

As Mary stood by me, she was also suffering from some recent trauma of her own, which I had shared with her, and between these two events I was developing an ever-deepening appreciation of my own life. Mary's story started on a visit to see her dying grandmother in New Mexico, who was passing away from Parkinson's disease. Parkinson's, as I am sure you are aware of, is a very debilitating disease that causes great suffering to its victims. One of the devastating final features of this horrible illness has major organs like the lungs filling up with fluid. For the more timid at heart or for those who hadn't made peace with themselves, a draining process could be repeated until it could no longer be tolerated or until the backed-up fluid accumulated so quickly nothing could stop it from killing its victim. But Mary's grandmother was a woman of tremendous character and strength who decided that she was not going to agonize through her disease any longer than she had to. So she made the decision to go out gracefully and courageously and just let the illness take her.

What that meant for Mary was that she sat by her grandmother's bedside for the entire five days it took for her to drown in her own fluids. This was very difficult for Mary, but she was at least thankful that she was with her grandmother during her final days. I had previously visited Mary's grandmother in New Mexico where she owned a beautiful Spanish-style cottage in a gorgeous suburb of the city. The whole family, including Mary, was staying at that very same house in order to be with this great matriarch during her final days. Mary and I decided it would be best for me to stay at home with our two dogs as things were very tight financially. But Mary did put her grandmother's ear to the phone a couple of times so I could say my goodbyes. I was always just a phone call away and made myself available for Mary whenever she needed me.

I was at work when Mary's grandmother finally passed on, so I took some extra time during my break to comfort her. But by that point, everyone in the family, including Mary, understood her grandmother's passing meant an end to her suffering. Because of the deep soul bonding that took place during her grandmother's final days, the kith and kin were in more of a frame of mind to celebrate their relation's life than to wallow in her loss. The whole ordeal served as a profound bonding experience for the surviving family members who made dinner plans at a local restaurant that same evening. This was to be a ceremonial dinner, paying homage to an incredible woman who was the glue that kept the family together for many, many years.

You can imagine my surprise when I was interrupted during my shift a few hours later by a co-worker who was urging me to call Mary as soon as possible. I immediately ran to my car and called her. She was frantically crying, and I could barely understand a word she was saying. As I put bits and pieces of her story together, I started concluding that someone she knew had been struck by a train. Could this be true? Was anyone dead? Mary was hysterical. She was also very lucky because she had changed cars at the very last minute. The vehicle she switched out of ended up being the car that was demolished by the train. On their way to the restaurant, the family formed a caravan with her aunt and uncle's car being the last car in the convoy, followed by her other uncle who was on a motorcycle. Mary noticed the train approaching as her vehicle cleared the crossing. When she looked back a few seconds later, she observed a Walgreens truck stopping to talk with her aunt and uncle, who engaged the Walgreens driver, before they crossed the tracks. At that time, Mary didn't think anything of it. The driver was taking oxygen to her grandmother's house, and her aunt and uncle were informing the driver that the oxygen was no longer needed as their mother had passed away.

When Mary's uncle on the motorcycle arrived at the restaurant twenty minutes later, Mary asked him, "What took you so long?" He immediately informed the family that her aunt and uncle had been struck by a train. Mary was in such disbelief she jokingly said, "Yeah right," to which he exploded, "I'm not kidding!!! They were hit by a train, and they're dead!!!!" Later that evening the story would get even more bizarre. Distance wise, Mary's grandmother's house was about a mile from where the accident occurred. In a weird twist of fate, the train ended up pushing her aunt and uncle's car a whole mile down the tracks until it came to a complete stop directly behind her grandmother's backyard. Mary and her family watched the surreal scene unfurl from their back porch as emergency workers pulled her aunt and uncle from the wreckage. Her uncle was removed literally in pieces. Mary was traumatized by the event, which served as the final blow to our relationship. Mary didn't think I understood what she was going through when, in my heart of hearts, I did. I just dealt with death a little differently.

Ironically, the following week, another person was killed at that same railroad crossing. According to the locals, a certain number of people have to die at a railroad crossing before the railroad company will put up a crossing gate, especially on a private road to a community such as her grandmother's. Rick's passing made Mary think that I would sink into a state of despair that equaled hers, but I had just been through too much in my life to allow that to happen. Don't get me wrong. I was sad and grieving but not to the point where I couldn't function or go to work for three months. I came out of the whole thing having a greater appreciation for my own life and for Mary's, which made me want to pursue my happiness even more. And because I wasn't at Mary's side during her ordeal in New Mexico, it wasn't so shocking that she wasn't at mine.

Rick's funeral was scheduled on a beautiful summer day in the Hollywood Hills. The ceremony was to take place at Forest Lawn Cemetery near the Hollywood sign and was to bring out all of Rick's most esteemed acquaintances and hockey buddies. An email card was circulated throughout our group by Rick's wife, Diane, who was a dynamic woman. Rick never recovered from their breakup, and obviously Diane didn't either. We all expressed our deepest sympathies and told our favorite stories of Rick on the email card. On my way to the procession, something very unusual happened.

I drove almost the entire way to the funeral site with my radio barely audible. I spoke briefly on the phone with a couple of people, including Mary, but basically, I just wanted to be alone with my thoughts during my ride to the service. When I entered the road leading to the cemetery, Forest Lawn Drive, I had a sudden urge to flip through the stations to find a fitting song for the occasion. That's when I ran across "Time" by Pink Floyd, which I found to be more than appropriate. I sat in my car outside of the main office building to the cemetery as I listened to "the time is gone, the song is over, thought I'd something more to say." I kept the radio on until the very last note of the song played out in full. I then entered the cemetery hub to get directions to the Old North Church, where the commemoration was taking place. The Old North Church was a re-creation of the historic church from Paul Revere fame. I was greeted outside by many of our mutual friends, who were still in shock due to Rick's untimely passing. Rick just didn't seem like the type of guy who would ever die, let alone at a fairly young age.

I was sitting in my pew reading my program, which contained our comments from the email card that we had passed around online, when the first strange coincidence presented itself to me. Written on the back of the program were the lyrics to "Time." This caught my attention just as the service was about to begin. A small handful of Rick's closest friends and relatives spoke in his memory, which provided quite a few touching moments throughout the ceremony, but when Rick's wife took the pulpit, I was glued to her every word. Diane's story would unleash a larger message that was about to tie my recent coincidences together. Diane was with her best friend a couple of days before the funeral when a giant eagle landed in a tree in her friend's yard. Rick's favorite animal was the eagle, and Diane had never seen an eagle in the wild before. She was amazed by this coincidence, especially since eagles don't normally fly down into neighborhoods and land in people's yards. They are also very cautious and, for the most part, unapproachable.

This eagle for some reason allowed Diane to get fairly close. Her friend watched in awe as Diane stopped just a few yards away from this giant bird of prey and uttered the word, "Rick?" Immediately, the eagle squawked back while Diane patiently stood and listened. On the verge of tears, Diane was blown away as she gazed at this magnificent bird for what she said seemed like an eternity. Diane then expressed a few heartfelt feelings to the eagle, which passionately cackled back. When Diane finally felt it was time to say their goodbyes after their intimate exchange, she stated the following, "I love you, Rick, and I don't want to ever leave you, so I am going to take three steps towards you. When I take my third step, I want you to fly away." She took her first step and then her second with the eagle still in place, but when she took her third step, the gigantic winged creature flew off into the clear blue sky.

The very next day, Diane found a giant feather in her yard. Diane immediately called her friend to ask her if she had placed the feather in her yard to mess with her. When her friend told her no, she shared with us how she couldn't help but believe that it was another sign from Rick telling her that he would always be with her. Diane was the last speaker that day. She thanked us all for coming and announced that Rick's favorite song would now be played. And wouldn't you know it, the very song that came on the radio as I entered the cemetery grounds was now peacefully playing through the church speakers. "Time" was announced as Rick's favorite song and the one he used to get dressed to before every college hockey game. Diane's story was sounding eerily familiar to me, and all of these peculiar happenings were resonating with me as well. I broke down during the playing of "Time." I don't know why it all hit me so hard at once, but as tears rolled down my cheeks, one of my teammates reached over from the pew behind me and patted me on the shoulder. It was one of the simplest yet most powerful gestures of friendship that I have ever experienced. As the song played out, the celebration of Rick's life was moving to the Hall of Liberty. I remained in my pew until the very last note of "Time" serenaded the empty church.

Now why in God's name would Diane hold a Nancy Pelosi loving, big-government fanatic's funeral at a replica of the Old North Church, which was made famous during the American Revolution, and then host his ensuing reception at the Hall of Liberty? Maybe Rick was finally conceding through Diane that my political beliefs had merit, or he was simply supporting my cause from his enlightened place in the afterlife. Either way, whether these things were all just serendipitous occurrences or a sign from the afterworld, Rick is dearly missed and will live on forever in the memories of those he touched.

In regards to my own death, I made a shocking statement one night at the deli that surprised everyone, including myself. This comment blurted out of me as a group of co-workers were talking about legendary baseball manager Tommy Lasorda's wish to be buried under the pitcher's mound at Dodger Stadium. I immediately quipped back with, "I want to be buried under the soup station." This induced a good laugh from those around me, but upon further inspection, my comment possessed an eerie ring of truth to it. It left me fearing a lifetime of servitude at the deli. The thought of spending any more time away from my friends and family back in the mountains of eastern Pennsylvania just to chase some crazy dream was starting to weigh on my soul. I had gone out into life and given it everything that I had, even though it didn't turn out quite as I had planned. But, I was to the point where I could look at myself in the mirror and honestly say that I had given it my all. And that was more than enough for me. With the danger of an economic collapse around the corner along with the threat of forced vaccinations and martial law sounding off alarm bells to everyone in the freedom movement, I knew my remaining days in Los Angeles were limited.

Seeing the Light(s)

I once heard a not-so-famous comedian on the *Jay Leno Show* say that it takes ten years to make it in Hollywood. Well, I think that only applies to people who actually do make it in Hollywood. I don't think that pertains to the multitude of people who give up their entire lives to commit themselves to an industry that, for the most part, only acknowledges you if your next of kin is Francis Ford Coppola. I also think that because I marched to the beat of my own drum and didn't do things the way everyone else thought that I should do them I hurt my chances of making it. The more I thought about the term "making it," the more I thought it should be replaced by some other phrase like, "compromising yourself so much that you can't recognize who the hell you are by the time it is all said and done." I mean how many grown adults dressed up as giant hamburgers do we have to stomach before we turn off our televisions for good? These spirit-crushing roles were as hard to audition for as they were self-depreciating. I guess I tried to rationalize even going into these torture chambers by convincing myself that booking a national commercial and humiliating myself in front of an entire nation of people was the equivalent, pay wise, of getting humiliated every day for an entire year while waiting tables. At least with the former I would earn a whole year's salary for one day's worth of work, where in the latter I would put a lot more wear and tear on my body, not to mention my psyche, while working long, hard hours that would in turn cause me to miss valuable opportunities to advance my acting career.

But there was one last agonizing experience that would finally spark my decision to leave the entertainment business for good and never look back. It involved yours truly having to audition for a chewing gum commercial while playing the role of a man dressed in a beaver costume. I was told the wardrobe was a pair of tight swim trunks, sandals, and a t-shirt and I was to look like a gawky European tourist. In the waiting room, I was surrounded by a plethora of beautiful women dressed to the nines to play the part of the reporter while I, in the meantime, was dressed like an Israeli Richard Simmons. When I got inside the room, I wanted to strangle the casting director who recited with such glee exactly what this terrific piece was out to convey. She explained the blocking, then tied a child's Scooby-Doo costume around my neck. How I didn't bludgeon her to death at that point in time I will never know. The suit was so small it felt more like a Scooby-Doo cape. I went on to perform my interpretation of the material with Scooby-Doo's head propped up on top of mine. I guess the casting director thought that draping this mini cartoon dog on me would give the decision makers a better idea of what I'd look like in a beaver costume.

As I got up from the floor after the segment's grand finale where a tree falls on top of the beaver (a.k.a. me) and pins it (a.k.a. me) underneath it, I hoped and prayed to God that I would either just die or never be called in again. I was angry at myself for even playing along with such stupid crap. As I shot out the door as fast as humanly possible, the casting director practically jumped out in front of me to thank me. I kept right on going. I had already decided that I was hanging up the Scooby-Doo costume or whatever other costume these morons wanted to pin on me in order to preserve my dignity and self-respect. My agent was dumbfounded when I told her I no longer wanted to audition and that I was leaving the agency. She was disappointed because she thought that I was getting a lot of "nibbles" and that her big payday at my expense was just around the corner. Well, nibble on this, Hollywood. My integrity is much more important than dancing for you, a.k.a. "the man," in an undersized Scooby-Doo costume, no matter how much money you throw at me. Did I just say that?!!!

As all of these life realizations were hitting me at once, I suddenly got wacked upside the head with yet another one. Mary was leaving me after seven long, hard years. She was moving to North Carolina within the week. North Carolina? What? Why was she moving there? What wasn't she telling me? Did the cuckoos from her spiritual psychology school finally convince her to leave me? Each and every one of the people Mary befriended at this school for the emotionally distraught thought that he/she was the most insightful person in the universe and that he/she knew better than Mary what was best for her. Many of them, even though they lacked the necessary battle scars in real life to have any sort of common sense, thought that because they were in spiritual psychology school, they suddenly had the answers to all of life's problems. I met most of them, and all of their wisdom combined couldn't find the prize at the bottom of a Cracker Jack box. They thought Mary's time would be better spent doing the things they suggested rather than what we decided as a couple. And so she went along with it.

But I also believe that Mary just didn't want to put any kind of real effort into the relationship. After teaming up with her on a theatre show and a movie and after witnessing the numerous jobs she either quit or got fired from, I knew hard work was not in her blood. As a matter of fact, having her pick up a quart of milk from the supermarket was asking for a miracle. And as sad as I was to see her go, I had already seen the writing on the wall. Maybe this is awful to say, but I was a bit relieved when Mary gave me the heave-ho because I was simply exhausted from all of the arguing over why she couldn't drop off a letter at the post office, even though she was going there in five minutes anyway.

But Mary's moving out meant that I would have to find a roommate to make up for her half of the rent, plus utilities. And this person would have to be accepting of the two best things that came out of our relationship, our two dogs Tai and Charlie. Both dogs were strays Mary rescued. Tai was found in a rice paddy in Taiwan in an area where people were dumping their garbage. Her friends at the time told her about a cute little white puppy they had seen on a hike, which also seemed to be in pretty rough shape. The gentle and nurturing side of Mary, which kept me attracted to her for all of those years, sent her on a quest to find the dog. When she arrived at the location, she searched the area by calling out, "Here puppy, puppy." Finally, a tiny white puppy, typical of the breed that flooded the streets of Taiwan, came crawling out from under a pile of wood. When Mary took Tai to the vet, Tai was on the verge of death. It was discovered that she had a large tapeworm inside her stomach and that she was severely undernourished. Mary nursed her for many days and eventually got her to regurgitate the worm. Tai returned to good health within a few weeks, and when Mary's military husband at the time was finished with his assignment, Mary brought Tai back to the states.

Charlie on the other hand, was a different story. He was discovered while Mary and I were together. Mary had pulled off the I-5 in central California to reluctantly find a number for me that she had written in her address book. She was returning home from her traveling sales job when she entered a rest stop along the interstate. As she pulled onto the off ramp, before her eyes was a gorgeous Australian cattle dog that was darting through traffic and jumping up on passing cars. It appeared someone had dropped him off there, and the dog was simply trying to find his owner. Mary's heart melted. After asking around and then locating a man who lived in a nearby trailer who also fed "Charlie," she learned that Charlie had been left there for over a week. The man didn't mind leaving some food out for Charlie but in no way, shape, or form wanted to keep him. So Mary brought him home with her.

Mary introduced me to Charlie by telling me that she had somewhere to take me. Shortly after, we exited the house and jumped in her car. As we pulled out from the driveway, I felt something cold and wet bump my elbow. It was Charlie's nose. He was in the backseat, and I didn't even realize he was there until I felt his friendly little nudge. It's instinctive for cattle dogs to push with their noses because it's how they round up cattle. Charlie was incredibly cute and was quite the surprise, but Mary and I had a hard enough time keeping up with Tai and our three cats. More important, our lease agreement stipulated that we could only have one dog living in the house with us so we decided to try to find Charlie a home. Mary searched online for Australian cattle dog owners who lost their pets, and we also had Charlie checked to see if he had an RFID chip under his skin so we could obtain his previous keeper's contact information. In both instances, we came up empty.

When we got back to our quarters, getting Charlie to enter our house turned out to be a real chore. It appeared he had been abused by his previous owner and was most likely never allowed to enter his last place of residence. Charlie was also afraid of men, especially tall guys like me. He refused to come inside and frantically resisted any attempts to bring him in through the patio door. So, as a result, Charlie slept out in the garage for a few days. In the meantime, we left the sliding patio door open so he felt at ease to enter the house whenever he was ready. Finally, after taunting Charlie with some food and then placing it just inside the door he cautiously entered. He started to feel more and more at home until we eventually moved him in. When we brought a friend over to meet Charlie for a possible adoption situation, he immediately recognized how comfortable Charlie was around us. When he made the suggestion, "Why don't you keep him?" his question deeply resonated with us. From that point on, we made up our minds that we were going to keep Charlie, no matter what.

When the topic of having kids came up between Mary and me, the emotional aspect of it was very appealing, but the reality of it scared the daylights out of me. If Mary was incredibly reluctant to split the cleaning duties with me, how would she react when one of our kids needed a ride to piano lessons or baseball practice? Her behavior was already stroke-inducing enough, and I can't even imagine what raising a child with her would have been like.

And because of her flighty nature and her own traumatic past, I always felt there was a very real possibility that Mary could just pick up and go without thinking twice, leaving me with a bunch of screaming kids and no explanation. When Mary was able to leave our two dogs behind without any apprehension, my suspicions were confirmed. I wasn't complaining and actually felt that Mary had given me a wonderful gift. Besides, I was still living in LA, and Tai and Charlie were excellent watch dogs. Mary was moving into an apartment where dogs were not allowed, and because of her sudden decision to leave everything behind her and start a new life in North Carolina, taking them with her would have been next to impossible.

So along with the fifteen hundred dollars a month rent I had to come up with entirely on my own, I was also facing a very significant rise in water prices, electricity prices, phone service, Internet, and food prices that were tattooing the state of California. Our dollar was really starting to feel the effects of irresponsible government and corrupt central banking policy. But on top of that, the evil tyrant Sardine was just looking for a reason to send me home … for good.

Another threat rearing its ugly head was that of forced vaccinations. There was talk that the swine flu could become a worldwide epidemic, and the mainstream media were trumpeting their firestorm of fear-inducing propaganda, warning us all that death from a killer virus that would infect over half of the population was imminent. Martial law had also been discussed during the bailout crisis when Henry Paulson threatened Congress that he would send our country into a state of national emergency if the bailout money was not approved. Talk about extortion. It appeared that our so-called leaders were frantically searching for any reason they could find to drop the heavy hand of government upon us. Only those paying close attention, which certainly didn't include any of my apathetic co-workers who were more concerned about the score of the Lakers game or who they thought would win *American Idol* than they were about the clear and present danger lurking amongst us, recognized it.

I documented in a journal the ever-expanding list of infractions Sardine was committing against me. I also kept tabs on who witnessed these abuses of power so that if I ever was punished or dismissed after one of our blowouts I would be able to retrace the problem back to the chain of events that caused it. I had already gone to the corporate office regarding Sardine's inappropriate behavior on several occasions, but the little slaps on the hand that she received did nothing to prevent her from getting on my very last nerve. I decided that as long as she wasn't affecting my earnings I would put up with her insults and harassment. But if she ever once tried to dip into my pocket, she'd be playing with fire and she knew it.

In order to cover all of my new expenses, I started working double shifts. The restaurant was having a hard time holding onto people who were willing to do the hard work necessary to survive in that job, and I jumped at every chance I could to pick up more hours. I was getting caught up, financially, but on the creative side, I was getting further and further away from the real reason I had moved to LA. I was slaving away more and more in a business that was slowly dying due to a sluggish economy. This financial decline also left my dream of producing my own screenplay hanging in the balance as raising the required capital was turning out to be a monumental task.

Because of the economic downturn, many of the investor contacts I had established throughout the years were seeing their resources dry up, and/or they were losing their businesses. The studios had already shown me what they thought of me and my work. They liked my work but didn't give a damn about me, so they stole what they wanted and left me for dead. The final infringement on my work came when an outwardly reputable but internally sleazy management company by the name of Millstone-Green jacked the storyline from one of my scripts and tried to use it as a vehicle for one of their "stars." They even had the gall to enlist this very famous but scraggly actor to play the role of the buffed character described in my story. Unfortunately for me, I think someone within the organization came to his senses and realized the scrawny puke they had in mind to play the role would have turned this dramatic film into an all-out comedy romp. So they abandoned their original idea and brought in a more traditional tough guy to star in the film. That said gawky actor then became a producer on the movie instead. Although the film was recognized during awards season, it fell disgustingly short of the original vision I had conceptualized for it. Thank God for Hollywood inadequacy. As the sitting co-director of my project and I restlessly sat through the Hollywood rip-off version of my story, this co-director named Tommy assured me, "Dude, you have nothing to worry about." And as much as I struggled with the stolen lines of dialogue, the similar character names and traits, and the identical scenes and story arches, I had to agree there was nothing to fear but fear itself. I still believed that I would get to make my movie one day the way I had originally intended.

But maybe LA wasn't the place from which to make it happen. I grew up on the East Coast, and I knew a lot of people back that way. Plus, the mountains would make for a nice getaway spot if the economy bottomed out, so I was starting to stick one foot out of the proverbial Hollywood door. Although part of me still felt the need to be around the industry for its many resources, that fact alone was taking a back seat to all of the other factors pressing down on me like a Chinese acupuncturist. I had plenty of loose ends to tie up, so I decided to find a roommate to help split the costs of living at the house. I was scared to death to put an ad on craigslist because I didn't know what kind of riffraff would show up at my door, and many of the people who I thought would make excellent roommates were already established in their living arrangements.

There was, however, one guy whom I worked with who was having trouble with his living situation. His name was Kip, and his roommate, Rich, was a fat, middle-aged, gay man with a foot fetish. The mere fact that Kip landed himself in this predicament raised a few red flags for me. But it was ultimately Kip's odd behavior that gave me all the justification I needed to keep my roommate search out of the work place. After a solid month of searching on roommates.com, which was referred to me by a very reputable member of our wait staff, my search was getting more and more desperate. Not one person had called me back from the roommates.com site. I also left no stone unturned as I asked every decent person in LA if he/she was looking for or knew of anyone looking for a roommate.

I thought I got lucky when Frank from the *Living with Uncle Ray* movie referred me to a friend of his who had a great paying job as a traveling computer specialist. Could there be a more ideal roommate? But this man never returned my calls. Flo and a few others knew that Kip was unhappy in his present situation, and although Kip didn't have a car or a computer, they thought he was a decent guy who would make a pretty good roommate. I know, why would I listen to them? Well, I'll tell you why, because I needed to save up enough money to get the hell out of LA. So, I decided to offer Kip the opportunity to rest his feet in a safe place at night.

I left nothing out as I gave Kip the full rundown of how I would soon be jumping ship. He didn't seem to mind as he was just simply tired of waking up with his roommate standing at the edge of his bed tickling his feet. Rich was also getting tired of Kip's loud music, and the situation was reaching a boiling point. And because I just wanted someone to split the bills with, I offered Kip a deal that was too good to be true, $650 per month for rent, instead of paying half which would have been $750, and we'd split the utilities. This was a better deal than he was receiving with Rich, and the house we were living in was much nicer and more spacious. Plus, he seemed to prefer me over his roommate, personality wise. I mean, of course; who wouldn't? So, as long as he didn't touch my computer, which I warned him not to do, and as long as he didn't grow pot plants in the backyard, which I also warned him not to do, we'd be fine. Or would we?

The first week or so was a marriage made in heaven. We even hung out together once. Kip didn't seem to be the burden I thought he would be in regards to wanting rides to and from work, and he basically stayed to himself. He appeared very friendly and was even helpful with the housework, which was a complete 180 after living with Mary for seven years. Things were moving along fine. As Kip felt more and more comfortable around me, he even began to loosen up a little. What a delight it was when Kip finally felt at ease enough to disclose the details of his admission into a mental health facility and the ups and downs of his past struggles with cocaine addiction. Insert the scratching record sound here. I calmly digested these shocking revelations as Kip rambled through his questionable life history. But I decided everyone deserves a second chance so I elected to brush off these blinking warning lights, despite the fact that the computer guru had finally called me back to see if he could stop by to check out the place. Kip was my guy, and nothing would change that. Or would it?

In the meantime, a random event would also enter a new factor into my life. A girl that I adored in high school and who had had a crush on me since junior high named Megan called me out of the blue one day just to say hi. We remained pretty good friends growing up but, for one reason or another, never dated. When she mentioned that she was married once but was currently single, my ears and my entire outlook on life perked up. The feeling seemed to be mutual when she learned of my recent split with Mary. What started out as an isolated incident turned into a budding phone romance that had us speaking on a daily basis from nearly three thousand miles apart. It was killing us not to see each other, and Megan even booked a flight to come out and visit me in California. She also sent me a few recent pictures via email in which she looked even better than she had in high school. My hormones were raging. My plan included taking her to Catalina Island, where we'd spend a beautiful weekend of fun and romance together.

But like everything in life, good things just don't seem to last. Not only was Kip now violating my one sacred rule of never touching my computer, he was now exhibiting some very odd behavior. Each day that I lived with this guy was one more day that I couldn't stand waking up in the morning. He had a new surprise waiting for me every twenty-four hours, and a typical day began with his startling me out of bed mid morning with music that was blasting out of MY stereo. And what was turning into his odd stunt of the day was now getting under my skin like a bad rash. One day I would come home to find a desk in the front yard. The next day I would pull up to discover one of his shirts drying in a tree. The day after that, I'd go onto my computer only to notice my tool bar flipped sideways. I mean who was I living with, Pee Wee Herman? The sad thing is I don't think he was doing it to mess with me. I just think he was so disheveled that he had no way of controlling his behavior.

Speaking of behavior, Kip was starting to really gross me out as well. One night out of complete boredom, he took a metal necklace and shoved it up his nose. He then pulled one-half of the chain out through the other side of his schnoz and began tugging on it from both ends until it moved up and down through each nostril. He went on to explain to me how he had burned a hole through the center of his nose as a result of all the cocaine he had done throughout the years and that surgery was required to mend the wound. That wasn't his only problem.

One night while Kip and I were riding home from Islands Hamburgers, where we had stopped for a bite to eat, he started blowing chunks out of my passenger side window. I hate anything to do with bodily fluids, especially when they're spewing out of someone I don't particularly like. So when we got home Kip immediately darted into the house for some cleaning supplies and rapidly returned to give the door a good wiping down. Kip assured me that very little hit the inside or outside of my car door and promised me that he cleaned up the little bit that had. But, of course, when I went out to run an errand the following morning streams of dried vomit lined the inside and outside of my passenger door. That was the first and last time I took Kip anywhere.

But, I couldn't stop him from eating at home. And just a few nights after Kip was tossing cookies out of my passenger-side window, he came running at me with his face turning purple. Seconds prior, we were having a normal conversation from two adjacent rooms. I was sitting in the living room trying to relax while he was standing in the kitchen inhaling a steak that he had prepared. Then, out of nowhere, he came rushing towards me like an infant being strangled by its own umbilical cord with chunks of steak falling from his mouth. Then he started pointing at his throat. My first instinct was to punch him in the face. But after quickly analyzing the situation, my next impulse was, although I hate to admit it, to let him choke to death. It wasn't until he aligned himself directly in front of me and into the Heimlich position that I even began to feel the urge to help him. I guess he made it so easy for me to unblock his airway that I really had no choice. After a few quick thrusts, a slab of meat came shooting out of his mouth and onto the hardwood floor that I had just cleaned. He wiped the slobber from his face and then thanked me profusely for saving his life.

When he started telling everybody at work about my heroics that evening, I started to question the legitimacy of the entire incident and began wondering whether he had planned the whole thing out just to use it as some sort of manipulative tool against me. So after that little episode, I began watching his every move. I latter surmised, after witnessing a few more of these harrowing experiences, that Kip had some sort of digestive problem. Great, just what I needed, an annoying roommate who spits up more than a newborn baby. Megan's visit couldn't come soon enough. It would at least give me an excuse to get out of the house for a few days.

I grew up in a smoking household, and the one thing that I despised more than anything was secondhand cigarette smoke. Of course, what new pain-in-the-ass roommate would be complete without violating your every household rule, especially the one of not smoking in the house, especially in the room next to yours while you're sleeping only to deny it the next day? Kip also put on a good front when it came to pretending to like the dogs. Whenever I was around, Kip would joke with them or try to pet them, only to receive nasty snarls in return. This served as an ominous warning to keep a very close eye on this guy.

I got to witness the true Kip in action one day when my car was at the shop and I was hunkered down in my room. Kip stumbled in from God knows where that day only to be met with persistent barking from the two best judges of character I had ever met in my life, Tai and Charlie. The dogs were super sensitive to people's energy, and Kip was a walking negative vortex. As the dogs told Kip what they thought of him, Kip screamed at them to "shut the f@#k up" along with many other angry remarks. The more he yelled at them, the more they barked. By the time they had completed just a few exchanges, I had already quietly made my way to a spot in the hallway where I could see Kip but where he couldn't see me. I don't know if Kip sensed my energy or if he just decided to back down out of frustration, but when he spun around to head towards his room I caught him by surprise. Suddenly Kip's demeanor drastically changed, and lo and behold, he was the fun-loving Kip again. Kip also knew that I kept a loaded .357 in my room and that I was just crazy enough to use it. When I pressed him as to why he was acting so nastily towards my dogs, he told me that he just didn't like dogs but that he didn't want to tell me at first because he didn't want it to affect our friendship and/or our potential living arrangement. The more this guy opened up to me, the more I wanted to shut him up … for good. I made a deal with myself that if I ever caught Kip smacking one of my dogs, no matter how hard or on what part of their body, he would not be making it in to work for the rest of his life due to personal reasons.

As his daily routine of tampering with my things and getting his destructive hands on projects that took me years to establish, like my garden, wore on, Kip had gotten on my very last nerve. It didn't matter that Megan's trip was less than a month away or that the Republican Central County Committee was splitting in two due to the illegal tactics used by establishment insiders to drive the pro-freedom representatives from their positions. My time was up.

And it couldn't have come at a better time. The WHO (World Health Organization) had just declared the swine flu a level six pandemic, and all of the intelligence that I had been receiving about martial law and forced inoculations was becoming a very real possibility. My decision to leave the entertainment capital of the world and head for the hills of Pennsylvania was further encouraged by the fact that I didn't want to be trapped in a city of fifteen million people when all hell broke loose. So, within the span of a day, I made my decision to leave Los Angeles by the end of the week.

The first person I notified regarding my escape from LA was Kip, who I anticipated would cry like a baby, which he most certainly did. But to this idiot's credit, even though, during our initial agreement, I had explained to him that I would be leaving LA at some point in time, this was a very unfair last-minute notice. So what I did to compensate for my abrupt proclamation was pay the ensuing month's rent in its entirety to give Boy Blunder enough time to either (a) meet with the landlord and upon my recommendation stay in the house or (b) simply find another place to live. But with the way Captain Crack Head was destroying the house even with me in it, I was caught in the conundrum of sticking it to Kip by not giving him a referral, which I am sure would have led to his destroying the place after I left, or giving him a referral with the hope that he would be unable to find a roommate, which would leave him short on cash and, therefore, unable to sign a new lease. Either way, I didn't want to screw over the landlord, who had been very good to Mary and me, by pawning this nut job off on him. Fortunately for me, it was the landlord's insistence on a credit check that consequentially drove Kip to a new address.

But in the end, thank God, I was leaving when I was because another month or two of Kip and I would've been sitting in LA County Jail on homicide charges. And unlike Kip, who was given a one-week notice of my departure, Sardine received word the night of my predetermined last shift. I knew that I would never in a million years work with the likes of Sardine again, which made me feel incredibly vindicated in sticking it to the man (well, sort of).

I had an impromptu yard sale scheduled at the house for my last three days in town. The goal was to sell as many memories of Mary and me as I could while accumulating enough gas money to drive off into the sunset. And what moving sale would be complete without a tweaked out roommate named Kip throwing a temper tantrum during my most robust day of business? First of all, Kip had the oddest sleeping patterns of anyone I had ever met. He would stay awake for three days straight and then suddenly crash for an entire twenty-four hours. Once he was asleep, not even an act of God could wake him. There was no rhyme or reason for his sleep deprivation, but he would become extremely irritable whenever he heard even the smallest noise while in the midst of a sleepless spell. But yet he could blast MY STEREO or play his guitar through his amplifier at any hour of the day or night, no matter who in the neighborhood wanted some piece and quiet, including me.

Kip had made arrangements to sleep at a friend's house while I conducted my clearance sale. And anybody who's ever had a garage or moving sale knows that the most serious shoppers always arrive first thing in the morning to find the best buys. This is especially true when the Hispanic community gets involved. The proceeds from my three-day bonanza were to pay for the U-Haul trailer that I needed to hitch to my car and for the overnight pet hotels I planned to bunk in. The first day of the sale went okay, but since it was a Friday and hence a workday, I was anticipating a much larger turnout the following morning. As it turns out, my prediction was accurate. Even before the official start time of 8:00 a.m., cars and trucks were slowly passing by the house. Knocks at the door came as early as 7:45 a.m., and although I wasn't quite ready to unveil my showroom, I let these early birds in anyway.

Cash was flowing, and product was moving as the items from my once fully furnished house were disappearing rapidly. As I was helping a customer carry a dresser to his car at around 8:30 a.m., I had to do a double take at what came staggering down the street towards us. It was a bare-chested Kip, stumbling through the neighborhood in a pouring sweat while angrily announcing to the whole block how he couldn't fall asleep at his friend's house. So now, out of nowhere, Kip wanted complete silence in the middle of my moving sale so he could rest. Nice time to tell me, jackass!! I currently had a Mexican family there buying everything but the kitchen sink (and only because that was securely fastened to the floor and wasn't mine to sell). But they did buy my futon couch, my futon bed/chair, the ottoman for the futon bed/chair, patio tables, patio chairs, lawn statues, kitchen appliances, clay pots of various sizes, a TV, a dresser, a few bookshelves, and my guitar to name a few. They even made an offer to buy all of the fruit trees in the yard.

The only vehicle they had to haul what had to be three rooms worth of furniture was a mini Toyota pickup truck. To this day, I have no idea how they were able to pile so much junk onto such a tiny vehicle. As they rode off, I could hear the banjos in my head strumming the theme song to the "Mexican" *Hillbillies*. The pile had to be three stories high, and if at anytime during their transit home they traveled under an overpass, I'm sure their newly purchased merchandise was found smashed to pieces all over the roadway. And, of course, during the entire negotiation process with these bargain hunters, Kip kept emerging from his den, violently demanding that we keep it down. He was moody because he was working nights and wasn't able to fall asleep, which he blamed on all of the activity at the house.

Due to my spontaneous decision to move my entire life across the United States within the next five days, I had an incredible amount of work and planning to do. The short version of the story is that Kip wasn't the only one not getting any sleep. But sleep, at this point in time, was a luxury rather than a necessity. The necessity was getting the hell out of Los Angeles and as far away from Kip as possible. With the welcoming arms of family, friends, and the woman I fell in love with over the phone on the other side of the country, I would have pinned my eyelids open and overdosed on caffeine before I risked staying in Los Angeles another day. And because I gave Sardine and company a one-day notice as a last "screw you for making my life a living hell even though I did everything humanly possible to offer each and every deli customer the best dining experience possible," I had no qualms about skipping out on a going-away party organized by the very same people who were ready to bury me alive underneath the soup station.

My last day in town was spent selling the remainder of my things that weren't nailed to the floor or crammed into my U-Haul trailer. I bought dog food along with lots of dog treats for Tai and Charlie and jammed my giant stuffed gorilla, Chet, into the passenger-side floor space to serve as a makeshift airbag for whichever dog served as co-pilot. I had plenty of blankets to act as comfy beds for the animals, and all I had to do was wake up the next morning in order to leave a long and difficult ten-year chapter behind me.

The following morning was shaping up to be the type of beautiful spring day that had attracted me and so many others to the Golden State to begin with. It was hard to drive off as the smell of the spring air triggered the many fond memories that I had of my decade-long stay there. For the first time all week, I second-guessed my decision to leave the City of Angels behind me. But it wasn't long until I was cruising on the open road with the two best travel companions a man could ask for, Tai and Charlie. I had Megan working the logistics of our trip from her central command post in Eastern Pennsylvania simply because I didn't have enough time to properly plan the whole voyage out. The idea was to put in as many miles as I could each day and, about an hour or so before I couldn't stand driving any longer, Megan would search for a pet hotel within a sixty-mile radius of our location. From there, she would make the arrangements for us to stay the night. There were a minimum number of mandatory miles that we had to travel each day in order for us to make it home in time for my birthday, which was just four days away.

Things went well on the first day of our nationwide tour except for Charlie trying to jump out of the car during an emergency pit stop along a busy highway. This happened after I pulled over to let a whining Tai out to go pee. I stopped on a steep, curvy mountain in Utah after Tai's whimpering became intolerable. I reached into the backseat to put on Tai's leash, and as I got out of the car to let her out, Charlie made a break for my door. I was barely able to stuff him back in as the worst possible scenarios raced through my mind. After that experience, I made a commitment to myself that no matter how bad they cried or regardless of how much they moaned, there would be no potty breaks along major highways. If push came to shove, they could just do their duty in the car. After just my second day on the highway with these two road warriors, I knew my fears of their misbehaving out of restlessness were all for naught. The character, poise, and patience they showed during our treacherous trip, especially on day two, cemented our friendship forever.

Because it was a typical spring day in western Utah, a state that I had never been through before, I wasn't quite aware of how dangerous driving through this canyon country could be. As we entered the mountainous region known as Bryce Canyon on day two of our cross-country extravaganza, I had roughly three quarters of a tank of gas. I was enjoying the scenery immensely as we weaved in and out through the many spectacular views. But the further we got into the canyon and thus the desert with our little trailer in tow, the higher the temperatures climbed, and the more I started realizing that we were running out of gas. I hadn't driven across country in fifteen years, so I guess I assumed every nook and cranny of our country was just a hop, skip, and a jump away from major civilization and hence a gas station. In this case, I couldn't have been more wrong. Although the dogs patiently rode along, the oppressive desert heat was pressing down on them like the gravity on Jupiter, causing them to pant heavily. I did my best to comfort them and made every effort I could to give them plenty of water. Tai, the older of the two, was getting so delirious that she kept licking the air instead of putting her tongue into the water bowl that I had repeatedly placed in front of her. And the canyon, which at first seemed spectacular and mesmerizing, now appeared vast and never ending.

And as hot and unsafe as it was for the dogs to be exposed to roasting temperatures inside the car, not to mention the anxiety they experienced just from traveling, running the AC would have put a major strain on our fuel supply. I started to panic. Everything I owned was attached to our car, and the dogs were looking at me like, "Please, turn off the heat." Being stranded on the side of the road would have completely stressed them out, especially the older dog, Tai, who was now around fourteen. As our gas needle dropped below empty, I started to feel that I would never forgive myself if anything happened to the dogs. As I looked off in the direction that we were heading, the horizon seemed to go on forever with no end in sight. But, finally, after proceeding a few more miles down the road, my prayers were answered when a blue highway sign containing the picture of a fuel pump appeared at the last possible moment. As we drifted into the parking lot of that lone desert gas station just shy of noon, I was quite relieved to know that my sidekicks and I were temporarily out of harm's way. But as fate would have it, there was more to come.

So onward we went. Fueled up, nourished, and hydrated, we took to the highway with new vigor. It seemed as though we had managed our way through the canyon part of our survivor course and were now entering the extreme desert portion of the terrain. As we topped out at around seventy miles per hour, the car seemed to be handling a little funny, but I assumed this was due to the weight of the trailer coupled with the hot scorching surface we were riding on. As I hit my accelerator to climb up over a slight little incline that we were rapidly approaching I got nothing. We had enough momentum to carry us up over this tiny hill but that was about it. The car had stopped accelerating even though I was gunning it full throttle. I immediately began to freak out, and in crisis mode called Megan. We slowed to a crawl as I vented to Megan about how our engine was spent and that we were now in big trouble. I only had enough money to make it back home under the assumption that there would be no major glitches. Even just one major mechanical failure would have left us stranded in the middle of nowhere with the little bit I didn't sell in LA fair game to the first opportunist to cross our path. I was also carrying a few valuable items that were mixed in with my everyday belongings, and we weren't nearly close enough even to the halfway point to have someone drive out to meet us.

As the doomsday scenarios played out in my mind, I was hemming and hawing to Megan about how there was no way I was going to make it home. I was now on the side of the road, and as I attempted to put my car in park, I realized that the gear stick had been bumped into neutral and that my sudden rise in blood pressure was all for naught. I deduced that Charlie probably hit the consol while shifting around on the front seat. Or Chet, being that he was crammed into the passenger-side floor space, may have also been responsible for this accidental shifting of the gears. But because of the sense of security

Chet provided for the dogs as they snuggled up to him during our long days in the car, Chet would remain put.

Well, once again we were back on the open road. And besides the sparks that were shooting off the chains that we were dragging along the road to secure our trailer to the hitch, we traveled approximately twenty miles before something else started going wrong. The car was pulling right. I tried to ignore this warning signal, but after traveling another fifteen miles or so down the interstate, a couple passed us urgently pointing downwards towards the back of our car. This could only mean one thing, the international sign for a blown tire. Again, my heart jumped to the middle of my throat. We were smack dab in the middle of a blazing afternoon, cruising through bum f%ck Egypt, and we now had a flat tire. Freaking great! I didn't have a spare or a tire iron, and I was beginning to think that this would be the crushing blow that thwarted my plans to make it home anywhere near my birthday. We stopped at the first two-horse town we came to, which was roughly another ten miles down the road.

I maneuvered our rig into the first gas station I could find. As I got out of the car, Tai and Charlie were looking at me like, "Oh God, now what?" I ran into the service center only to find out that they did not have a resident mechanic on their payroll. Getting some basic information out of any one of the three inbred tellers behind the counter was proving to be a real task. I thought I was going to need a local interpreter to translate from mumbled redneck to English and then back again. As I held up the long line that was forming behind me, I finally endured enough snide remarks from the local yokels during the Children of the Corn's fifth version of their garbled up directions to get me in the general vicinity of the tire shop. There was no time to lose as these snickering service workers gave me my last piece of advice, "Ya better hurry; they close in fifteen minutes."

I blasted out of the storefront so fast the townsfolk barely had enough time to gather their pitchforks for my public lynching. I quickly filled the damaged tire with air and began to follow the scribbled down directions that were written onto the back of a crumbled up sales receipt by one of the tellers. I prayed during my entire scenic tour to the tire shop that my tire would at least maintain enough pressure to keep me from doing any further damage to my car. I also hoped that the tire shop would still be open so I could fix the problem and get right back on course.

After making a few wrong turns which resulted in the pups and me circling the town square multiple times, we finally made it to the tire shop as one of the mechanics was pulling the first of three garage doors shut. I urgently explained our dilemma to the gentleman closing up for the evening who reluctantly agreed to assist us. But I couldn't help but think that this whole ordeal was going to turn out like the scene in *Vacation* where Chevy Chase's character asks the man at the desert garage how much the repairs are going to cost and the man responds, "How much do you got?" At that point, Chevy's character is left no choice but to give the man everything in his wallet in order to get his car back. I especially got this feeling when the very large man assisting us started jacking up the car with the dogs still inside. When the car hit its maximum height on the portable lift, I sheepishly asked the man, "Can I please take my dogs out of the car, sir?" to which he responded, "I don't know. CAN YOU?"

At that point, I thought the service charge alone was going to cost me an arm and a leg, leaving it up to Charlie to operate the pedals as we drove homeward. But as Hillbilly Jim and I talked about dogs and women, we actually started to bond a little, even though he did have a few dozen more than me. And yes, I am referring to both the dogs and the women. This opened the door for a more serious conversation that ranged from the state of our country to the fact that he had eight kids from three different wives. As this grizzly bear of a man put the finishing touches on my tire, he not only gave me the great news that no damage had been done to my tire or to my axle, but that he was only charging me nine dollars for the plug. He also informed me that I would not need a new radial because the patch he affixed would last throughout the lifetime of the tire. Once again, God was watching out for me and me mutts, allowing us to circumvent yet another setback that day. The guys in the garage even offered me a cold bottle of water for the next leg of our journey, to which I gladly obliged. I tipped the man an extra ten dollars for his help, and the perros and I were on our way once again.

It was around sunset when we entered the Rocky Mountains way behind schedule. Had I put any kind of serious thought into our travel plans and even slightly considered the ginormity of the Rocky Mountains, I would have never taken the I-70 through Colorado. After ten years of easy living in California, I would have never in a million years guessed that I would encounter a snowstorm in the first week of May. But as we approached the base of the Rockies, a light snowfall began sticking to the ground. As we continued our ascent up this monster of a mountain, I nervously watched from my rearview mirror as our tow-along trailer slid out of view and then back again. The climb up the Rockies was breathtakingly beautiful but also incredibly steep and lengthy. The more we climbed, the harder the snow fell. The road was getting so treacherous that if at any point we would have stopped our upward momentum, we would have gotten stuck. Charlie was sensing my anxiety and was looking at me like, "Please, get me down off this mountain." I entertained the thought of lodging in Vail, but I would have spent my entire expense fund on one night's stay there, and the dogs would have been forced to sleep in the car. We had no choice but to get past the Rockies. Besides, we had only traveled a couple of hundred miles that day, and we had some serious ground to make up. So we continued onward.

We stopped for a bathroom break at the summit, where I enjoyed watching Tai and Charlie's first interaction with snow. I made a quick call to Megan to say, "You are not going to believe this, but I am standing in a cloud with my shorts on in the middle of a blizzard." We then jumped back in our car and, in a serious race against time and Mother Nature, commenced forward. We cautiously scaled back down the other side of the mountain, and after a couple hours of driving, I was finally able to let out a sigh of relief as we dismounted this large beast. I had no idea what was in store for us next.

We weaved through a small village and then rounded some turns when, lo and behold, we were abruptly climbing again. I truly did not think I had it in me to tempt fate once again as a thick blanket of snow fell from the cold, dark sky. And just like during our first ascent, the higher we scaled, the more hazardous the conditions grew. I was now having a hard time seeing the road, and the wind felt as if it was going to rip our trailer from the hitch and throw it over the mountain. The large surface area provided a friendly target for the strong gusts of wind that were pelting our trailer. My fear was that the trailer would be tossed over the guardrail, pulling the car along with it. Even the dogs jumped every time a powerful blast of mountain air shook our motorcade.

Again, we gradually made it to the top of the second peak, but the situation was much more precarious. The entire mountain was pitch black, and there were no street lights lining the highway. From what little visibility I had, I could tell that we were riding next to some very terrifying drops. As we crept along, I could no longer tell where the road was as the white and yellow lines were completely covered with snow. Big rigs were zipping past us on our way back down Colossus, rattling our car as they stormed by. I found these truckers to be insane but figured they must be so used to this throughway and the treacherous conditions that they weren't even fazed by them. I still couldn't rein in the horrifying scenarios that formed in my mind's eye as I imagined big rigs flying off the side of the mountain and dropping thousands of feet until they burst into flames at the bottom of this large abyss. By the time we crawled back down to the base of this second behemoth, I was a nervous wreck. My fingernails were embedded into the steering wheel, and I was on the verge of tears. If we would have stumbled upon a third climb I would have jumped out of my car and buried myself alive in a snowbank. As we barreled towards the middle of Colorado, I couldn't wait to put that day behind us.

On our way towards the next hotel Megan had picked out for us, I somehow made a wrong turn, and we ended up about a half-hour off course. We had already been driving for about fifteen hours, and I couldn't take another minute behind the wheel. I was tired and delirious and considered just sacking out on the side of the road. But that's when Megan phoned back after consulting with a friend as to the error of our ways. She immediately got us back on track to the hotel, which was now about an hour away. At that point, I felt the best thing to do would be to hang up with Megan to conserve energy. This turned out to be a huge mistake. I could barely keep my eyes open, even with all of the windows rolled down and the radio blaring. Soon after, we entered a new and eerie stretch of isolated highway, and I started losing it. I called Megan back and caught her just as she was going to bed. I began crying from the incredible amount of pain I was in due to the long, nerve-racking day we had just had. I now severely needed Megan to keep me awake … and sane. Between my acting experience and my ten years of waiting tables, I had the heart of a lion and the skin of a rhinoceros, but I just couldn't take any more of this.

That particular length of road we were on was frighteningly creepy, and I couldn't tell if I was hallucinating or there were actually witches on broomsticks flying around our car. These witches were also accompanied by a maniacal laugh that sent a chill down my spine. Was I going crazy? And were these witches harassing me? I began screaming into the phone. I must have scared the daylights out of Megan, who was a friend from high school but one with whom I hadn't talked much in the past twenty years or so. Her soothing nature did calm me down a bit, and I was clinging to her company for dear life. It wasn't until we were about thirty miles from the hotel that I began to figure out what had been haunting us since entering that black hole of a highway. It was tumbleweed, bunches of tumbleweed that were blowing across the plains and getting stuck in our wheel wells, thus creating the high-pitched squeals. That stretch of road was one of the darkest and dreariest I had ever been on, and the dumpy motel Megan was guiding us to was a welcome sight for my bleary eyes.

After having a nice continental breakfast at the Bates Motel, I saddled up the dogs for day three. We shoved off in the direction of the highway that just eight hour's prior had grabbed hold of my darkest fears. As we meandered towards that barren stretch of pavement once again, I spotted a sign along the road that urged drivers not to stop for hitchhikers as there was a prison nearby. No wonder I was having such a strong visceral reaction to the highway from hell. My instincts were trying to tell me something. The rest of the trip would not even come close to the torturous experiences my two best friends and I had just put behind us on day two. But there was yet another dangerous scenario that unfurled around us as we gathered steam towards Pennsylvania.

This event came in the form of a tornado warning that trumpeted over our car radio as we proceeded through Indiana. The report warned motorists to immediately pull off to the side of the road if they were traveling within a certain county. Well, I had no idea what county we were passing through as I was just following a small black and white map of the United States that I had printed off Mapquest. I urgently called Megan who, for the first time throughout this entire endeavor, was at work and was unable to take my call. I finally reached a living person at my cousin's house in Virginia (the same cousin who had mailed me the picture of Erik Estrada). His wife jumped on her PC and asked me to recite the names of the towns that we were approaching so she could figure out where in the hell we were. Once she pinpointed our location, she was able to guide us away from the storm's destructive path. In the middle of saying our goodbyes, Megan was calling on the other line.

Poor Megan was probably as stressed out as we were because anytime there was a crisis on the road she was indirectly experiencing everything that we were going through. As we put more and more of these trials and tribulations behind us, I began to feel that nothing could stop me from holding Megan in my arms. As we moved from west to east, I developed a whole new respect for the open road. I now knew firsthand how many perilous situations one could find himself in while traveling alone across country with two dogs. The earlier tornado scare in conjunction with the severe thunderstorm that was currently pummeling our car gave me the incentive I needed to stop prematurely for the evening, even though we were still a few hundred miles short of my goal for day four. This also meant that we were not going to make it home in time for my birthday. But by that point, I just wanted to make it home alive.

During her last day as our crosscountry tour guide, Megan made contact with a man named Jimmy B, who worked for a hotel chain in Indiana. When Megan instructed me to call Jimmy B to let him know where we were so he could guide us to his flophouse, I quipped back, "What? Jimmy B? Are you serious?" I mean I just wanted to find some comfortable lodging for my pooches and me, not a pimp daddy named Jimmy B who could set us up with drugs and hookers. When I finally got in touch with Jimmy B by phone, I realized that I had never talked to a more enthusiastic hotel professional in all my life. He quoted me the price of a room and then gave me the play-by-play directions on how to get to the facility.

When I pulled into the parking lot, Jimmy B was awaiting our arrival. He began directing us into a premiere parking spot with a flashlight as if I was taxiing a jumbo jet into O'Hare airport. When I got out of the car, Jimmy B immediately whisked us off for the fifty-cent tour of a room that he had already picked out for us. He refused to check us in until he was absolutely certain that I was completely satisfied with the lodging unit that he had assigned to us. What he didn't seem to realize was at that point I would have slept on a bed of nails.

When we entered the spacious room, he flipped on the TV, which was already set to a porn station. He then lay the remote control onto the arm of the recliner that was lined up with the TV and asked me if I wanted a beer. I was a tad overwhelmed by this high level of personal service, and to be quite honest, I was a bit skeptical. But he did go right to the porn station, and it had been a long trip thus far, so what would one beer hurt me? As we marched across the parking lot and into the suite warehousing the beer, I thought I had just entered a distributorship. The room was packed wall to wall with alcohol. Jimmy B then explained to me that the Indy 500 was only a week away and that he was stocking up for the big race. He kept emphasizing that when you do good things for people, they return the generosity. I saw this as an indirect way of asking for a tip, but when I offered him a five spot, he absolutely refused.

After ten years of living in LA, this type of erratic behavior now had me on guard. We ventured over to the main office where he began digging underneath the registration desk for my paperwork. In the meantime, he rambled on about how pet owners love the grounds because of all the green grass the animals have to roam on. He was right about that. The hotel felt as if it was built on a golf course and had more green grass than any other overnight inn I had ever been to. Then, I finally realized why Jimmy B had broken out all the bells and whistles and went out of his way to roll out the red carpet for us when we arrived. When he quoted me the price at the front desk, it was fifteen dollars more than the amount he had quoted me over the phone. Also worth noting is the fact that Jimmy B was both the manager and the proprietor of this fine establishment. Being on a tight budget, my initial reaction was to resist this price gouging, but I quickly decided that this wacky experience alone was well worth the extra fifteen dollars. I knew that Jimmy B and his zany antics would leave a lasting impression on me, and since it was the last night of a very long and eye-opening journey, I simply agreed to pay the inflated amount he quoted me.

With the weight of the trip really starting to wear on me, I decided to sleep in the following morning, causing us to get back on the road just a little later than normal. As we closed in on the Keystone State, the landscape began looking increasingly familiar. As we weaved in and out and up and down the mountains of Pennsylvania, the anticipation was killing me. I was finally nearing the town where I had so many fond memories growing up as a kid. I could barely wait to see everybody. I had been through so much since leaving this small town almost fifteen years ago. My previous life here seemed like a distant memory. I came back a changed man who had gone out into the world to pursue his dreams only to end up falling a little short. I knew upon returning, however, that it wasn't the fact that I came back empty handed that mattered. It was the fact that I went out into the world and gave it everything I had, a lesson that will benefit me until the day I die. I am very excited to start this new chapter of my life, and it will all happen as the matzo ball turns.